VENGEANCE

VENGEANCE

HEATHER BURNSIDE

HEAD
ZEUS

An Aries Book

ISBN (PB): 9781801107990
ISBN (E): 9781801107983

Cover design: Matt Bray

Typeset by Siliconchips Services Ltd UK

Printed and bound in Great Britain by
CPI Group (UK) Ltd, Croydon CRO 4YY

Head of Zeus Ltd
First Floor East
5–8 Hardwick Street
London EC1R 4RG

WWW.HEADOFZEUS.COM

For Phil and Baz.

I

'What can I get for you?' asked Hannah, leaning across the bar at The Gilded Cage nightclub and giving Russ Cole a full view of her tantalising cleavage.

Hannah was deliberately flirting with Russ, one of the club's regulars. She couldn't help herself; it helped to pass the time and made the job more interesting. And Russ didn't seem to mind. In fact, she knew he enjoyed it. It was obvious from the way he was assessing her.

The bar Hannah worked behind was the most popular of the two housed inside the nightclub. Russ often took up a seat there and watched Hannah as she worked, striking up conversation whenever she got a free moment. She liked Russ a lot. He was great company and he had something about him.

Although Russ wasn't conventionally handsome, he had strength of character and a raw masculinity, which made him difficult to ignore. This was accentuated by his height, at over six feet tall, and his well-built, muscular physique. He was around thirty, making him only five years older than Hannah, but he had a level of maturity suggesting he'd already had a full lifetime of experiences. And that intrigued Hannah.

'Fuck's sake, Hannah. You nearly had my eyes out then,' he said, grinning.

Hannah smiled back as she straightened up again and flicked her blonde, highlighted hair, which was mid-length and hung about her shoulders in messy layers. Tonight, she was wearing a black vest with a midi-length skirt, which had a small black and cream print and a slit up the side. The vest was plain, but it was fitted, and that was all Hannah needed to show off her 34F assets.

'They shouldn't have been so wide open then, should they?' she teased.

'You know what you're doing,' he said, laughing.

'I've not got a clue what you're talking about,' she said, flicking her blonde tresses again and gazing at him seductively. 'Anyway, what did you call me over for? What do you want?'

'Now that's an invitation.'

'You know what I mean, cheeky. Do you want the same again?'

Russ chuckled. 'Yeah, go on, a pint of lager.'

She made her way towards one of the pumps, but as she did so, she became aware of a customer leaning over to catch her attention and thrusting his chin forward.

'Hey, what the fuck?' he shouted. 'There're customers waiting here y'know. Why are you serving him?'

'He's been here ages,' said Hannah, calmly.

'Yeah, but he's not been waiting to get served, has he? He's just hogging the fuckin' bar! He's only just asked for his pint, and I've been trying to get served for ages.'

'I'll serve you next,' said Hannah, holding a pint glass under the pump.

'No, you fuckin' won't! Why should he get served first just 'cos he knows you? He should wait his fuckin' turn like everyone else.'

Hannah ignored him as she poured the pint.

'Bitch!' he yelled, causing Hannah to look up in shock.

Straightaway she noticed the anger on Russ's face. 'Who are you fuckin' talking to?' he yelled. 'Don't you dare speak to her like that!'

Hannah stopped what she was doing and held up her hand, signalling to Russ to let it go. But she could see from his expression that it was too late.

'I'll speak to her how I fuckin' like!' complained the other man.

Russ jumped off his stool and launched himself at the customer. For a few moments they traded blows. As Russ was bigger and stronger, he was getting the better of his opponent till two more men joined the fracas. Hannah assumed they were friends of the troublemaker as they surrounded Russ and attacked him. He tried to put up a bold defence, aiming practised punches in response to their haphazard blows, but there were too many of them.

When one of them landed a particularly savage thump, which opened a cut on Russ's forehead, Hannah screamed at the sight of the blood. To her relief the bouncers soon appeared. With Russ's help they overpowered the men, then the bouncers marched them out of the club.

Calmly, Russ straightened his shirt and hopped back onto the stool as though nothing had happened. The rest of the bar area had cleared so he was the only person there for the moment.

'Oh my God! Look at your face,' she said.

Russ fingered the cut on his forehead then gazed at the blood on his fingers. 'It's nowt. Just a small cut. Probably looks worse than it is.'

'Come into the back and let me clean it up for you,' ordered Hannah.

She opened the gate that separated the staff from the public and motioned for Russ to follow her. Then she led him to a small kitchen behind the bar area. Hannah grabbed a clean tea towel and ran it under the hot water tap, then encouraged Russ to sit down while she wiped the blood away with shaking hands.

Despite the hours she had spent chatting to Russ at the bar, she'd never been this close up to him before and her actions felt intimate somehow. If she was honest with herself, she loved the way Russ had jumped to her defence. She found his manliness a massive turn-on, but at the same time, the violence had shaken her.

'Your shirt's ruined,' she commented, trying to take her mind off the way she was feeling.

Russ looked up at her, his gaze lingering on her breasts. 'Great view from here,' he quipped.

Hannah tutted. 'Is that all you think about?'

He noticed she was shaking, and he asked, 'Eh, are you OK?' Without waiting for a reply, he took hold of her free hand. The motion took her by surprise, and she felt a frisson of excitement. 'Don't worry about me,' he continued. 'I'm not hurt, not really. I can easily handle a bunch of dickheads like them.'

Looking at his damaged clothing and the cut on his head, Hannah wasn't so sure, but she didn't say anything. Her mind had now switched to concerns about what sort of person Russ must be to keep so calm after he had just been viciously attacked. Then another thought occurred to her. 'Eh, how come the bouncers threw them three out but left you alone?'

'Because I wasn't the one in the wrong. I suppose the bouncers must have known that.'

'I suppose it helps that you're a regular, too,' said Hannah.

'Yeah, well, I talk to the guys and the boss, Jez, too. They've seen that I'm alright, haven't they?'

Hannah laughed and said, 'They don't know you like I do then, do they?'

Russ smiled. 'That's another thing I like about you. Your banter.'

'Ooh, there's more, is there?' teased Hannah.

They carried on in that vein for a few more minutes until the bleeding of Russ's forehead had stopped and Hannah had finished cleaning him up. Their banter helped to take the focus off the spark of electricity that sizzled between them. Hannah wondered whether Russ had noticed it too.

Then she returned to her work while Russ took up his seat again and guzzled the fresh pint that Hannah poured for him.

An hour later, Russ left the nightclub, and Hannah began serving a young woman. She was blonde, tall and slim, in fact, not dissimilar in appearance to Hannah. She had finished ordering a round of drinks, and while Hannah handed her the card machine, the woman lowered her voice as she addressed her.

'He's bad news, y'know.'

'Who is?' asked Hannah.

'Russ Coles.'

'Oh, you know him, do you?'

'Yeah, very well, actually. I used to go out with him until I found out what he was like.'

'What do you mean?'

'I mean, he's involved in illegal activities. I saw what went on before. Why do you think the bouncers didn't throw him out?'

'Well, because they knew it wasn't his fault.'

'Do you really believe that? Usually when there's trouble, they throw the lot of them out no matter who started it.'

'What are you getting at?' asked Hannah.

'He works for Jez Reilly, the owner, and he's as bent as he is. If I were you, I'd give him a wide berth.'

Thinking they were the words of a bitter, jilted woman, Hannah said, 'It's not like that; me and Russ are just friends.'

The girl let out a puff of air. 'Huh, you could have fooled me. I've seen the way you two are with each other.'

'So what?' said Hannah, becoming irritated. 'What's it got to do with you?'

The girl took her credit card and the receipt and put them inside her handbag. 'Just don't say you weren't warned, that's all. I'm doing you a favour.' Then she picked up the drinks and walked away.

Hannah was left wondering why the girl had told her all that. Was it just jealousy or was she genuinely trying to warn her? She decided not to challenge Russ, just in case the girl was right. It was best to keep the information to herself for now.

2

It was late when Hannah got home to her one-bedroomed flat, but she wasn't quite ready for bed. She was often wired after a night at the club and preferred to have a bit of relaxation when she got home. She grabbed herself a cup of tea and plonked down onto the sofa. Despite the late hour, she could hear her next-door neighbours engaged in a screaming row, the man letting out a barrage of expletives and foul-mouthed insults.

The flat was in a more rundown part of the city than Hannah had been used to previously. It was the type of area where residents either worked in non-skilled jobs or, as was the case with the majority, lived on benefits. As with many rundown areas, crime rates were high, and Hannah had invested in secure locks and bolts on her doors and windows. She worried about Kai growing up there as she didn't want him getting into bad company. It wasn't the sort of area she would have aspired to live in, but it would have to do for now.

The flat was sparse but modern, and it was all she could afford at the moment. Inside the lounge was the two-seater sofa she was currently occupying and an armchair her parents had given her. They were different colours, and the sofa had a tear on one of the arms, but she had used matching slate blue throws to cover them. The walls were painted in a pale grey, apart from one, which was papered in an art deco design in shades of blue, grey and cream.

There was a TV in the corner, not quite as big as she would have liked, but it was alright, and it was mounted on a set of shelves her stepdad had made for her. Although the flooring was cheap laminate, there was a rug in the centre of the room, in colours that complemented the rest of the décor.

Hannah didn't switch on the TV. She was too busy mulling over the events of the night. After the girl had left the bar, it had become busy, and Hannah hadn't had chance to dwell on what she had said. But now, as she sat in the silence of her flat, the girl's words came back to her.

If Hannah was honest with herself, she was massively attracted to Russ. Even though she wasn't in the right frame of mind to start a relationship, it had been fun flirting with him. After everything she had been through, that feeling of mutual attraction had lifted her spirits, buoying her like a mighty tide of burgeoning self-esteem. But now she decided to back off a bit.

If the girl in the club had been telling the truth, then Hannah couldn't help but wonder why Russ had kept his connection to Jez a secret. For the few months she had worked at the club, she had thought of him as just another customer. She had had no idea he worked for the manager, and he had said nothing to make her think otherwise.

The only reason she could think of for keeping it secret would be if, as the girl had said, both Russ and Jez were involved in something illegal. And if that was the case, then

Hannah wanted to be as far removed from the truth as possible.

Hannah awoke from a fitful sleep and gazed across at her bedside clock. One o'clock in the afternoon. *Bloody hell!* She had agreed to be at her parents' for twelve. Stumbling out of bed, she reached for her mobile and gave her mum, Jill, a quick call. Jill was understanding as always and told her it wasn't a problem. By the time Hannah had taken a quick shower and driven the short trip to her parents' house, it was almost two o'clock.

Unlike her own flat, her parents' home was in a more affluent area of the city with properties situated on tree-lined streets and occupied by professionals. She wouldn't have expected anything less from Pete, her stepfather, who was fiercely ambitious and aspirational. Hannah missed the area herself, but she valued her independence too much to move back in with her parents.

'I'm so sorry!' she gushed when Pete answered the door. 'I should have set the alarm, but it was late when I got home, and I just forgot. I bet I've held you up with your shopping, haven't I?'

Pete had been with her mother for ten years and married for eight of those. It had been difficult to accept him at first, as Hannah still had powerful memories of her loving father who had passed away when she was just a kid. But Pete's affable manner had soon won her round.

As time went on, she'd learnt that Pete was quite an old-fashioned man who believed in looking after his wife and kids, and he could be quite protective at times. But Hannah accepted that. He was of another generation, and at least it showed he cared.

'No, we went this morning,' answered Pete, smiling at her question about the shopping.

'What? When you were looking after Kai? How?'

'He came with us. He was as good as gold. So, stop fretting, everything's fine. They're in there.'

Hannah smiled and went through to the lounge where she found her mother on the sofa with Hannah's three-year-old son, Kai. Like Hannah, Kai had blond hair and blue eyes. He was a cute and endearing child who captured the hearts of anyone he came into contact with. There was a dinosaur jigsaw spread out on the coffee table, which they were both focused on until Kai spotted his mother.

'Mummy!' he shouted running over to her and hugging her legs. 'We had choccies.'

'Erm, only after he'd eaten his lunch and been a very good boy in the supermarket,' Jill reassured her.

Hannah stroked his head affectionately. 'Good boy,' she said and was rewarded with a chuckle.

For the next half hour, Hannah and her mother made small talk while Pete made her a cup of tea and a late lunch. It was just like him to home in on the fact that she'd left her flat in a rush without having anything to eat and then make sure she was fed. Not for the first time, Hannah realised how lucky she was to have such wonderful parents who had been there for her through some dreadful times.

Once Jill had waved goodbye to Hannah and Kai from the front door, she returned to the lounge to find her husband watching sport. He paused the TV as she sat on the vacant armchair across from him. It was as though he instinctively knew she had something to say.

'It's not doing our Hannah any good working in that nightclub,' Jill began. 'She looks shattered. She's not eating properly either.'

Jill had expressed the same concerns with every part-time job Hannah had undertaken over the last two and a half years: from waitressing to bar work and even a short spell at a casino. She couldn't help worrying about her daughter.

'I know,' said Pete. 'But what can we do?'

'We should tell her to pack it in. But you'll have to back me when I tell her, otherwise she'll take no notice.'

'Jill, you know as well as I do, she can't afford to pack it in, not unless she lives off the state, and that wouldn't suit Hannah. You know how independent she is.'

'What about if we help her?'

Pete looked taken aback. 'We can't afford to. Not since we took on a bigger mortgage to have that extension done.'

'Fat lot of use that is. It's standing bloody idle.'

'I know. I know. But things were different when we had it done, weren't they? Hannah was still at home then. We had no idea she was going to get pregnant and then up sticks.'

'If it hadn't been for that Greg, she'd have still been here now,' said Jill. 'Cheeky swine, impregnating her then rushing off to London to pursue his career while Hannah had to put hers on hold. She was doing well, too, working as a finance officer with that technology company. It wouldn't have surprised me if she'd ended up doing better than Greg once she'd finished her accountancy exams. But there's no way you can hold down a pressurised job like that while you're trying to bring up a toddler without the support of a partner. So now she's having to work in a bloody nightclub to make ends meet.'

'We don't know that she'd have stayed here, do we?' said Pete. 'If she hadn't got pregnant, she might have left anyway to set up home with him. She was never going to stay forever. She's twenty-five for heaven's sake!'

'Well thank God she didn't end up living with him anyway. At least getting pregnant made her see him for what he is before she ended up lumbered with him.'

'Yes, but let's not forget, Jill, it's also the reason she had to put her career on hold to look after Kai.'

'I know that. I know the situation isn't ideal. None of us would have wanted her having to bring Kai up on her own.'

'Yes, well, now it's happened, we just have to make the best of it, don't we?'

Ignoring his last comment, Jill said, 'Well, assuming she won't move back in with us, there is another alternative.'

'What's that?'

'If we downsized, we could help her. The bills would be a lot lower, and we'd have a lot more disposable income.'

This statement seemed to antagonise Pete. 'What? And give up everything we've worked for?' he said.

Jill supposed he did have a point. They'd both worked all their lives to build something up for themselves, she in the offices of builders' merchants and he at various estate agents. And now they had finally got their home just as she liked it, she was reluctant to give it up.

'I suppose you're right,' she said. 'Hannah wouldn't want that. You know what she's like. And it's only till Kai's in school. Then she'll be able to go back to her career in finance.

It doesn't stop me worrying about her in the meantime though. I don't like her living on that bloody rough estate. And it's not as if we don't have the room.'

'But it's not what she wants, is it? I've told you, she's independent. And even if she moved in with us, she'd still want to do some sort of work. And, seeing as how she can't work in the week while she's looking after Kai, it doesn't leave her a lot of choice, does it?'

Jill was becoming exasperated now and just wanted the conversation to end. They'd been over this time and time again, or something along similar lines: Hannah's job, where she lived, the fact that they didn't have a social life of their own because they looked after Kai every Friday and Saturday night. But their discussions made no difference. They couldn't change the facts; all they could do was hope Hannah's situation changed in the future.

With that in mind, Jill said, 'Anyway, things could change. She might meet someone nice and move in with him.'

'Not in that bloody seedy nightclub, she won't,' grumbled Pete, bringing an abrupt end to the heated conversation.

3

Russ was outside Mulberry's, a popular bar in one of Manchester's more salubrious areas. It had been open for almost a year, and from the outside, it looked inviting, the amber glow of the interior spilling out onto the pavement. The large windows had frosted panes with the word *Mulberry's* written across the entire width in clear glass and a fancy cursive script.

Surrounding the windows was plain charcoal grey wooden panelling creating a modern feel, and the name of the venue was reiterated in the gold lettering above the door. Russ let out a low whistle, thinking about how much the design must have set the owner back. No wonder Gareth Smith was still in debt to Jez Reilly.

Russ peeped through one of the clear glass areas, checking how many customers were still inside. He thought of them as customers, but, in actual fact, they were Gareth's cronies who regularly stayed after hours. From the information Russ had gleaned, these after-hours soirées were free of charge to a select few. The alcoholic bar owner was only too glad of someone to share his expensive pastime with when his long-suffering wife became bored of it. And he enjoyed lording it over everyone as the proud owner of such a prestige establishment.

Russ could see that only two customers remained. Gareth was saying something to them while clearing their empty glasses and placing them behind the counter, ready to wash in the morning, Russ presumed. One of the two men was now without a drink and was looking at his friend who seemed to be draining the last of his. When Russ saw the two men turn away from the counter, he knew they were on their way out.

Russ took up position next to the door and waited till he saw it open, then he approached them as though he had just arrived. Politely waiting for them to step outside, he nodded amiably then stepped into the bar, loudly announcing, 'Hi Gareth, me old mucker. How are you?'

It was a ruse to fool the two men. But Gareth wasn't fooled. He had followed the two men to the door, and when he caught sight of Russ, he began to protest. Russ, anticipating his alarm at being greeted by a stranger, launched himself at Gareth, who stumbled to the ground, where Russ used his body weight to pin him down then slapped a hand over his mouth.

'You'll keep your fuckin' gob shut if you know what's good for you,' said Russ.

Gareth's eyes grew wide with shock and terror, which amused Russ in view of the way in which Gareth had been strutting around earlier that evening playing the hard man. Russ knew because he'd conducted a recce beforehand.

'Fuckin' nice place you've got here, Gareth,' he said. 'Only trouble is, you still fuckin' owe Jez for it, don't you?

He was generous enough to set you up in business, but, little scrote that you are, you can't be arsed paying it back. You're two instalments behind now on the loan.'

He uncovered the man's mouth to let him respond, grasping his throat instead, ready to tighten if he tried anything. 'I-I have been paying it back,' he protested, and Russ caught a nauseating whiff of his vinegar breath, a sure sign of an out-of-control alcoholic.

'Not for the last two months you haven't, and Jez wants payment.'

'But, but … takings have been down.'

'That doesn't fuckin' surprise me considering you're giving it away to all your deadbeat pals.'

'I'm not I …'

'Shut the fuck up!' yelled Russ. 'I don't wanna hear it.' He covered Gareth's mouth again, then continued. 'Right, what I want you to do is take me to the safe and hand over the last two instalments.'

Gareth tried to protest, but it was impossible with his mouth covered.

'I don't want any fuckin' excuses,' said Russ. 'Just give me whatever you've got, and if it's not enough, I'll come back for the rest. And don't dare make a fuckin' sound 'cos I don't want you waking your missus up. If you do anything to try to warn her or if you try anything, I'll fuckin' do the pair of you.'

He eased his weight from Gareth. 'Right, now get up! And do as I say.'

Gareth rose to his feet unsteadily, and Russ guessed that the number of pints he had sunk had something to do with that. Russ was about to follow him to the safe, but to his surprise, Gareth swung a right-hander at him. The punch was ineffectual, missing its target by several centimetres, and Russ was soon on him again. Within seconds he had Gareth back on the ground, but this time Russ wasn't going to let him off with a warning. He set about him, his fists sinking into Gareth's beer belly and trying to find his head and face, which Gareth was shielding with his hands.

When Gareth started squealing for mercy, Russ covered his mouth again. 'Right, I'll stop, but only if you promise to shut the fuck up and hand over the money you owe.'

Russ allowed Gareth to get up off the floor again and this time Gareth didn't put up a fight.

Jez Reilly was a small man in his mid-forties with a big ego and even bigger ambitions. He stood at only five feet five but didn't let that deter him from his missions in life, which included bedding as many beauties as he could and making money – loads of it.

He'd started out as a small-time drug dealer who had invested his cash wisely until he eventually bought his first business. Now he had a string of pubs and clubs across Manchester as well as a taxi firm. But he still wasn't happy. He wanted to be somebody, a man who was respected and admired.

He was currently in the room at the back of The Gilded Cage, which he used as an office. Spread out on the desk was a street plan he had obtained from a mate who had a dodgy contact at the council. Jez loved studying the plans and dreaming about his lucrative scheme. If everything went well, he would become a very rich man. But there were a lot of hurdles to get over first.

When he heard a knock on the door, he quickly folded the plans up so they couldn't be seen. He'd come back to them once he'd got rid of whoever had disturbed him.

'Come in!' he shouted, and Russ Coles entered.

He didn't need to ask Russ if he had the money; he already had it in his hand, which he now passed to him across the desk.

'There you go. It's all there, apart from my cut, but you can check it if you like.'

Jez did check the money. He always checked. You never knew who you could trust in business, and he'd come across plenty of unscrupulous characters over the years.

'Great stuff,' he said once he'd finished counting. 'Did you have any trouble?'

'Nothing I couldn't handle. The guy fancies his chances a bit, but I don't think he took account of the twelve or so pints he'd probably had earlier. He was off his fuckin' tits.'

'I told you, didn't I? The bastard's drinking all the fuckin' profits, well, him and his piss-head mates. But I'll make sure I get everything that's fuckin' owed to me before that business goes down, don't you worry.'

Jez stayed quiet for a moment, assessing the man in front of him. Russ Coles was a handy man to have around, there was no doubt about that, which was why he wanted him involved in his future plans. And he felt sure Russ would want a piece of the action. After all, who else would employ him?

'There's something else I want to discuss with you,' he said.

Jez outlined his plans including the part he expected Russ to play in them. Then he sat back in his oversized office chair and puffed on a cigar while he awaited the other man's reaction.

4

Hannah swung into Rovener Street in her battered old Mini. She'd had the car for years after it had already been passed down through the family, but she refused to part with it. The Mini had never let her down, so she didn't see the point in getting rid.

When she reached her nana Pat's mid-terraced house, she parked outside and looked across at her son, Kai. He had noticed the car stop and excitedly announced, 'Nana!', the name he used to refer to his great-grandmother so that he wouldn't confuse her with his actual grandma: Hannah's mother.

'Yes, that's right. We're at Nana's house. Come on, let's get you out of that car seat so we can go and see her.'

Picking up on her son's eagerness, she raced round to the other side of the car and lifted him out and onto the pavement. As Kai raced to Pat's front door, Hannah smiled in amusement. Pat was at the door before they had chance to knock, and Hannah guessed she was as excited as Kai.

'Hello, little man. How are you today?' asked Pat, who was in her early seventies but still vibrant and young for her age.

Kai responded with a wide smile before dashing inside.

'Look what I've got for you,' said Pat, taking a packet of chocolate buttons off the coffee table and holding them up for Kai to see.

He reached his little hand up. 'Want them.'

'Er, what do you say?' prompted Hannah.

'Please, Nana.'

'That's a good boy,' said Pat, ripping open the packet and passing it to Kai.

Then she turned to Hannah, saying, 'Come on, I'll make you a cup of tea, then I'll show you what I've bought.'

After making a fuss of Kai, Pat selected a children's channel on her Freeview player and left him watching it while she and Hannah went to the kitchen. There she took a carrier bag out of a cupboard and extracted the contents.

'What do you think of that?' she asked. 'It's a belter, isn't it?'

It was a carriage clock, a bit old-fashioned for Hannah's liking, but there was no mistaking the fact that it was a quality item. It was solid brass and gleamed under the light streaming in through the window. The round face was white with black Roman numerals and was surrounded by gilt brass in an intricate pattern. The columns at either side were of a fancy design, framing the clock with added splendour.

'Bloody hell! That's lovely, Nana. Where did you get it?'

'From that shop at the end of the street. I was just having a mooch, and I couldn't resist. It was a bargain as well. Only thirty quid.'

'What shop?' asked Hannah.

'The one that sells second-hand goods. It's between the off-licence and the hairdresser's. You must have seen it on your way here. It's been open for a while.'

Hannah recalled the row of only three shops at the top of her nana's street. She remembered the off-licence and hairdresser's but thought the third shop was a bookmaker. Then again, she hadn't passed them for a while.

'No, I don't come in that way, do I?'

'Oh yeah, I didn't think. Anyway, it's a good shop. I mean, I say second-hand, but you wouldn't think it. He has some lovely things there. A lot of them look nearly new.'

'What sort of things?'

'All kinds. Clocks, watches, phones, computers. You name it, he's got it.'

'What about furniture and things like that?'

'A bit, yeah, but mostly smaller items. It's worth taking a look.'

'It sounds good, Nana. I'll have to check it out sometime,' said Hannah, thinking of the things she still needed for her flat, but hadn't been able to afford.'

'Yes, you should.'

They went through to the lounge where Kai had finished demolishing his treat, his face and fingers now smeared in chocolate.

Hannah laughed. 'Look at you, you mucky pup.'

She took some wipes from her bag and cleaned him up while her nana walked into the room with her carrier bag.

'Now that you've seen it, I might as well put it on display,' she said.

Pat took the clock and placed it on the mantelpiece, standing back and admiring it. Hannah caught the satisfied smile on her nana's face and smiled back. The clock looked well inside her nana's home, and she was right, it was a bargain. Hannah made a mental note to check out this shop as soon as she got a chance. If it was selling quality goods at bargain prices, then that sounded like too good an opportunity to miss.

Russ stared over at the diminutive man sitting on the opposite side of the desk to him, looking smug as he puffed on his cigar. He felt like wiping the smugness off his face but knew he couldn't. Jez Reilly knew too many people, and if Russ attacked him, it would be like signing his own death warrant. The man obviously thought he had him over a barrel, but Russ wasn't too willing to concede defeat.

'I'm not doing it,' he said. 'It's my livelihood.'

'You can always set up elsewhere.'

'No, I can't. It's hard to find decent rental properties now unless you want to pay an arm and a leg.'

'Then you can take me up on my second offer.'

'Not a fuckin' chance. No way am I doing summat like that!'

'Why not? It's not much different from what you do for me now.'

'Yes, it is. It's way fuckin' different. The people I collect from now are arseholes. They're all alkies and druggies.'

'They're still people,' said Jez calmly. 'Anyway, it wasn't a request. It was an order. You'll do as I say or else suffer the consequences. And you know what that means, don't you?'

Russ squirmed, thinking of the last person who had crossed Jez and ended up in the infirmary for a week thanks to Jez's henchmen. For a moment he considered Jez's proposal, but then decided against it. He couldn't. He wouldn't. He might have operated on the wrong side of the law for the past few years, but he was still a man of principle. And what Jez was asking him to do was a line he wasn't prepared to cross.

By the time Russ left Jez's office, Jez was no longer calm. He let out a barrage of threats to Russ's retreating back, screeching abuse at the top of his voice. Russ kept walking. He'd made his decision, and he was going to stick to it. Why couldn't Jez find somebody else to carry out his dirty work? He had plenty of people to choose from.

But Russ was seriously worried because, despite his refusal, he had no doubt that Jez would follow through on his threat. Maybe it would be best to stay out of his way for a while.

5

Hannah was having a rare night out. She had booked the time off work, and her parents had kindly agreed to have Kai overnight, so she didn't have to rush home. It was her old school friend Taylor's birthday, and Hannah was determined to enjoy herself.

The two girls had started off at Hannah's apartment drinking a bottle of wine before going on to Manchester to meet some of Taylor's other friends. They were a mixed group, mainly people who Taylor worked with. Hannah didn't know any of them well as she rarely got the chance to go out these days.

One of the lads in the group insisted that they all have shots, and Taylor and Hannah were happy to partake. By eleven that night they had visited several bars and Hannah was feeling very drunk. She hadn't yet reached the point where she had lost all sense of reason, but she was certainly starting to lose her inhibitions.

While Taylor was chatting to some of her work colleagues, Hannah slipped away to top up her makeup in the ladies'. On the way she spotted someone she knew. Russ Coles. Despite convincing herself that he was bad news in light of what his ex-girlfriend had told her, Hannah couldn't help but feel a flutter of excitement in her stomach, remembering how he'd fearlessly jumped to her defence a week previously. They exchanged smiles as she passed, and by the time Hannah emerged from the ladies', Russ was alone.

'Hi Hannah, how are you?' he asked. 'How come you're not working tonight?'

'It's my friend's birthday,' she slurred.

'Bloody hell. You're having a great time by the sound of it.'

'Yeah,' she said. 'Brilliant. What about you? How come you're not in the club tonight?'

'Oh, I er, I just fancied a change. I don't always go there. I have to say though, you're a lot friendlier tonight than the last time I saw you in there.'

Hannah felt a stab of conscience. She knew she had been keeping him at a distance since the warning from his ex-girlfriend. Although she had decided to keep it to herself, now that she was intoxicated, she thought differently. If the girl was accusing him of something, then it was only right that he should be given the chance to explain himself.

'Well, I didn't know what I was dealing with, did I?' she teased.

'What do you mean?'

She smiled and said provocatively. 'I heard you were a bad boy.' Then she added, 'And I don't wanna get involved with a bad boy. I don't wanna get involved with anybody.'

'Who told you that?' asked Russ, furrowing his brow.

'Your ex-girlfriend.'

'Huh, Simone?' He laughed but it was a forced laugh. 'She's just bitter because I'm not with her anymore.'

'She's a pretty girl. Why did you two finish?'

'Simone's the jealous type. She was always giving me grief. What did she tell you about me anyway?'

Despite being drunk, Hannah hesitated over her answer. Instinct told her not to mention the connection to Jez. He'd only deny it anyway, and it might not be a good thing to admit she knew her boss was corrupt.

'Oh, she just said you're bent and into all sorts.'

'Ha! That sounds like just the sort of thing she would say. But, talking of bent, you need to watch Jez.'

The mention of her boss's name took her by surprise, considering she had just been thinking about him. 'Jez? Why?' she asked.

'Well, he used to run girls out of the back rooms until the cops got wind of it.'

'You're joking! How do you know that?'

'Let's just say I hear things.'

'Well, how come he didn't get into trouble for it?'

'Rumour has it he's got cops on the payroll. One of them gave him a tip off and he cleared out all the girls before the cops could get to him. God knows where he keeps them now or whether he's even running them anymore.'

Hannah didn't know whether she believed him, but she also noticed how he'd conveniently deflected from the subject of himself, so she asked, 'What sort of things are you into anyway?'

'What do you mean?'

'Well, your ex reckons you're bent and into all sorts, doesn't she?'

Russ tutted. 'I told you, she's jealous and bitter. She's obviously seen how well we get on and feels threatened.'

27

'Why? Should she be?' asked Hannah. She couldn't seem to help herself when it came to flirting with Russ and hadn't realised he'd actually deflected again.

Russ smiled enigmatically and asked, 'What do you think?'

When Hannah failed to respond, Russ gazed at her, their eyes locking for several seconds. She felt weak under his gaze, his rugged features doing things to her. Then he smiled again. This time it was a cheeky grin, which enhanced his average looks into something attractive and intoxicating. It was as though he knew the effect he had on her.

Russ broke their gaze, taking hold of her hand and saying, 'Come on, I'll get you a drink.'

He led her to the bar, and Hannah followed meekly, the feel of his hand giving her a warm glow. Her eyes travelled up his arm, noticing his biceps which were bulging out of his tight-fitting t-shirt. As people stood aside to let them through, she sensed the power of him. He was so manly and vital, and though she hated to admit it to herself, she had always had a thing for macho men.

The night flew by, Hannah becoming increasingly drunk. She remained in the company of Russ, oblivious to everyone around them as they chatted, flirted and revealed details of their lives. At some point later that evening, Taylor came over to tell Hannah she was going home.

'Will you be alright?' she asked.

'Oh yeah, 'course I will. I'm with Russ. He's great.'

Hannah held her glass out drunkenly, as if raising a cheer to Russ.

'Are you sure?' asked Taylor, looking concerned.

Hannah wanted to reassure her friend but somehow the right words wouldn't come out. 'Yeah, yeah, I told you ...'

'It's alright,' Russ cut in. 'I know her from The Gilded Cage. I'm one of her regular customers. I'll make sure she gets home OK.'

Then Taylor was gone, but Hannah was past caring. She was with Russ, the man she had fancied for ages. And everything was wonderful.

Hannah awoke the next morning with a massive headache, a racing heart and a dry mouth. Unaware of where she was at first, she gradually raised her throbbing head from the pillow and assessed the room where she lay. *A hotel room? What the fuck? No, not a hotel room.* There were several items of clothing hanging outside a wardrobe at the end of the bed and the room had a lived-in feel. She turned to find Russ looking back at her wearing a massive grin and nothing else.

'Shit! What the hell? You bastard! You took advantage of me,' she yelled, knowing deep inside that she had promised herself she would never stray from anything other than innocent flirtation with Russ. And now here she was, in bed with him. His bed presumably.

Russ held up a hand in defence. 'Hang on a minute. I didn't take advantage at all. It was you who seduced *me*. Do you not remember what you were like in the taxi? You were practically ripping my clothes off till the taxi driver told you to turn it in or he'd throw us out of the cab. And then when we got back here, you couldn't keep your fuckin' hands off me!'

'Shush, shush. Enough!' said Hannah, covering her thumping head with her hands. 'I don't fuckin' believe you anyway.'

Then a recollection from the previous night hit her, hazy at first but gradually taking shape in her mind, and she flushed with shame. They were in Russ's hallway. She had pounced on him, kissing him ardently while she ran her hands up the inside of his t-shirt, caressing his muscles and practically begging him to take her to bed.

And when he did take her to his bedroom, she was so drunk she had lost her inhibitions, doing all the things with Russ that she had wanted to for ages. And he was good! He'd brought her to multiple orgasms till they both collapsed, exhausted, and fell to sleep.

'I kept asking you if it was OK,' he said.

She didn't reply. She knew he was right.

He broke the silence, that cheeky grin lifting his features again. 'If it's any consolation, we had a great time.'

'Bastard!' she yelled, thumping him playfully but quickly returning her hands to her sore head.

He stepped out of bed, and she couldn't help but admire his toned physique. 'I'll get you a cuppa and some pain killers,' he said. 'You look like shit.'

While Russ was out of the bedroom, Hannah took the opportunity to assess the situation. She was full of regret and remorse, not only because of what Russ's girlfriend had said but also because she'd sworn off men for a while. She had a son, and he was the main focus in her life. And she didn't want any complications to cloud things.

By the time Russ returned, she had rehearsed what she wanted to say. 'Russ, I'm sorry but I made a mistake. This can't go further. I've got a son and …'

He laughed. 'I know, he's your pride and joy, you told me last night about a dozen times.'

'This isn't funny, Russ. I'm trying to be serious here. There can't be a repeat of this. I won't let it happen.'

He flashed that cheeky grin again then held up his hands in supplication. 'Fine, have it your way. If that's what you want. If that's what you think you want. But you and I know that you're only fooling yourself. Anyway, you don't have to worry, I won't be coming in The Gilded Cage anymore, so you won't have to resist me. I'm done with that place.'

6

Hannah had taken Kai to visit her nana again. He loved going to see her as she always made a fuss of him and gave him treats. On this occasion, Hannah found Pat dressed ready to go out.

'Oh, do you want to go straightaway?' asked Hannah, who had arranged with her nana to visit the second-hand shop she had told her about.

'We might as well, so we get the best of the bargains. We can always have a cuppa and a catch up when we get back.'

'Oh, alright,' said Hannah. As the shop was only at the top of the street, they walked to save the hassle of having to park the car. Pat insisted on holding Kai's hand as they made their way up the road, but Hannah didn't mind at all.

'I'll go on ahead, shall I?' said Hannah, eager to find some bargains and knowing it would be easier without Kai.

By the time Hannah reached the shop, Pat and Kai were some distance behind. She knew they would get there at Kai's pace and her nana would relish the time alone with her great-grandson, so Hannah decided to go inside the shop alone and let them catch her up.

As Hannah approached the shop, a car stopped at the edge of the pavement and three men got out. They were young, wearing hoodies and larking about as they carried two boxes into the shop. She hung back, allowing them to enter ahead of her. When she got inside, she noticed that they had gone straight to the counter.

Hannah stopped to admire a tall columnar stand, which had a magnificent display of watches and jewellery behind a glass exterior. She knew she should be concentrating on the household items as she couldn't really afford to buy luxuries but there was no harm in looking. As she checked out the goods, she overheard a conversation taking place at the counter.

'We've got some fuckin' well smart gear here,' came a voice.

'Come on then, let's have a look and I'll tell you what they're worth,' said a second man, presumably the shopkeeper. The voice sounded vaguely familiar, but she wasn't sure where from.

Silence for a moment and then she heard, 'Right, I'll give you twenty for that and thirty for that one. Show us what else you've got.'

'Hang on a minute. They're worth miles more than that. You should have seen the fuckin' house they come from.'

She heard someone say 'Shush,' loudly and assumed they must be dealing in stolen goods. Hannah was in a bit of a predicament. If she came out from behind the stand now, they would know she had overheard the conversation. So, she stayed where she was and waited. The conversation that took place made her even more certain that the shopkeeper was dealing in stolen items. Hannah therefore made sure she wasn't seen by the men when they left the shop.

As the men walked out, Pat and Kai walked in. Hannah

met them at the door so the shopkeeper would think she'd only just entered. She would have preferred to have left, given what she had overheard, but Kai was overexcited by a toy he had spotted in the window. Pat was determined to treat him to it, and it was his birthday soon, so Hannah had no choice but to go with them to pay for it.

She had almost reached the counter when she couldn't help but notice the shopkeeper, who was standing with a wide grin on his face ready to greet them. The smile died on his lips when he noticed her. It was Russ Cole. *Jesus!* Hannah thought. *He gets everywhere.*

For a moment she was taken aback, her heart hammering inside her rib cage, not only because she'd slept with him but because she now realised that his ex-girlfriend had been right. He was corrupt. She had no doubt he was dealing in stolen goods and dreaded to think what else he might be involved in. And she had willingly slept with him when she had been pissed. The thought made her feel sick.

'Hi, Hannah. Fancy seeing you here,' he said casually.

There was no turning back now. She had no choice but to put on an act. 'Hi, Russ. I had no idea this was your shop.'

'Yeah, been here for a while now.'

At that point, the conversation stalled, but Pat butted in. 'Ooh, fancy you two knowing each other.'

She flashed her eyes at Hannah, who quickly quelled any suggestions of anything more than friendship. 'He's one of my regular customers at the club.'

'Yeah, that's right,' Russ agreed.

Pat nodded. 'Oh, I see. Well, he's a very nice young man and he sells some lovely goods.'

'Ooh, flattery will get you everywhere,' joked Russ.

He received a smile and a friendly tap on the hand from Pat. 'He's cheeky as well,' she said.

'Only with my special customers,' he added.

'Will you two give it a rest?' said Hannah, who was becoming exasperated.

She didn't like Russ being overfamiliar with her nana, especially considering what she had just learnt about him.

Russ shrugged. 'No worries. I'm only teasing. Pat's one of my best customers. How do you two know each other anyway?'

'Ooh, Hannah's my granddaughter,' said Pat proudly. 'And don't worry, I don't mind a bit of teasing, especially at my age. I'll take all I can get.'

She giggled then threw Hannah a sideways glance as if she wasn't happy at her spoiling her fun.

When they were outside, Pat whispered to Hannah so that Kai couldn't hear. 'What the bloody hell was wrong with you? Russ is a nice lad. Eh, you could do a lot worse than him,' she added suggestively.

'You don't know him, Nana,' Hannah bit back.

'Why? What's he done?'

Hannah didn't like to go into too many details, fearing the conversation might lead to the night she had spent with Russ, so she said, 'There's just rumours about him in the club, that's all.'

'What kind of rumours?'

'Oh, just that he's a bad un and involved in crime.'

'I can't see that myself. What kind of crime?'

'I don't know. I'm just repeating what I've heard, that's all,' Hannah snapped, putting an end to the conversation.

★

When they got back inside Pat's house, Hannah noticed how Pat's eyes were drawn to a letter on the mantelpiece.

'Oh, I keep meaning to mention that to you,' said Pat. 'I've had it a few weeks. It's from a developer. They've offered to buy the house. Apparently, they want to redevelop the land for commercial use.'

Pat often kept letters on the mantelpiece, stood up behind the clock, so Hannah hadn't noticed that one in particular. 'How much for?' she asked. 'And what is this "commercial use"?'

'A hundred and fifty thousand. I don't know what they're going to build. The letter didn't say, it just said "commercial use".'

'It's not a bad offer,' said Hannah.

'Well, Maureen from number four reckons she'll get even more out of them. Apparently, her son says it's in a good location because it's near the canal where they've done the redevelopment and built all those new expensive apartments. Prices are high these days, and she said that if they wanted the land badly enough, she could probably get them to pay another ten or even twenty thousand. She's seriously thinking about it.'

'What about you?'

'No, I'm happy where I am.'

'Not even if they offered you another ten or twenty thousand, and all your friends moved out?'

'No, a lot of them won't move. They like it here as much as I do. Don't forget, I've lived here over fifty years, and I've got to know a lot of people. It's a happy street. Everyone looks out for each other.'

'I know, but if the builders keep improving their offers, your friends might be persuaded. And the street won't be the same once they've all moved out.'

'Well, they won't bloody persuade me, not over my dead body. The only time I'll be moving out of here will be when they carry me out in a wooden box.'

7

Russ hadn't been in The Gilded Cage since Jez had threatened him for refusing to carry out his orders, and he was doing his best to lie low. He should also have kept away from the shop on Rovener Street since Jez had demanded that he vacate the premises. But the stubborn side of Russ refused to be forced out of the place he loved so much.

He'd worked hard to build it up, and it was now known in the area as somewhere to offload hot goods as well as a place to buy cheap quality items. He knew running the shop was risky, but if the police should call, he would simply tell them that he had no idea where the goods had come from when people came into the shop offering to sell them to him.

The other risk was that he might have a visit from Jez's men. But Russ had been cautious of anything suspicious. He had a camera mounted outside the shop and a screen on the counter where he could monitor things. If he saw anyone dodgy, he'd quickly lock up, drop the shutters and escape through the back door.

But this day he'd dropped his guard. It wasn't far off closing time, and one of his customers was admiring a necklace in the display cabinet. When she asked him if she could try it on, he came over, his attention half on the customer and half on the outside of the shop. Once she'd tried the necklace on, she asked to look at another. But as she tried to undo the necklace it became entangled in the back of her hair. Russ could see she was struggling to free it.

'Here, let me help,' he said.

His focus was now fully on the necklace as he tried to extract it from the woman's hair. The action felt quite intimate, and for a moment, he imagined himself back with Hannah, running his hands through her hair as they kissed passionately. But this woman wasn't Hannah, and he quickly brought his attention back to the matter in hand.

As soon as the necklace was freed, he remembered that he'd taken his attention off the street outside. His head swung round but he was too late. By the time he caught sight of three men wielding baseball bats, they were already inside the shop.

Hannah was having some alone time. She had dropped Kai off with her parents and was watching a bit of TV before making herself something to eat and getting ready for work. But she couldn't focus on what was happening on the screen because her mind was on Russ.

She hadn't seen him since she had called in at his shop a week before, and true to his word he hadn't been inside The Gilded Cage. Nights there had become less interesting since Russ had stopped going in. She had got used to him sitting at the bar watching her, and she especially missed the flirtation and banter.

But, in a way, it was a good thing. She had dreaded facing him after the one-night stand. The encounter in his shop had been bad enough, but at least it was soon over. If he was still sitting at the bar in The Gilded Cage, she would find it difficult to work, knowing he was watching her, his eyes filled with desire once again.

That wasn't the only reason it would have been difficult. After that night, Hannah had wanted more, and it would have been hard to resist. She wished he hadn't turned out to be crooked. Otherwise, she could have seen herself falling for him despite having sworn off men.

But then she wondered why he hadn't been in the club. When he had mentioned his intention not to visit anymore, she had been so consumed with feelings of guilt over her night of passion that she hadn't taken it in. She'd just thought it was a casual comment, perhaps meant to let her think that he was no longer interested. But she'd fully expected that it was only a matter of time before he turned up there, knowing as well as she did that the attraction between them was too strong to resist.

She remembered that night so clearly, and as thoughts of it went over inside her head, she couldn't help but feel aroused. His flat was in Rusholme and would only take about ten minutes to reach by car. She looked at the clock, wondering whether she'd have time to get there and back before she got ready for work.

Her intention was not to go inside the flat or even to knock at the door. At least, that's what she told herself. She was just curious about him and wanted to get another glimpse of the man that had seduced her. The first man to penetrate the steely barrier she had built round herself since Kai's father had left.

It wasn't long before she was dashing up the road where Russ lived. She couldn't remember the number, but she did remember that it was above a hairdresser's. She passed the hairdresser's, then turned back and parked the car on the opposite side of the street. And watched.

Hannah thought about how sad she must appear to anyone who spotted what she was doing as she sat inside the car hoping to catch a glimpse of him. Her eyes travelled from the hairdresser's up to the window of Russ's flat. The curtains were open wide, and yet there was no light inside, even though it was now getting dark. Hannah waited for a few minutes, hoping he might come to draw the curtains. And then she'd see him.

Hannah jumped when a knock on the passenger side window caught her attention. She looked round to see an elderly man peering through the window. He was saying something, but she couldn't pick out his words, so she wound the window down slightly.

'Do you mind if I ask what you're doing?' he said. 'Only, I'm a member of the local neighbourhood watch, and if you don't mind me saying so, you're looking very suspicious. I notice you've been watching that flat for a few minutes.'

Hannah panicked. 'Oh, I, er … I'm a friend of Russ's. I was just checking whether he was in. I thought I might pay him a visit.'

She was thinking about how she'd have to knock on Russ's flat to make her words sound convincing and was deciding what she might say when he opened the door. But then the man's words took her by surprise.

'You'll have a job. He left two days ago. Melissa from the hairdresser's saw him getting into his car. When she tried to chat to him, he said he was in a rush and had to leave the flat, or something. He didn't say anything more, not even goodbye but she said he did seem panicked. And nobody's seen him since.'

Russ dropped the necklace in shock as soon as he saw the men. He knew from the masks they wore that they meant business.

'Do yourself a favour and fuck off,' one of them ordered the customer, his voice muffled under the mask.

The woman didn't hesitate. She was straight out of the door. The man followed her, bolting the door and pulling down the blinds. The other two didn't wait for him to return before setting about Russ. He tried to put up a defence, diving at the smaller of the two men and grabbing at the baseball bat. But it was no use. As he grappled with him, the other man attacked from behind, bludgeoning his head and back.

Russ could feel the dull aching thud of the bat again and again. But he fought on desperately. The smaller man refused to give up his weapon, dragging it from Russ while booting his shins. Then the third man joined in. A shroud of pain enveloped Russ who was still trying to prise the bat away. If only he could get it off the man! Then he might be in with a chance.

But his rival held on tight. While he fought with Russ for the bat, one of the others hacked at Russ's hands till he drew them away, the pain unbearable. Then his instincts kicked in. He raised his hands again to protect his head despite the throbbing of his fingers. But it wasn't enough. A blow to the back of his skull stunned him and he fell to the ground.

'Enough!' ordered the man who had locked the door and seemed to be the leader. 'Right,' he continued, giving orders to the other two. 'Stuff as much of that jewellery as you can inside your pockets. But don't go to the car yet. I want that fuckin' door to stay locked.'

Russ still lay on the ground, his face beginning to colour and blood seeping from his nose and mouth. As he tried to regain his senses, he spat out a tooth and licked at the metallic-tasting residue that coated his lips.

'We've got a message from Jez,' said the man as the other two ransacked the shop. 'He wants you out. After today, the fuckin' boards are going up, and you won't be coming in this shop no more.'

Russ didn't argue. There was no point. He had already lost. He'd tried in vain to keep hold of the shop, but it was impossible. Even if he managed to prevent them boarding it up and carried on trading tomorrow, the men would be back. Besides, with the way he felt at present, he doubted he would be up to running the shop for some time.

But the man wasn't finished yet. 'Jez still wants you to do that other work for him. He needs someone to put the frighteners on a few people, and we're not gonna be around for much longer, so that leaves you. In fact, you haven't got a fuckin' choice. He'll give you a week to go and see him. If you haven't been by then, we'll be back. So, do yourself a favour and keep him sweet.'

They left the shop as quickly as they'd entered. The whole thing had lasted only a few minutes. Russ guessed they wanted to escape before anyone alerted the police. He struggled to his feet, his head pounding and every part of his body tender.

As he stood there unsteadily, Russ surveyed the damage both to himself and to his precious shop. His hands were already starting to bruise, and from the pain he felt, he guessed that the rest of him would look just as bad. He glanced around the shop in despair. It was a mess. They'd smashed a couple of the display cases in their eagerness to get to the most valuable goods, and many unwanted items were left strewn about the place.

Why? Why was Jez doing this to him? Why did he want him out of the shop so desperately? Then it came to him in a moment of clarity. It was connected to the job Jez had wanted him to do, intimidating residents out of their homes because he wanted the land for development. It hadn't occurred to Russ at the time that Jez was referring to the same land where his shop was situated: Rovener Street.

But Russ had other things to think about at the moment. He was still unsteady on his feet. The beating had been brutal, and he knew he needed medical attention. He grasped at the phone tucked inside his pocket, his swollen fingers struggling to press the keys, and called 999. Chances were the police would arrive as well as an ambulance. But he would tell them nothing. He just wanted his broken bones mended and his wounds stitched. There was no way he would report Jez's involvement in this. It was too risky.

Despite his fear of repercussions, Russ knew he wouldn't be visiting Jez within the next week either. He wasn't prepared to do the other thing Jez was asking of him. So, he had no choice but to make himself scarce once he'd visited the hospital. And he prayed that Jez and his men would never find him.

8

Hannah was sitting inside her parents' home. She had just called to pick up Kai and was enjoying a cuppa and a chat before leaving them.

'Have you spoken to your nana recently?' asked Jill.

'Not for about a week. Why?'

'Well, you know about them developers offering her money for her house, don't you?'

'Yes, and she's adamant she's not moving.'

'That's right. But she's received an increased offer now. An extra ten thousand.'

'She's not changed her mind about selling, has she?'

'No, she's still adamant. She says it makes no odds to her at her time of life. She's happy where she is so why have all the hassle of moving?'

'It's a good offer,' said Pete, joining in the conversation. 'And if all her friends are leaving the street, there might not be much to stay for. She could go into a retirement apartment. It'd be a lot less work for her, and she'd meet lots of new people her own age.'

'But she's happy where she is,' said Hannah.

Pete shrugged, but her mother said, 'Yeah, you're right.

But listen to this: all the other residents have received increased offers as well, and all three shops have shut.'

Hannah was startled to hear this, especially after recently discovering that Russ had vacated his flat. 'What do you mean shut?'

'They're no longer trading,' said Pete. 'The shutters are up.'

'Really?' asked Hannah, not letting on about her connection to Russ.

'Yeah, it's gonna be like a ghost town on that street.'

'It's all very strange. It sounds as if they want the whole street. But how did they manage to get the three shop owners to sell up?'

'The shopkeepers didn't own the shops,' said Jill. 'They only rented them, and from what your nana says, the same company owns all three.'

'Ah right. Is that the same company that are trying to buy up all the houses?'

'We think so, but nobody actually knows.'

Thoughts of Russ were going over in Hannah's mind now. It struck her as strange that not only had he stopped going inside The Gilded Cage, but he'd also left his home and business. It was as though he wanted to get away, which made her suspect even more that he was involved in something illegal. She regretted now that she hadn't thought to ask him why he'd decided not to go in The Gilded Cage anymore.

'Are you alright, love?' asked Jill.

'What? Oh yeah, sure,' said Hannah. 'I'm just thinking about why the developers would want everyone out of the houses and shops.'

'Don't know,' said Jill. 'But it's worrying. If they're so keen to get rid of everyone, then Mum might have a job hanging on to her house.'

Hannah's brow furrowed. 'Yeah, you're right. I hope she'll be OK.'

It was apparent to her that this was about more than just Russ because he presumably had no connection to the other two shops. The shopkeepers of those two had been there for years. So why would they suddenly up sticks, unless the firm that was hoping to buy all the houses also wanted the shops? If the shopkeepers were only renting, then it would be easier to shift them than it would the houseowners, which was probably why they had gone first. And like her mum had said, these developers seemed pretty determined, so all of this would adversely affect her nana as well as the other residents.

Hannah couldn't help but wonder where all this left Russ though. How did he make his living now that he didn't have the shop? And if he was hiding out, then why? And where the hell had he got to?

Hannah was behind the bar of The Gilded Cage when she overheard Russ's name. The mention of the man she had feelings for drew her attention, and she tried to listen to what was being said. But the club was packed, and the discussion was taking place somewhere in the crowd.

She couldn't just stop what she was doing. There were too many customers waiting to be served. But she did pick out the words 'been arrested'. She returned from the optics at the back of the bar to find that the conversation had changed. She didn't even know who had mentioned Russ's arrest, but that was definitely what she had heard.

No wonder he hadn't been in the club. He was obviously otherwise occupied and, although she missed Russ, the revelation cemented her resolve not to get involved with him.

Hannah was glad to be going home when her shift finished. It had been a long night at work. She'd been so busy that she'd hardly had time for a break, and her feet were aching. As she made her way to the staff entrance, she said goodbye to two of her colleagues then approached the door. One of the doormen swung it open and she glanced outside.

Then she remembered something. One of the girls had brought some makeup into work for her. She worked as a part-time sales rep and sold her goods to the other bar staff. Hannah had left it in a carrier bag in the club. She could risk waiting till she was next in work, but it might disappear. There was no telling who might visit the place before she was back on shift. *Damn!* She'd have to go back for it.

'Be back in a minute,' she said to the doormen, then she turned and made her way to the makeshift staffroom where the staff kept all their personal items.

To get to the staffroom, she had to pass Jez's office. She could hear him on the phone. The door was ajar, and as she approached, she could hear some of what he was saying.

'I didn't think you'd be up at this fuckin' time.' A pause. Then, 'Rovener Street? Yeah, all in order. Don't worry about it.'

Hannah was shocked. Rovener Street! That was where

her nana lived and where Russ had had his shop. Why would her boss be talking to someone about it?

Jez must have heard the sound of her heels on the laminated corridor because he then said, 'Hang on a minute.'

By the time she had reached his office, Jez had hold of the door. He swung it wide open and said, 'Yes? What do you want?'

His tone was irate, which surprised Hannah as she'd never seen that side of him. She guessed that whatever he had been about to discuss was something he didn't want her to overhear. Instinct told her not to refer to his telephone conversation. She'd keep it to herself for now.

'Oh, nothing much,' she said in as casual a tone as she could muster. 'I left a bag behind, and I need the stuff that's in it.'

'Go on, get it, and hurry up!' he snapped. 'It's about time you were on your way home.'

Hannah was perturbed by his angry manner, but she didn't want to challenge him. That wouldn't be a wise move. There was no-one about and it was late. Recalling now what Russ had said about Jez previously running girls from a back room at the club, she suddenly decided she didn't want to be here alone at this hour. So, she would exercise caution and act as though nothing was amiss. She dashed to the staffroom, grabbed her bag and was soon on her way.

But what Hannah had witnessed tonight had left her curious. The way Jez was acting told her that he had something to hide. And whatever it was, it was somehow connected to Rovener Street.

9

Russ had been avoiding Jez for the past few weeks. As the men had ordered, he had left his shop straightaway, arranging for a trustworthy friend, Chris, to gather the remaining goods and put them into storage for him. He hoped that one day he might be able to set up trading again elsewhere.

It had taken a while to recover from his injuries. He had suffered from cracked ribs and concussion, as well as severe bruising to his torso and minor cuts on his face and arms. In fact, he still had the odd twinge from his ribs, but at least the pain was subsiding.

Not only had he not set foot in Rovener Street since that day, but he'd also kept away from The Gilded Cage. Jez had a reputation, and Russ didn't feel safe about him knowing where he was. He'd already moved out of his flat before he was forced to vacate the shop. Fortunately, it was rented rather than owned, and Chris had fixed him up with somewhere else to live.

The problem for Russ was that Jez wanted something from him, even if it was only his services as hired muscle to intimidate innocent people. And although Jez could easily find someone else to do his dirty work, the fact that Russ had refused would rankle him. Knowing the sort of man Jez was, Russ doubted whether he would let it rest, especially as Russ knew so much about what he got up to. That would have been fine if Russ had still been working for him, but not once he had become an adversary.

With Jez out of his life, things weren't too bad for Russ, apart from the situation with his old man and the fact that he missed Hannah. He liked her a lot more than he'd let on, especially after seeing her in his shop with her child and her grandma. It was obvious how well thought of she was by her family. And even though Hannah had given him the brush off, he was finding it hard to forget about her.

And as for his old man, Russ's namesake, he'd been arrested for a warehouse robbery. It had upset Russ a bit, but he'd tried not to focus on it. His dad had always been on the wrong side of the law, but where Russ drew the line at certain activities, his dad had no moral compass. That was why he no longer saw much of him.

Aside from all that, Russ was thinking about his future now his injuries were mending. He had been checking out other shops away from the city centre where he could sell his goods. It would take a while to build up his suppliers again, but he had no doubt that it could be done.

He was also focusing on his social life. Chris had introduced him to his local pub, The Bush, which was a few miles from both the nightclub and Rovener Street, so Russ felt safe to go there for a few pints.

Tonight, both Russ and Chris were in The Bush enjoying a drink. Chris was a good mate. They went back some years and had mixed in the same circles. Like Russ, Chris hadn't always stayed on the right side of the law, but he'd done alright and had a business supplying fruit machines to pubs and clubs. He had the sort of good looks that drew women in, but that didn't bother Russ. He was confident of his own charms, and besides, there was only one woman he was interested in.

While Chris was away chatting to a girl he knew, Russ saw a familiar face. He couldn't place him at first but knew he'd seen him around somewhere. It might have been in the club or in his shop, which meant he could be connected to Jez. Russ was therefore wary of letting the man see him. He stood out of view while he tried to recall where he had met him. Then it came to Russ. He had been one of his customers at the Rovener Street shop.

Russ felt a sense of panic as the man walked towards him. There was nowhere Russ could go without being seen. For a moment Russ debated whether to make a run for it, but then he noticed the state of the man and curiosity got the better of him. He couldn't help but stare at his swollen and bruised face then their eyes met, and Russ received a smile of acknowledgement. Deciding that at least he was being friendly, Russ stayed where he was.

'Hello, Russ. How are you?' he asked.

'I'm not too bad. Sorry, I can't remember your name.'

'No worries, mate. You probably had a lot of customers at the shop. It's Roger.'

'Oh, hi Roger. How are you? You don't look too clever.'

Russ noticed a twitch in Roger's eyes. 'Yeah, I er … I was jumped.'

'Jumped? Who by?'

'Dunno?'

'What were they after?'

'Dunno.'

'Did you catch sight of any of them?'

'No. They were wearing masks, both of them.'

Russ had picked up on the fact that Roger was being evasive, and it made him question why. He decided to push for more information. 'Shit! That sounds bad. Where did it happen?'

'Just near where I live. It's getting bad there now.'

'Why's that?'

'Well, I'm not the only one that's been attacked. And then there's the shops. They're all boarded up now. What happened anyway? Why did you move out of the shop? It seemed strange as the other two closed around the same time.'

'Really?' asked Russ. *Jesus!* he thought. Jez obviously meant business, which was even more reason why he didn't want him to know where he was. And if Roger gave away Russ's whereabouts, he'd be in deep shit. For a moment he was lost in his thoughts. Roger must have picked up on his obvious worry because he continued to question him.

'Am I to take it that you didn't want to leave the shop?'

Russ hesitated before responding, 'Well, let's just say I was persuaded. But I'd prefer it if you didn't let on that you'd seen me here. The people who forced me out of the shop are not very friendly and I'd like to keep a low profile.'

A look of recognition crossed Roger's face. 'I think you and me have been done over by the same people, mate.'

'What do you mean?'

Roger sighed. 'I do know what my attackers were after. I just didn't know if I could trust you, that's all. But it sounds like me and you are in the same boat.' He sighed again before adding, 'They're trying to force me to sell my house to them, but I've told them no. I'm beginning to think I should though. The bastards could set about my wife and kid next. She's had to go to her parents while I'm out so she won't be in the house without me.'

'Shit!' said Russ. 'I'm sorry to hear that, mate. It sounds like they're keen to get you out. But I wonder why?' He didn't let on to the man that he knew Jez was behind his own attack and therefore probably forced the other two shops to close too.

Roger lowered his voice. 'It looks like these men are connected with the firm that offered to buy our houses. A lot of the residents caved in when they received an increased offer, but we chose to stay because my daughter's happy at the local school. There are only a handful of us that haven't accepted the offer, and now it looks as though they're gonna intimidate us till they get us out. Oh, and don't worry mate, there's no way I'll let those bastards know where you hang out.'

Russ was relieved that he could rely on Roger to keep his whereabouts a secret, but at the same time, he was stunned. He hadn't realised things had got so bad. When Jez had asked Russ to get involved with intimidation, he hadn't known at first that it related to Rovener Street. But now it was all slotting into place. If Jez had forced him out of his shop and presumably the other two shopkeepers, then he was probably behind the firm that was pressuring people to sell their homes too.

And the work that Jez had wanted Russ to do involved applying pressure to people who were standing in his way. Those people must have been the residents of Rovener

Street. Russ was glad he had turned it down and risked the consequences. There was no way he would want to be part of anything like that.

'What's the name of the firm buying the houses?' he asked.

'Pake Holdings Ltd.'

Russ tightened his lips and shook his head. He wasn't familiar with the name at all and particularly not in connection with Jez. But then something else occurred to him.

'Which residents are left?'

Roger reeled off a list of names and Russ was disconcerted to hear that Pat Bennett was among them. Hannah's grandmother. *Shit!* That meant she was also under threat from Jez's heavies.

10

As Hannah drove into Rovener Street on her way to see her nana with Kai, she was surprised to see how many houses were boarded up. A few months had elapsed since her nana had told her about the offer from the property developers, and Hannah knew from her parents that some residents had taken them up on their generous offers, but she hadn't realised just how many.

She arrived at Pat's house, and it took her grandmother a while to answer the door. When she did finally open it, Hannah was surprised at the state of her. She looked to Hannah as though she had aged ten years in the past couple of months, and Hannah wondered whether it was because the street had changed so much. After all, Pat had lived in the street a long time and changes like this were unsettling for someone of her age.

Kai was bouncing up and down excitedly, presumably expecting the treat he usually got whenever they visited Pat. But there was nothing.

'Go and play with the train set I've put in the living room, that's a good boy,' said Pat, but her tone was lacklustre.

Kai raced ahead of them and as they walked slowly

behind him, Hannah said, 'What's wrong, Nana? You don't seem yourself.'

'Oh, it's all this carry-on with the developers. I've just been talking to that family at number seven, and you wouldn't believe what they've told me.'

Hannah could see now that the lines on Pat's face weren't just down to old age: they were worry lines. Her nana had lost her usual vitality and instead she seemed troubled.

'What is it?' she asked, concerned.

Pat shook her head from side to side and tutted while inhaling sharply. 'Let me get us a cuppa and I'll tell you all about it. But we'll have to be quiet, so Kai doesn't hear us. I don't want to be upsetting him.'

Hannah was shocked at what Pat had to say. 'There's only a few of us staying. Most of them have taken the developers up on their offers. And of the ones that haven't, well, according to that family at number seven, two of them have been attacked.'

'Attacked? Why?'

'Because they won't sell.'

'You're joking! How do your neighbours know the developers are behind the attacks?'

'Because the attackers said as much. They threatened them worse was to come if they didn't agree to the developers' offer.'

'Well, haven't they reported it to the police? Surely, they could do something about it.'

'One of them was too frightened to, but the other did. The police told him there was nothing they could do, though. The buggers wore masks so the victim couldn't identify them. And, of course, the developers would just deny that it was connected to them. There's no proof, is there?'

'God, Nana, I'm so sorry. Do you still see your friends?'

'Not as much, although we still make the effort to go out for regular meals. It's not as easy when you don't live in the same street anymore though, is it? I used to see them nearly every day.'

Hannah thought her nana's eyes had misted over at that point, but she hid it well, turning away and plumping up cushions. Hannah didn't know what else to say to her. What could she say to make things better? This entire situation was getting out of hand. She thought about everything that had happened recently, trying to piece together what exactly was going on:

The eagerness of the developers to buy up all the houses on the street. Her suspicions that Russ was criminally connected to Jez, according to what his ex-girlfriend had said. Discovering that Russ was dealing in stolen goods from his shop. Russ's disappearance and the fact that all three shops were now empty. Russ's arrest and the conversation she had overheard when Jez had mentioned Rovener Street.

And now she had found out that people were being attacked for not selling up. She was convinced that Jez was involved in this scheme to buy all the properties, and maybe Russ too. But how did she prove it?

Then she thought of something else. 'Nana, what did you say was the name of that company that offered to buy the house from you?'

'Pake Holdings Ltd. Why?'

'Aw, nothing. I just thought I might see if I can find out anything about them.'

'Eh, you be careful. These are dangerous people from what I can make out. I don't want you to go upsetting anyone.'

Hannah could hear a tremble in her voice and see the fear in her eyes. 'Don't worry, Nana,' she reassured her. 'I will be.'

After visiting her grandmother, Hannah dropped Kai with her mum and stepdad as she was working that night. Before she went to work, she had a chance to do a bit of research. She entered the company name 'Pake Holdings Ltd' into the Companies House website to see what she could find out.

It didn't take long to find details of the company directors. They were listed as Samuel Sweeney and Thomas Markham. After what Russ's ex had told her about Jez being bent and then overhearing him mention Rovener Street on the phone, she had suspected that he might be behind the company. But just because he wasn't a director, that didn't mean he wasn't still involved in some way. With Russ, on the other hand, she hadn't really expected to find his name because he struck her as being employed by Jez rather than being the main man.

Maybe she had been mistaken. Perhaps Jez wasn't involved at all, and his mention of Rovener Street had nothing to do with all this. Or maybe he was involved, and he was very good at covering his tracks.

II

That night as she drove to work, Hannah was still preoccupied. In fact, she had been so busy finding out as much as she could about Pake Holdings that she was running late. Unfortunately, her search hadn't come up with much. The company had been set up in the last few months, and at this point, there wasn't even a website. The nature of business was listed on the Companies House website as 'Development of Building Projects', and the registered office address was somewhere in Warrington. In addition, she knew the names of the two directors, and that was it.

She parked her car in the usual street, which was essentially more of an alleyway that led to the back entrance of The Gilded Cage. As she walked at a brisk pace, she continued to go over everything in her head. Hannah wished there was some way she could help her grandmother. But she couldn't think of anything. She could hardly confront Jez; she didn't even know for certain whether he was behind what was happening.

A part of her wanted to jack her job in. She no longer felt comfortable working for a man like Jez. But what if she was wrong about him? Then she would have jacked in her job for no reason. And, at the moment, she needed the money.

Hannah was so deep in thought that she wasn't aware of what was going on around her. She was passing a doorway two buildings down from the nightclub when a man's hand reached out and grabbed her, pulling her towards him. Hannah tried to scream but he had covered her mouth, his other arm fixed firmly around her waist and pinning her to his body.

Jez had the plans for Rovener Street and the surrounding areas laid out on the desk in front of him again. As he studied them once more, he automatically rubbed his hands together. There was no doubt that Rovener Street was in a prime location close to a thriving town centre with a busy shopping precinct. It was crying out for new upmarket restaurants and bars. He couldn't wait to get started with the development, knowing he'd make a killing, and hospitality businesses would be lining up to be part of it.

He was imagining the types of restaurants and businesses that might get in touch when his phone rang. Jez was a bit irritated when he grabbed it out of his pocket. The bloody thing never stopped these days, and its tinny ring tone had broken him out of his reverie. But then, he supposed the numerous phone calls were only to be expected. It was a busy time and there was a lot to sort out.

'Yes!' he barked into his mobile.

For a moment he listened to what the caller had to say, before responding, 'Right, well we need to push harder.' He paused while the other person spoke, before adding, 'Yeah, I know the old woman's an easy target but leave her for now. Don't worry, once she sees what we've got lined up for some of the others, she'll easily cave. It's the more stubborn ones we need to concern ourselves with.'

He listened again before saying, 'No, leave it for now. Don't worry, we'll get to them all eventually. But, before that, I've got something more urgent that needs attending to.'

He paused before conveying his latest instructions. 'Russ Cole. I need you to find him, and when you do, I want you to bring him in. The bastard knows too much. Since we've been targeting the residents, he's bound to connect that with the job I wanted him to do for me, especially as I persuaded him to leave the shop as well.'

There was a sarcastic edge to his voice as he said the word, *persuaded*. When his employee asked for more details, Jez said, 'I can't afford to let him go free. The bastard's already proved awkward and refused to do any more work for me, so there's no telling what he might do, especially when we escalate things. Come back to me and let me know when you've found him.'

He allowed his employee to speak again before responding once more. 'OK, make sure you do. I want him gone and then we'll start stepping things up with the residents. Rovener Street won't know what's fuckin' hit it.'

It had been a frantic night for Russ. He'd started by having a couple of pints early doors, hoping they'd calm him down a bit. His head was frazzled with troubled thoughts that had been plaguing him for days. Ever since he'd seen

Roger, he'd been riddled with guilt. He'd wanted to warn Hannah about the danger Pat was in, but after the hiding he'd had from Jez's men, he'd been too worried.

Then he'd seen Roger again and that had made his mind up for him. Roger had told him that he'd reported the attack to the police and told them Pake Holdings were behind it, but the police had said they couldn't prove it. Subsequent to that, a second resident had been attacked, and it had left him so shaken that he refused to go to the police. If people were being attacked, then there was no way his conscience would let him leave it without at least warning Hannah about what was going on.

Unfortunately, before he had got chance to leave The Bush, Chris had called in for a pint. 'Oh, hi, mate, I was just off,' said Russ, swilling the few remaining drops of beer around in his glass.'

'Aw, stay for one, at least.'

'Sorry, mate, I can't. I've got to go somewhere.'

Chris had grimaced. 'What can be so important that you can't have a pint with an old mate?'

Russ hadn't wanted to tell him. He might have been an old mate, but Russ wasn't taking any chances. The less people knew what he was up to, the better as far as he was concerned.

'OK, I'll stay for one,' he'd agreed.

Chris had been chatty tonight, but Russ was in a rush. He finished his pint in record time then told Chris he was going to get another round in. As soon as he was out of view, he had given him the slip. This was too important to leave. He'd think up an excuse to give Chris next time he saw him.

*

Hannah felt the first signs of panic as she fought to break free. Her pulse was beating rapidly, and a tremor of fear rose from her gut to her throat, constricting the airflow till she was struggling for breath.

The man spoke. 'Calm the fuck down, will you? It's me. Right, I'm gonna take my hand away. But don't say a fuckin' word or we'll both be in the shit.'

She recognised the voice. 'Russ! What the hell?'

'Shush,' he whispered. 'If anyone finds out I'm here, I'm a dead man.'

She looked at him, confused, then lowered her voice. 'What the hell is going on, Russ?' she hissed. 'Why are you fuckin' attacking me and where the hell have you been all this time?

'Shush,' he repeated. 'Sorry, I didn't mean to scare you. But it was the only way I could get your attention without anyone knowing I was here.'

'How about you just go inside the club and speak to me while I'm there like any normal person would?'

'Because I can't be fuckin' seen, that's why. I've been keeping a low profile, staying with a friend, but please don't tell anyone. I can't risk being found.'

She threw him a curious glance, her eyebrows knitted together. Hannah was becoming irritated now. She was in no mood for a game of cat and mouse. 'Look, what's this about, Russ?' she said. 'I'm already late for work as it is.'

'OK, if you've got to go then let's arrange a meet-up, but whatever you do, don't fuckin' tell anyone. I've got to talk to you.'

'Why? Why would I want to meet you?' she asked.

She was about to list all the reasons why she'd prefer to never set eyes on him again including her discovery that he sold stolen goods and the rumours of his arrest. But he cut in before she had chance.

'Because it's fuckin' important!' he said, and she could hear the desperation in his voice. 'Your grandma is in danger. So am I. Jez is behind it all so, whatever you do, please don't tell anyone I was here.'

She could see the fear in his pleading eyes now as he stared at her while slipping something into her hand. Hannah opened her palm and gazed at the piece of paper he had placed there.

'It's my phone number,' he said. 'Don't give it to anyone. Call me. I'll explain.'

Then he slipped away.

12

Late morning, Hannah went to collect Kai from her parents' house. She was surprised and pleased to find her nana there too.

'Hi, Nana,' said Hannah, going over to her and planting a kiss on her cheek. 'Ooh, you smell lovely,' she added, pulling away.

'It's my best perfume,' Pat replied, smiling.

Hannah noticed that she was also smartly dressed in a pair of formal trousers and a bright flowery top with a Bardot neckline. It was a bit of a bold choice for someone in her early seventies, but with her youthful looks and slim figure, her nana pulled it off.

'You *look* lovely too,' Hannah commented, before turning to her parents, who were also dressed smartly although a bit less flamboyant than Pat. 'You two are all dressed up as well. What's happening?'

'We're taking your nana to lunch. We thought it might cheer her up.'

'Why, what's happened?' asked Hannah, heedful of Russ's words last night.

'Oh, nothing in particular. Just the carry-on with these developers.'

Hannah got the impression her mother didn't want to go into any more detail, perhaps to spare Pat's feelings. At that moment, she picked up on her nana's body language. Despite the forced smile, smart clothing and makeup, she could tell that Pat was on edge, so she decided not to press the matter but hoped nothing further had happened in relation to Rovener Street.

'We're going away too,' Jill added. 'It's one of those over fifties' holidays. Mum's been at us for a while to try one, so even though I'm not quite there yet, we'd thought we'd give it a whirl since Pete's had his big birthday.'

'Yeah, I might grab myself a toy boy while I'm there,' Pat chipped in, and Hannah caught a glimpse of her playful side, which had been lacking recently.

'We booked it at the last minute,' Jill continued. 'We go in a week's time.'

'A week? Bloody hell! That *is* last minute.'

'I know. It's not a problem, is it? Will you be alright here on your own, love?'

'Yeah, 'course I will,' said Hannah. 'You go and enjoy yourselves.'

'What about Kai? Will you have anyone to mind him?'

'Oh, don't worry, I'll probably take a couple of nights off work. I'm well due some holidays. Where are you going anyway? Anywhere nice?'

'Menorca,' Jill and Pat chorused.

'Great,' said Hannah, thinking that if her nana was in danger as Russ had said then it was best that she was out of the way for a bit.

In the meantime, Hannah would try to keep an eye on her, but she wouldn't tell any of her family anything yet. She didn't want to worry them. For all she knew, Russ might have been piling on the drama to get her attention. So, until she knew exactly what was going on, it was best to keep her mouth shut.

It was Sunday evening, and even though the club was shut, Jez was in his office making a series of calls and tending to some of his emails. It was the place where he got most things done, unlike home where the nagging wife and screaming kids often got in the way. Aside from that, he didn't want his wife knowing too much about his shady business interests.

Jez's associates and employees were aware that this was the place where he could be found most days, unless he was out schmoozing one of his business contacts. He always had a man on the back door while he was there so he could vet visitors and make sure they were kosher.

While he was going through some of the paperwork, which was usually locked away overnight in his filing cabinet, he heard a knock at his office door. 'Yes!' he called, slipping the paperwork inside a file so it couldn't be seen.

'Joel Barton to see you, boss.'

Recognising the voice of his doorman, Jez said, 'OK, send him in.'

The door opened and in walked Joel Barton. He was a young man of around twenty-five, tall but not particularly buff. But what Joel lacked in physique, he made up for in brains. He was smart, which was why Jez employed him. That, and his ruthless streak. Once you assigned him a task, he was like a Rottweiler with a juicy bone. He wouldn't ease up till it was done. Jez was surprised to see him so soon though. They'd only spoken on the phone two days ago. That was quick even by Joel's standards.

'So, what have you got for me?' demanded Jez. 'Have you found out where Russ Coles is yet?'

Joel shook his head but didn't speak. Instead, he remained stony faced.

'What the fuck are you doing here then?' asked Jez. 'I told you to come back to me once you found out where he was.'

Any hopes Jez had of intimidating Joel were wasted. The younger man stayed calm as he responded in a steady voice. 'I ain't found Russ Coles, and I don't know where he is, but I've found out summat that could lead us to him.'

Jez sprang forward in his seat. 'What? Come on, don't fuck about. Out with it.'

'There's someone who knows him. We could use him to get to Coles. But it's not gonna be straightforward. The guy's gonna take some persuading.'

'Nothing that can't be dealt with, I'm sure,' said Jez.

He nodded at Joel, willing him to give the details so they could get to work on finding this man. Then, once they'd found him, they'd do whatever was necessary to make him divulge Russ Cole's whereabouts.

13

Hannah pulled into the car park of a country pub, miles from anywhere, the nearest town being Knutsford. It was a family pub with a play area for children. Its remoteness together with the child-friendly aspect were the two reasons for coming here in particular.

She helped Kai out of the car, and they walked indoors where Hannah bought a soft drink for each of them before going through to the outdoor area. There she found Russ sitting on a bench overlooking the playground.

For days Hannah had debated whether to meet him or not. There were a lot of reasons why she shouldn't. But she was worried as to why he thought her nana was in danger, so she had finally rung him and arranged a meeting. Her curiosity extended to Russ's strange behaviour, including the fact that he didn't want anyone to know they were meeting or the location. Aside from that, she was still drawn to him, making it difficult to keep away.

He stood up when she arrived and patted her on the arm. 'Thanks for coming.' When Hannah scowled, he turned his attention to Kai. 'And this must be your son,' he said, ruffling his hair. 'What a big strong boy you are. What's your name?'

Kai smiled and told him. She got the impression Russ was good with kids, and she could tell Kai had taken an instant liking to him, the lack of a father making him responsive. For a moment she was wistful, but she soon gathered herself together. Even if she was to find a baby daddy, it wouldn't be someone like Russ.

Her son turned back to her, 'Can I play, Mummy?'

'Erm, what do you say?'

'Please, Mummy.'

'OK, but promise me you won't leave the play area. Give me your drink to mind and then you can go.'

Kai beamed a smile and then trotted off.

'Nice kid,' Russ commented.

'Yeah, well. He's been brought up properly, and he knows right from wrong.'

'Ouch! You're taking no prisoners today, are you?'

'Just tell me what's going on, Russ, and why you've brought me here. What's all this about you and my nana being in danger, and what's Jez got to do with it?'

'OK, well, it's to do with the street your nana lives in. Jez is intimidating the residents.'

'I already know they're being intimidated. Two of them have been beaten up. But why do you think she's in danger? Are they going to attack her next? And what makes you think Jez is behind it?'

'It's not just her. It's all the residents. He's not gonna stop till he gets them out. Believe me, I know what he's capable of.'

'I'm sure you do, seeing as how you used to work for him. Is that why you were arrested?'

'I haven't been arrested. Where's that come from?'

'Someone in the club. They said, and I quote, "Russ Coles has been arrested." That's you, isn't it?'

Hannah observed his look of comprehension before he replied. 'Ah, I see where you're coming from now. That's not me, that's my dad. I was named after him, my grandad too. My mum had this daft idea of keeping it in the family.'

'OK, so are you telling me your dad has been arrested?'

Russ nodded, shamefaced.

'It looks like you're from a family of bloody criminals. Jesus Christ! Why did I even agree to meet you?'

Russ held out his hands in a placatory gesture, 'OK, admittedly I'm not perfect, but can we not make this about me?'

'But it is about you, isn't it, Russ? You used to work for Jez, doing something illegal from what your ex told me. Then I see you taking stock of stolen goods at your shop. Then you do a disappearing act. And now you're trying to tell me Jez is behind the intimidation of Rovener Street residents. Why would I believe you, Russ, especially when you used to work for him? Is this just a ruse to get back in with me? Because, if it is, it's a pretty low blow, using my nana as an excuse.'

She paused, awaiting his response.

'Will you let me speak now?' he said, a note of irritation in his voice. 'Right,' he began, 'I might have done some dodgy stuff, but there are some lines I won't cross. And I know Jez is involved in the intimidation because he tried to recruit me.'

'No, you're wrong,' she cut in. 'Jez isn't even behind the company that are trying to buy up the houses. I know because I checked. He's not one of the directors.'

'He might not have his name listed as a director, but believe me, he's behind it. Who do you think owns the three shops? I rented one of them from him. That's how he managed to get me to do some of his dirty work in the past because he knew he could pull the plug at any time. And I'd built up a successful business. I didn't want to let it go.'

'An illegal business!' she snapped.

He ignored her barbed comment and continued, 'Jez sent three of his guys to beat me up so that I'd leave the shop. They've also beaten up two of the residents, like you said. I met one of them, Roger. He said they're trying to force him to sell up.'

Hannah recalled Jez's mention of Rovener Street when he was on the phone, and suddenly everything Russ was saying started to make sense. 'But why did you go into hiding if he's already got you out of the shop?' she asked, mellowing towards him now.

'Because I refused to be involved in the intimidation. Jez won't like that. He's used to people doing what he wants. And, apart from that, I know too fuckin' much. Jez doesn't like to leave any loose ends. Believe me, I know what he's like. Now I'm not working for him, he's got no use for me. My fuckin' life's at risk, Hannah.'

She could tell he was becoming exasperated, but she still wanted answers. 'So why are you telling me all this?' she asked.

'Because, like I said, your grandma is in danger. If I was you, I'd get her to move out. It's not worth it. Things will get a lot worse. I'm telling you; he won't stop till he's got rid of all the residents. I don't like what he's doing but I can't do anything about it 'cos I can't fuckin' prove anything.'

His words shook Hannah, who was beginning to realise that if all this was true then her knowledge could endanger her too. She told him as much.

Russ shrugged. 'I'm sorry, that's not my intention. I think a lot of you, Hannah, and I wouldn't want any harm to come to you. But I felt you should know because of your grandma and because you work for the guy too.'

Hannah didn't thank him for the information. She still wasn't sure what to think and for a few minutes they sat in silence. Eventually, she decided it was time for her to go and she called Kai over to them.

'Don't make a fuss of him,' she said. 'I'd rather you didn't. I just want to get out of here.'

'OK,' said Russ, standing up. 'I'll leave you to it, but please promise you won't tell anyone you've seen me. And, whatever you do, don't let Jez know what you've found out.'

Hannah switched her attention to her son who had just arrived in front of her. When she didn't reply to Russ, he walked away, his head hung low. She looked up at his retreating back.

'Don't worry,' she called after him. 'I won't.'

14

The next time Joel Barton came to see Jez it was the early hours of the morning, and he had two men with him. One was another of Jez's employees called Dom Slater, but there was a third man who Joel pushed roughly inside the office. He and Dom then flanked the man on either side.

'About fuckin' time!' said Jez. 'Is this what I have to do to get you to visit me?'

As he spoke, he looked directly at the man, whose face was swollen and puffy beneath each eye, tarnishing his otherwise perfect looks. 'If you'd have come when I fuckin' asked,' he continued. 'I wouldn't have had to get my boys to send for you. But now that you're here, you can tell me where Russ Coles is holed up.'

'I've told you; I don't know.'

'But that's not fuckin' true, is it? Now, tell me what you know and spare yourself any more grief.'

'It *is* true. You can do what you want but it won't make me tell you 'cos I don't fuckin' know.'

Jez laughed. 'Trying to save yourself from another hiding, are you?'

'No! I can't 'cos I can't tell you owt. So, you'll have to do your worst.'

Jez saw the man stiffen as he prepared himself for the oncoming assault. Not wanting to disappoint, Jez gave Joel and Dom the go-ahead.

For several minutes, he watched in wry amusement as Dom held the man back while Joel struck him in the guts several times till he was bent forward fighting for breath. Jez called a halt and allowed him to straighten up before addressing him again.

'Right, has your memory returned yet?'

The man shook his head from side to side, so Jez ordered his men to resume the attack. After several rounds he still refused to speak. By now, the white of his bi-coloured polo shirt was stained red with the blood that flowed from his nose and mouth.

'Are you ready to speak yet?' Jez urged again.

'No!' the man spluttered as a claret stream gushed from his mouth.

'OK. Well, there are more ways to skin a cat,' said Jez who then addressed his two thugs, 'I think he's had enough beatings for now, don't you lads? But I want you to stay while he hears what else I'm going to propose. Because I've got a feeling he won't like it.'

Since her meeting with Russ a few days prior, Hannah had thought about little else. She was tempted to go to the police, but what proof did she have? Jez wasn't even listed as a director of Pake Holdings, and even if he was, one of the people who had been attacked had previously reported it to the police and got nowhere. Besides, how could she reveal the source of her information? She had promised Russ she would tell no-one.

She wanted to warn her grandmother, but what could she tell her that she didn't already know? Pat was aware of the attacks on residents, yet she was still determined to remain in her home, even though she was really shaken by what was happening.

If Hannah was to divulge any of the other information Russ had given her then she would have to tell her nana about his illegal connection to Jez and the reasons for him going into hiding. She'd thought about telling her she'd bumped into him in the club, but that wouldn't be convincing; why would he be hanging about in the club if he was afraid of repercussions from Jez?

Hannah had considered presenting Pat with a diluted version of events once she was back from her holiday. But anything Hannah told her would lead to further questions. And it would be impossible to furnish Pat with enough answers to make her believe what Hannah was saying.

In the end, Hannah decided to stay quiet for now but to keep a watch on things. For the same reasons, she wouldn't say anything to her mum and Pete either. She didn't want any of them to be more alarmed than they already were, not unless it would achieve anything, such as persuading her nana to leave her home.

The other thing Hannah was conflicted about was her work at The Gilded Cage. She hated the thought of working for a criminal who was involved in intimidation, violence and God knows what else, if Russ was to be believed. But there were two reasons she had decided to stay.

The first was because she needed the money, and the second was because it might help her remain vigilant. She had already overheard Jez mention Rovener Street and hoped he might let something else slip, something that might give her the proof she needed.

Russ was enjoying an evening drink with his mate, Chris. They were both standing near the bar area of The Bush, chatting. But Russ couldn't help noticing that Chris wasn't his usual self tonight. Not only was his manner a bit off, but he'd turned up with his face a mess, and when Russ had asked him what had happened, he'd told him he'd been jumped. But the tale wasn't convincing.

Eventually the conversation turned to football, but when Chris still seemed tense, Russ cut the discussion short to ask for the second time, 'Are you alright, mate?'

'Yeah, 'course I am. Why shouldn't I be?'

'You just seem on edge, that's all.'

'No, I'm fine, honest.'

'Well, you don't fuckin' look fine. You've been twitchy all evening. I don't think you've been listening to a word I've been saying. You're fuckin' miles away, mate. Is there summat going on? Is it to do with you being attacked?'

'Nah, it's nowt really. Just a bit of work pressure.'

Russ spluttered into his beer. 'Work pressure? You're fuckin' joking, aren't you? All you do is flog fruit machines to a few pubs and clubs. What's pressurised about that?'

Chris seemed affronted. 'I don't flog them, I rent them out. And I have to make sure I have plenty of customers wanting to rent them. I had a few returned last week, and I need to get new customers.'

His last few words tailed off as something behind Russ caught Chris's eye. Russ was just about to ask him what he was looking at, but Chris quickly refocused on him, making Russ think that he may have been imagining it. Ever since the attack by Jez's men, he'd been wary.

But Chris remained on edge, and Russ thought there could be something else going on. Suddenly it occurred to him what that might be. Had Chris noticed somebody he knew in the bar? And if so, why hadn't he mentioned it to him? An uneasy feeling settled on Russ. He didn't mention it to Chris because a gut instinct urged caution.

His eyes drifted to the bar area where he knew there was a mirror at the back. Then he noticed their reflection. They were standing some distance behind him. Two guys who worked for Jez: Joel Barton, whose bright ginger hair and sly features made him difficult to miss, and a big ugly guy Russ knew only as Dom. Russ had always got on well with Dom in the past, but that was obviously before he'd been on Jez's payroll.

Russ realised there was no way his mate wouldn't have noticed them, and Chris knew as well as he did who they worked for. So, he hadn't been imagining it. That was obviously what had caught Chris's attention. And yet he hadn't said anything.

Guessing at the reason for that, Russ tried to act casual and pretend he hadn't seen anything. But he had noticed, which made him realise with a sinking feeling that his friend had betrayed him. And now he needed to stay calm and see if he could find a way out of this.

'I'm going for a piss,' he announced to Chris. 'Back in a minute.'

Then he walked away, careful not to rush so that his pursuers wouldn't realise he had spotted them.

15

Joel sped across the pub, heading for Chris, who felt a tremor of fear as he watched him approach with Dom. Where Joel was skinny, Dom was well built with bulging muscles displaying the hours he put in at the gym. No matter how intimidating Dom was, though, it was clear to Chris who was the leader of the two.

'Where the fuck is he going?' Joel demanded.

'It's OK,' Chris cajoled. 'He's only gone to the toilet. He's not clued up about anything, I promise. I ain't said owt.'

'Go and check he's still there while I keep an eye on this one,' Joel ordered Dom, taking hold of Chris's arm to show he meant business.

'It's alright, the windows in there don't open,' said Chris. 'And there's no back entrance. He can't get out.'

Dom hesitated for a moment, awaiting further instructions from Joel. 'Fuckin' make sure,' he reiterated, and Dom dashed in the direction of the mens'.

'You better not be fuckin' lying,' threatened Joel, squeezing Chris's arm before following Dom out of the bar area.

Once they were gone, Chris gazed around, self-conscious

when he spotted a few people looking at him, concern etched across their features.

He brushed his sleeve where Joel had pinched his arm. Then he tried to act casual as he took a massive slug of his lager. His heart was hammering. Those two bastards were scary, and he hoped to God there was no comeback from this. But what he had said was true; the toilet windows didn't open and there was no back door, just a private door that led to the kitchen.

Chris felt bad for dobbing his mate in, but he hadn't had much choice. Jez had vowed to destroy him, and he couldn't risk that. Chris supplied fruit machines to several of Jez's bars, and he had threatened to terminate all Chris's contracts unless he gave Russ up. Jez had already sent a few of his machines back to show he meant business.

Not only would he cancel his contracts, but he would also put the word out to all his associates to make sure they no longer dealt with Chris either. Jez had a lot of contacts in the hospitality industry, people who owned bars, clubs and pubs. Most of them had no idea of Jez's reputation. But Jez had influence, and Chris had no doubt that he could come up with a convincing story as to why they shouldn't continue to deal with him.

Thinking now about his long-time friend, Russ, Chris worried about what would happen to him once Jez's men caught up with him. And he felt like an utter shit.

Pat got off the bus at the top of Rovener Street and made her way towards her home. She was smartly dressed in a fitted jacket with a midi-length flowing skirt that had a slit up the side. Her dyed platinum blonde hair was styled to perfection, and she was heavily made up.

She had been out for tea with her friend Gwen, an ex-resident of Rovener Street, along with two of Gwen's other friends. The four of them regularly took advantage of the early bird menu or the pensioner's special at one of several restaurants and gastro pubs they frequented.

It was eight o'clock by the time Pat got off the bus, but that didn't usually bother her. Nights were light at the moment and the bus stop was only at the top of her street – a street where she had lived for years and knew all the residents.

Having recently returned from her week abroad and sporting a healthy tan, she was feeling good after a nice get-together and a giggle with her friends. But as she made her way along Rovener Street, her mood soon changed. On her way out she had failed to notice the number of empty properties, maybe because she had been in a rush to catch the bus. But now, in the stillness of evening, the bleakness of the place was strikingly apparent.

As she walked along, she took a mental note of the houses that were now abandoned. Number thirty-five – boarded up, number thirty-three – boarded up, number thirty-one – occupied, number twenty-nine – recently vacated, the empty interior now visible through the windows.

Her curiosity prompted her vision to stray to the other side of the road where it was a similar story. Numerous homes were boarded up, and others were empty but awaiting the arrival of the developers with their planks of wood and hammer and nails.

Suddenly, Pat became aware of how deserted the place now seemed. It was eerie and she found herself feeling nervous. She'd never felt like this before, not in her own street. But now, as her tiny heels echoed on the pavement, she could hear other sounds. Footsteps from behind. Dense and heavy. Wait... No. Two sets of footsteps. One clumpy, the other heavy.

Pat's heart rate sped up as she quickened her pace, hoping to bridge the gap between her and her followers. But she could still hear them. She risked a glance back, dreading the sight of masked thugs. Terrified that she might be the next on their hit list.

But it was just a young couple. The girl was wearing high heels, the man, tall and stocky, was in some sort of brogue. She smiled with relief and turned back round. But the nervousness still hadn't left her, and she focused on getting inside her own home as soon as possible.

She was almost there when she caught sight of someone. It was the lady from number seven, Gemma Brady. She was carrying a child's car seat, and while Pat watched, she clicked the key fob to open the car door.

Pat was relieved to see a familiar face. 'Eeh, are you having a job getting the little-un to nod off?' she asked, knowing that the couple sometimes took the baby out in the car of an evening so that the motion would lull him to sleep.

Gemma turned and smiled. 'No, he's well away, thank God, but I'm just getting things ready for tomorrow, trying to get a head start. It's going to be a busy day.'

'What do you mean?'

'Oh, sorry, I didn't have chance to tell you with you being

away. But, well …' Gemma lowered her voice. Then, having placed the car seat inside the vehicle, she stepped closer to Pat. 'We're moving out tomorrow.'

'Really? Tomorrow? Bloody hell! I had no idea.'

'I know. We only decided a few days ago. It was after that letter and then the call.'

'What call? What—'

'The call came a couple of days ago,' Gemma cut in. 'And the letter was over a week, maybe a fortnight ago. It was just before you went away, but I didn't have chance to tell you. Proper nasty, it was. Threatening repercussions if we didn't move out. We told the police, but they said there was nothing they could do because it was typewritten so anyone could have sent it.'

'That's shocking. They should have followed it up,' said Pat whose anxiety levels were now spiralling.

'I know, but I don't suppose they have the resources these days. Anyway, we decided to ignore it, but then we got the call. It was bloody frightening!'

'Why? What did they say?'

'Oh, just … the same really.'

Pat heard the tremor in Gemma's voice and decided not to press any further. She put a reassuring hand on Gemma's arm. 'It's OK, you don't have to repeat it. But I have to say, I'll be sorry to see you go, you and your lovely family.'

Gemma forced a smile. 'What will you do?' she asked, her voice now steadier.

'Oh, I've told you before. I'm staying. I've lived here a bloody long time and I'm not having any developer turfing me out.'

'But aren't you bothered by the threats?'

'To be honest, I haven't received any.' Pat felt an icy trickle down her spine. She shuddered. 'And I hope to God I don't,' she quickly added. Then she changed the subject, not wanting to think about it but knowing inside that the more people moved out, the more she felt at threat. 'Anyway, like I say, I'm sad to see you go. Do pop in for a last cuppa tomorrow if you get a minute.'

Gemma lowered her head. 'I'll try.' Then she went back to securing the car seat.

Pat carried on to her home, hearing the persistent ringing of the phone as she approached her front door. She quickly turned her key in the lock and rushed to answer it, unaware at that moment of who or what it might be.

16

As soon as Russ was out of sight, he fled down the hallway that led to the gents'. But he didn't enter. Instead, he bypassed the toilets and sped through the next door, which was the staff kitchen.

'You can't come in here, mate,' said a man dressed in chef's whites.

Russ ignored him and headed towards the back door. By the time the chef realised what had happened, Russ had passed him as well as two girls who stopped and stared after him in astonishment.

'Eh, you can't go out that way!' shouted the chef.

But Russ was already running through the door and out into the beer garden at the back. He knew about the staff entrance; he'd taken note of it as soon as he started frequenting The Bush. Russ had become so paranoid since his attack from Jez's men that he had prepared himself for an instance like this. And now it had paid off.

He crossed the beer garden at speed till he reached the peripheral fence, which he climbed, lowering himself into the garden on the other side. Dashing across the garden, he vaulted over the gate that led onto the driveway. Then he sprinted down it and out onto the road.

It was a road he was familiar with, and he knew it was only a few minutes' walk from his home. Running would be even quicker. But he wasn't crazy enough to hang around, knowing that Jez's men would make it their next destination. No, he just wanted to pick up his car so he could escape.

By the time Jez's men realised that he had exited the pub through the kitchen and then had the nous to get in their vehicles and track him to his home, he would be long gone.

'I want you out!' Jez shouted into one of the burner phones that he kept hidden from staff. He allowed the person on the other end of the phone to respond before he added, 'Oh, we'll see about that. You either do as I say or …'

But then he realised the call had been cut. He stared at his phone with a wry grin on his face. She'd cut him off. *The cheeky old bitch!* He laughed to himself. She had guts, he'd give her that. But she obviously didn't know who she was dealing with.

'There's no way you're getting me out of my home,' she had said, but even though she had tried to resist, he had heard the fear in her voice. Well, she'd had her first warning. That was just a taster of what was to come. If she wanted to play hard then he was only too willing to oblige.

He sat back in his chair, a look of contentment now adorning his weaselly features. Jez loved making these calls. He could have got one of his minions to make them for him, but why would he do that when they gave him so much enjoyment? It was the feeling of power that gave him a kick, the knowledge that he was the one in charge.

And when the residents resisted, it made it all the more

fun. It was amusing knowing that they actually thought they could go against him. How he loved that sense of satisfaction when these people found out they couldn't.

He had no doubt it wouldn't take much more to frighten Pat Bennett out of her home. After all, the rest of the residents were leaving in their droves. He was now down to the last few, but he was confident that it wouldn't be long until they were out too.

Joel soon caught up with Dom, who was on his way back out of the gents' and claiming there was no sign of Russ. Joel sent him in again and this time he accompanied him. He knew Dom would have already checked the windows, but he wanted to see it for himself. When he saw the two frosted glass panes, fixed in place with no sign of a breakage, he decided to check the cubicles.

There was no-one inside and a quick glance upwards told him Russ hadn't secreted himself in the space at the top of the cubicles either. Neither was there any sign of a suspended ceiling or any tiles that could have been pushed up in an effort to crawl into the roof space. But then an idea came to Joel.

'Come on!' he yelled to Dom, dashing back into the corridor, then through the door marked 'PRIVATE'. 'He must have gone this way. There's no other way he could have got out.'

The two of them burst through the door to see the astonished faces of the staff.

'Eh, what the hell's going on?' yelled the chef who attempted to block their way to the back door.

Joel pushed him viciously to one side, but when the chef stepped forward and put up a fight, Dom stepped in, shoving him so hard that he careened into the oven top, which was occupied by several boiling pans. Joel didn't wait to see the outcome, but he heard the chef's agonised screams as they sped through the outer door.

He scanned the beer garden, but there was no sign of Russ. Knowing his target had had a head start while they had been scouring the men's toilets, he hammered his fist on a table in frustration.

'Bastard's gone!' he yelled.

'Let's check round the front,' urged Dom, dashing round the side of the pub.

Joel followed him but he knew it was useless. Russ would be long gone by now. When he entered the carpark at the front of the pub, he was tempted to get inside his vehicle and rush to Russ's home. But he suspected he wouldn't find him there either. Russ Coles was no fool.

So, instead, he decided to carry out the second part of the task they had been set.

'Come on,' he said to Dom, turning and heading back inside the pub. 'Leave Coles for now. Let's get the other one. And this time I'm taking no fuckin' chances.'

17

Pat was shaken after the call, but she was also angry. How dare they think they could intimidate her into moving! They might have got rid of the younger people in the street, as well as some of her friends, but she was made of sterner stuff.

She recalled how she had nursed her husband through cancer for over a year, until he had finally submitted to that horrible disease and she'd had to let him go. The man who had been her constant companion for over forty years. It would have been easy to let her sorrow take over, but she had refused to sink down that big black hole.

Instead, she had presented a calm façade despite her inner turmoil and set about rebuilding her life. Now, almost ten years since she had lost her Harry, she was happy on the whole. She had good friends and a wonderful family as well as an active social life and a lovely home. And she was buggered if she was going to let some greedy developer take it from her.

Spotting her shaking hands and feeling annoyed at herself for letting the phone call get to her, she poured a measure of brandy into a glass and sat down on one of her comfy armchairs. As with the death of her husband, she decided to remain outwardly calm. Tempted as she was to tell her family what had happened, she would keep it to herself for now. She didn't want to worry them.

Chris was surprised to see Joel and Dom walk back inside the pub and come straight over to him. He had expected them to still be in hot pursuit of Russ.

As soon as they reached him, Joel took hold of his arm, saying, 'Come on, we're going.'

Chris flashed a look of alarm. 'B-but I thought you'd have been at his flat. Didn't you know he lives a few streets away?'

'Shut your fuckin' mouth and keep moving.'

Dom moved behind Chris, and he felt a sharp jab in his back. 'Get moving,' he said. 'And don't fuckin' think of raising the alarm or this will go straight through you.'

Chris felt the breath catch in his throat, realising that Dom was holding a knife to him and had every intention of using it if he didn't do as they said. He put down his pint, watching it wobble as he let go of it with unsteady hands. He tensed, expecting it to crash to the floor and rouse attention. But thankfully it stayed upright.

They led him out through the door and shoved him inside their waiting Audi. Dom got into the driver's seat and pressed down on the central locking switch while Joel sat next to Chris on the back seat. Dom had now put the knife away, but the threat remained. Terror flooded Chris's veins as he questioned what more they could want with him.

'Do you need his address?' he asked, his voice trembling.

'No, we've already got that. You should know. You're the

one that gave it to Jez. But there's no fuckin' point going there now, is there? The bastard had a head start on us. He'll be long gone.'

'I-I didn't fuckin' give him the nod. Honest. I don't know how he knew you were there. I swear down, I didn't fuckin' tell him.'

'Shut yer fuckin' whinging!' growled Joel.

Fearing reprisals, Chris did as Joel said, and for a few seconds neither of them spoke as the car wended its way through the streets of Manchester, bypassing the place where Russ lived. Chris's face was moist with sweat and his mouth dry as the fear coursed through his body.

After a while he could stand it no longer. He had to know where they were taking him. 'I don't know where he is, I swear. What the fuck's going on? I kept to the bargain. I told Jez where he was so what the fuck's happening.'

'Shut it!' ordered Joel.

Two more minutes passed before Dom left the main road they had been travelling along and took a dirt track to the left. Chris was familiar with the location. The track led to a large park, an oasis in the desert of urban sprawl. But it would have shut hours ago. Panic swept over Chris as he drew his own conclusions as to why they would be bringing him here.

'Open the fuckin' doors!' he yelled, rattling the handle in a vain effort to open it. When it wouldn't budge, he pressed the window release catch but that was also locked. 'Let me out of this fuckin' car!' he yelled again.

'Shut the fuck up!' Joel shouted back.

Then the prod of a knife in Chris's side silenced him.

Dom stopped the car and got out of the driver's door. He

opened the back door and dragged Chris from the car while Joel helped to push him out. To prevent any further noise from Chris, Dom grabbed him from behind, and stuck a meaty hand over his mouth.

Joel stepped to the front wielding a hunter's knife, its huge blade menacing. 'Right, now I'll tell you why we've brought you here,' he said. 'You were the second part of the job.'

Chris stared at him, a look of petrified confusion on his face.

'Yeah, you heard right,' Joel continued. 'First, we were to get Russ, which we've not given up on yet. And second, we were to take you out once you'd served your purpose. There's no way Jez will let you live when you know so much. If you're gonna dob your best mate in, then Jez can't trust you not to dob him in to the cops too.'

Chris began struggling now, but Dom held on tight. Despite Dom being a much bigger and stronger man, Chris tried to slug it out. He was just starting to break free when Joel rushed forward, plunging the knife deep into Chris's gut. For a moment Chris stared in stunned silence, one thought now dominating his mind. The struggle was over. He was a goner.

18

Two days had passed since Pat received the threatening call. As she had done for the past two nights, she sipped on a glass of brandy to calm her nerves before she went to bed. And like the other two nights, she admonished herself for letting them get to her.

It was twelve o'clock when she finally surrendered to the sleepiness that had hit her two hours ago. She hadn't wanted to go upstairs too early, worried that they might think the house was empty and launch some sort of attack during her perceived absence.

Before climbing the stairs, she checked that she'd locked the back door. Pat knew she had already checked it twice, but she wanted to make sure. Then she did the same with the front door before checking all her window locks.

She went up the stairs, trying to talk herself into some sort of reassurance despite her mounting dread. At least it was only two more days before they came to fit her new burglar alarm. Then perhaps she'd sleep.

The following morning when Pat woke at eight, she had a mouth like sandpaper and felt groggy. Her night had been restless despite the brandy, which had left her with a mild headache as well as the dry mouth. She realised she must have overdone it and knew she couldn't carry on like that. But she wouldn't have to once she had her alarm.

Pat walked down the stairs, looking forward to the cup of tea she would make as soon as she got to the kitchen. She was almost at the bottom when she noticed an envelope on the doormat. *Strange*, she thought. The postman normally delivered around eleven.

She picked it up, noticing there was no name or address on the envelope, but the words Number 3 were typed. Despite her resolve not to be intimidated, her hands trembled a little when she opened the envelope and removed the letter that was inside. The tremble gained intensity when she read the words contained in it, and she raised her hand to her mouth in shock.

You've ignored your first warning, so now we'll have to step things up. Don't be foolish enough to think we won't. You've heard what's happened to some of your neighbours. Worse is to come. Move out before it's too late.

Like the envelope, the words were typed, and Pat knew that was done so there was less chance of the perpetrators being traced. Feeling her legs weaken, she lowered herself onto the stairs and sat with her head in her hands. As her eyes misted and worrying thoughts clouded her mind, all notions of a soothing cup of tea vanished.

*

When Hannah visited her nana later that day, she knew straightaway that something was amiss.

'What's up, Nana?' she asked, looking at her troubled frown. 'You don't seem yourself.'

'I'm fine, don't worry about me.'

But Hannah *was* worried, and she wasn't prepared to let it go. 'Has something else happened?' she asked.

'What do you mean?'

'With the developers, of course. There haven't been any more attacks, have there?'

'No, no, nothing.'

'OK, well, I couldn't help noticing that number seven looked empty when I passed. That's where that nice couple lives, isn't it? The one that told you about the attacks?'

'Yes, they've moved out.'

'Oh no! Why? Were they threatened?'

'Apparently, yes.'

Hannah could tell by Pat's evasiveness that there was something else and she guessed what that might be. 'Have you been threatened?'

Pat shrugged.

'You have, haven't you?'

'Don't concern yourself,' Pat snapped back. 'It's nothing I can't handle. It'll take more than a few choice words to get me out of my house and home.'

'Why? What did they say?'

'Oh, just the same old nonsense that they've been saying to everyone about moving out or else suffering the consequences. Anyway, I put the phone down on the bugger.'

Pat then changed the subject, but she still wasn't herself. Her whole demeanour was off, and her body was rigid with tension. Hannah also noticed the way her eyes kept wandering to the mantelpiece, but she pretended not to notice.

For a while they supped tea and made general chitchat until Pat got up, announcing that she needed to use the bathroom. Hannah waited until she was out of the room, then she seized her chance, going to the mantelpiece to see if there was any clue there as to what was wrong with her.

She spotted the letter straightaway. It was inside an envelope, which had been opened. Hannah felt bad for intruding on Pat's privacy, but she felt sure that whatever was inside that envelope was troubling her nana. She picked it up and slid the letter out, opening it carefully so Pat wouldn't know it had been disturbed.

When she read the words, she gasped in shock. *Bloody hell!* No wonder her nana looked worried. For a moment she stood there dazed, until she heard Pat coming back into the room. She hurriedly tried to push the letter back inside the envelope. But she was too late.

'What the bloody hell do you think you're playing at?' Pat demanded.

But, despite feeling bad for opening her nana's mail, Hannah wasn't prepared to let this go. 'I knew there was something wrong. Why didn't you tell me?'

'Because I don't want you all worrying about me. Give it here,' Pat ordered.

She snatched the letter out of Hannah's hands before she had chance to hand it back to her, then tore it in two.

'Stop!' said Hannah, reaching towards her. 'It's evidence. The police will want to see it.'

Pat stopped for a moment. 'Fat lot of good they'll do. They didn't do anything about the attacks, did they?'

'Only because they didn't have proof. Obviously, the more people report these threats to them, the more proof they'll have. Then they'll have to do something. You need to tell them, Nana! What if it's you that's attacked next?'

Pat shrugged it off again. 'We don't know that the attacks had anything to do with all this. It might be coincidence.'

Despite her bold words, Hannah noticed her lip tremble. 'But I thought your neighbours said it was connected.'

'Well, that's what they were told. But they might have got it wrong. Gemma could be a bit dramatic at times. I mean, look at the way they moved out after a couple of threats. I tell you, it'll take more than a couple of letters and calls to get rid of me. Now, let the matter drop, and whatever you do, don't tell your mother. I don't want her fretting.'

That evening, Hannah was at work when in walked Jez Reilly dressed in an expensive-looking suit and shiny shoes. Still reeling from her discovery at her nana's house, Hannah turned her back to him when he approached the bar and pretended to be wiping the sill underneath the optics.

'Good evening, ladies,' he said to the barmaids in general.

Hannah pictured him rubbing his hands together as he stretched himself up to his full height in an effort to impress, and she cringed.

'And I must say, you're all looking very lovely tonight,' he continued. 'Now then, I want you to make sure you're nice to the customers. I want them coming back for more. So, let's make this a good night. I want those tills ringing.'

Hannah heard a conceited chuckle, and she turned round just as he was walking away. She watched him as he went through the door marked 'PRIVATE', no doubt on the way to his office.

'God, he makes me sick,' she muttered to one of the other girls.

'Bloody hell! What's got into you?' the girl replied. 'He's not that bad.'

Hannah kept schtum. She couldn't risk telling her. Not yet. She had to keep her suspicions to herself for now. But, deep down, she knew he was the person responsible for the change in her nana. She only wished she could prove it.

19

Russ sat up on the back seat of his VW Golf, yawned and stretched his arms. He pushed aside the blanket that had been covering him and stepped from the car. Once outdoors, he stretched again and shook his legs one by one trying to bring some life back into them.

It was the fourth night he had slept in his car, and it wasn't getting any easier. But he had no alternative. Russ didn't know who he could trust, especially as his best friend had betrayed him. He tried not to think too much of the number of years they had been friends and all that they had been through together. Such thoughts only angered him. If he ever came through this, he and Chris would be having a serious talk. But he had other things to focus on now, such as survival.

At first, he'd worried that Jez might trace him through his car because, if the rumours were to be believed, Jez had police on the payroll. Likewise, he was anxious about using his bank cards, or whenever he went into a pub or café to charge his phone. But up to now there had been no sign of anyone trailing him.

That might have been due to his location. He gazed around him. All he could see were trees on either side of the dirt track. He was currently in Werneth Low but had been changing his location frequently, trying to avoid the urban areas where he and his car might be spotted.

It was getting more difficult though and he didn't know how much longer he could go on like this. Since he'd been on the run, he hadn't taken a shower or had a proper meal, just sandwich packs and other snacks bought from out of the way shops. And his money was running out.

Currently he was toying with the idea of ditching Manchester altogether but how could he make a start in an area where he knew no-one? What would he do for money, let alone somewhere to live? He was becoming desperate, thoughts and ideas whirling round inside his mind. But he hadn't yet reached a decision.

It was early morning and Hannah was on her way to visit her nana again, but this time she had Kai in the car. As Pat had requested, Hannah hadn't told anybody about the threats she had received, but Hannah was getting increasingly worried. She hoped she could find an opportunity to speak to her nana without Kai overhearing and see if she could persuade her to leave her home this time.

She turned into the opposite end of Rovener Street to where Pat lived, passing the row of shops. To her dismay, she noticed the number of empty properties. Then she noticed something else. Smoke. And it was coming from the direction of her nana's house.

Hannah pressed down on the accelerator in her haste to get to Pat's home and check she was alright. When she was almost there, she noticed that the smoke wasn't coming from her nana's house but from another property on the other side of the street.

Angry red and amber flames consumed the building, gusting out of the windows and devouring the roof beams, the smoke billowing from the burning mass and darkening the sky. When Hannah spotted a crowd of onlookers near Pat's home with her standing among them, she stopped the car. There were no spaces near to Pat's, so Hannah parked nearer to the burning building than she would have liked. She got out of the car and set about freeing Kai from his child seat.

Hannah could feel the heat rising from the wreckage that was once someone's home. The acrid air encircled her, invading her throat and lungs and making her cough. She threw her coat over Kai's head and face to protect him, then picked him up and raced towards her nana, holding Kai in her arms while she ineffectually tried to cover her mouth with her sleeve.

The small group were standing well back from the fire, and here the smoke wasn't quite as bad. As Hannah approached, she could hear anxious voices, but she didn't catch what they were saying, her concern for her son overriding anything else.

'Can we go indoors?' she asked. 'I don't want Kai to breathe it in.'

Pat said a quick goodbye to her neighbours and led the way inside her home.

'What the hell has happened?' asked Hannah once they were indoors and Kai was settled on the sofa.

'Nobody knows,' said Pat, her voice full of sadness.

'Roger spotted it when he got up to go to work. He thinks the developers are behind it, the same people who attacked him.'

'Oh God, no! That's terrible.'

As Hannah spoke, she heard sirens and guessed the fire brigade had arrived and perhaps the police too.

'Nana, would you look after Kai for a minute?' she asked, dashing from the house before Pat had chance to reply.

It had occurred to Hannah that if she wanted a word with Roger then she needed to do it before the fire brigade or maybe even the police occupied his time.

'Which one's Roger?' she asked as she dashed into the crowd.

'I am,' said a tall man of around forty.

'Hi, I'm Hannah, Pat's granddaughter. Do you mind if I have a word?'

Roger shrugged. 'Sure.'

Hannah led him away from the crowd before speaking. 'I believe you were attacked by someone connected with the developers,' she said.

'Yeah, that's right.'

'Are you sure it was connected with them?'

'Definitely.'

'Why? What did they say?'

'Oh, that there'd be more where that came from if I didn't take the offer from the developers, or words to that effect.'

'Do you know what they looked like?'

'No. They were wearing masks. Why do you want to know?'

'I'm just worried about my nana, that's all. I want her

to leave but she's refusing, and I'm worried sick she's in danger.'

'No more than the rest of us to be honest. I've stayed put up until now because I didn't want to drag my daughter out of a good school, but after this, I'm beginning to think it's not worth it.'

Hannah spotted two police officers alighting from their squad car, then noticed a woman pointing in their direction.

'Sorry, I need to go,' said Roger. 'They'll probably want a word with me seeing as how I was the one that called it in.'

Hannah trudged back to her nana's house.

'What was so urgent?' asked Pat.

'Sorry, I just wanted to find out a bit more off Roger.'

'Well, he doesn't know any more than I do. He'd only been there a couple of minutes when I came out. I smelt the smoke and went to see what was going on.'

'What about the people who live there? Are they alright?'

'Yes, thank God! Roger said they'd gone on holiday, so they probably won't know anything about it unless the police manage to contact them. Imagine having to come home to that though. It'll be a right bloody shock. The fire brigade has taken its time to arrive too.'

'Mummy, can I see the fire engine?' asked Kai.

Hannah frowned then forced a smile, thinking of how nice it must be to have such an innocent view of life. 'Yes, but only through the window.'

'No. Outside.'

'No, Kai, you can't go outside. It's very smoky, and it will make you cough.'

Kai pulled a face then ran to the window, where he stared

open-mouthed at the frantic activity that was taking place in the street. Meanwhile, Hannah couldn't help but worry. Russ had said that Jez wouldn't stop till they got everyone out of the houses. And now it seemed that he was right.

20

While Kai was occupied at the window, fascinated at the sight of the fire engines, the policemen and all the people standing looking at the big fire, Hannah decided to have another word with her nana. She hadn't failed to notice how much Pat had been trembling since she'd spotted her out on the street.

'How are you feeling?' she asked as they each sipped at the cups of tea Hannah had made.

'Not too bad considering,' said Pat, failing to meet her eyes.

'Not too bad? Nana, you haven't stopped shaking since I saw you.'

'Obviously it shook me up a bit, but that's to be expected, isn't it?'

'Well, what are you gonna do about it?' asked Hannah. When Pat shrugged, she added, 'Don't tell me you're still thinking of staying here after that?'

Pat shrugged again but this time Hannah saw her eyes fill with tears. She walked over to her, enveloping her in a hug. When Hannah spoke to Pat again, her voice was gentler this time. 'What is it, Nana? You know you can talk to me.'

Pat cleared her throat. 'I can't leave here.'

'Why not?'

'Because it's my home Hannah,' she said with a quiver in her voice. 'I've lived here over fifty years.' She took a deep breath then, but her voice was still shaking when she said, 'It's not just my home, Hannah; it was Harry's home too. Your grandad.

'Can't you see? It's full of memories. We spent all our married life here. Forty years together before he was taken from me. Memories are all I've got left of him now. And I'm buggered if I'm going to let some greedy developer take them away from me.'

'Oh, Nana,' said Hannah, squeezing her tighter.

It all made sense now. She could finally see why Pat had been so stubborn about not wanting to move. But she still thought she was being foolish. 'I know it's hard, Nana, but you need to think of the people who are still here. How would Kai feel if something happened to his Nana? Besides, you can take your memories with you,' she said, looking around at the ornaments.

Her grandad had collected toby jugs and other knick-knacks, which still adorned the mantelpiece and corner cabinet. Hannah had no doubt that the house contained many other memories too. They perhaps weren't so obvious as the tiny ornaments, but they were in her nana's mind, in the rooms and in the moments she and Hannah's grandad had shared, firstly as a young couple and then throughout the years until Harry was sadly taken from his family before he and Pat had the chance to enjoy their retirement together.

Hannah was about to speak again, to offer more platitudes in an attempt to get her nana to change her mind. But Pat beat her to it.

Pulling from their embrace, she straightened her shoulders then said, 'Sorry, but my mind's made up, Hannah. Let them do their worst. If my time has come, it's come. I'll just have to deal with it, but at least I'll get a chance to see my Harry again.'

The visit to her nana had left Hannah more troubled than ever. She knew now that it was a waste of time trying to get her to move. Her mind was made up, and that was that. Pat was also still refusing to let Hannah tell her parents what had happened, although word of the arson attack would probably reach them soon enough.

How could she confide in her parents about how she was feeling when she wasn't even allowed to tell them about the threats her nana had received? It seemed to Hannah that she had no-one to confide in about everything. But it was a dangerous situation and she supposed that the fewer people who knew what she knew, the better.

There was one person who might be able to help her though. Russ. She'd sworn to herself that she wouldn't get involved with him. He was shady and she didn't need someone like that in her life. But he knew a lot, and if she was to put a stop to what Jez was doing, then she needed proof. And having someone onside with Russ's knowledge of Jez's operations therefore had to be a good thing.

Hannah searched her handbag for the scrunched-up piece of paper Russ had handed her with his phone number on. She hadn't thought she'd need it again, so she hadn't even bothered entering it in her mobile. But it was probably about time she did, just in case.

Russ answered her call almost straightaway. 'Hannah, am I glad to hear from you! You haven't given anyone my number, have you?'

'No. Why would I?

'OK. Does anyone know you've called me?'

'No. Why? What's going on, Russ? Are you still hiding from Jez?'

'Yeah. But it's worse than that. The bastards came looking for me.'

'Where?'

'Doesn't matter where. A mate of mine put me up and I thought no-one would find me there. We were in the local pub having a drink when Jez's men came looking for me.'

'Jesus! How did you know Jez had sent them?'

'I recognised them. Let's just say I've seen them around. Anyway, I'm having to sleep in my car now. To be honest, Hannah, I don't know what to do for the best. I think a good friend of mine told them where I was, and now I'm not sure who I can trust, which is why I'm lying low.'

Hannah was surprised to hear him speak this way. He genuinely sounded scared. She had been hoping that he might be able to help her, but he sounded even more at a loss than *she* was.

For a moment she didn't know what to say, but then he asked, 'To what do I owe the call anyway?'

'It's about the developers. I think you were right, Russ. Jez, or whoever it is that's doing this, won't stop till they've got everyone out of the houses. I'm worried about my nana.

She's been receiving threats and, well, one of the houses was set alight while the owners were on holiday. It's in complete ruins. I'm worried it might be her next, but I can't persuade her to leave.'

'OK. What do you want me to do?'

'I don't know really. I somehow need to convince the police about all this, but I've got no proof that it's the developers, let alone that Jez is involved. I mean, the fact that the threats are aimed at getting people to leave their homes points to it being the developers, but without proof, the police can't do anything about it.'

'Right, well, to be honest, I don't have much more to go on than you. I know who came for me, but I've no proof Jez sent them, and because I escaped before they did anything, they could always say they were just having a drink in the pub. The guys that beat me up last time are long gone, and I can't prove that these two were sent in their place, so I don't really know what else I can do. It's my word against Jez's, like I said before.'

'Right, OK. Maybe I shouldn't have called. You've obviously got problems of your own.'

Hannah was preparing to finish the call when Russ said. 'No, wait. Let's have a meeting. We can put our heads together and see if we can come up with something. But you mustn't let anyone know you're coming to meet me.'

Reluctantly, Hannah agreed, out of desperation more than anything. She took details of the meeting place and time from Russ and was about to terminate the call once more when he stopped her again.

'Hang on!'

'What now?'

'I don't suppose you can get hold of a change of clothes for me and a nice hot meal, can you?'

Hannah laughed and cut the call.

21

Later that day, once her mum was home from work, Hannah dropped Kai off with her for the evening then drove to Werneth Low, telling them she was going to see an old friend. She could have saved herself some time by leaving Kai with her nana earlier that day, but Pat was troubled enough without having to cope with the demands of a three-year-old.

Aside from that, she was glad to get Kai away from an environment steeped in fear and suspicion, not to mention the thick smoke. During the afternoon she'd read to him, and they had both sat watching cartoons as Hannah tried to bring some normality back into his young life.

The meeting place was in a pub car park up in the hills of Werneth Low. Russ had given her a description of his car, and when she saw a dark blue VW Golf across the other side of the car park, she locked up her car and walked over.

Russ leant over the passenger seat and opened the passenger door so she could get inside. 'Quick,' he said, looking furtive. 'We'll go somewhere quieter where we can talk.'

Hannah got inside the Golf, and he started the engine then sped out of the car park. As soon as the door was shut,

Hannah noticed the smell. The stale stench of body odour was overpowering.

'Bloody hell, Russ! You weren't joking about needing a change of clothing, were you?'

He laughed. 'Do I look like I was joking? I've had the same bloody clothes on for four days. I don't suppose you've brought that hot meal I was after either, have you?'

'No, sorry,' said Hannah.

Russ didn't say anything, but he looked crestfallen. Despite her mixed feelings about Russ, seeing him unshaven and slightly grubby-looking made her realise what a hard time he was having. He might have sailed on the wrong side of the law from time to time, but she wasn't without a heart, and she felt guilty that she had let him down by not bringing the things he had asked for.

She changed the subject by asking the question she had already broached on the phone. 'How did Jez find out you were in the pub?'

'I think it was my mate that told them, the same one that found me a place to live.'

'But why would he do that?'

'I don't know. Chris has always been a good mate. I've known him for years. Jez must have got to him somehow. Anyway, I managed to twig what was going on, and I did a runner before they could get to me. I've been sleeping in the car ever since.'

'Jesus! You do mix with some dodgy people, don't you?'

Russ shrugged again. 'It is what it is.'

She could tell by his aggrieved tone that now wasn't the time to lecture him about his lifestyle.

'Anyway, why did you want to meet up?' he asked.

Hannah was beginning to wonder whether he really was the person to ask for help, given his current situation. 'I'm worried, Russ. My nana's started to get threats now and one of the resident's houses was torched. I spoke to Roger, and he thinks it's the same people who attacked him.'

'I told you Jez would step things up, didn't I? I take it your grandma's gonna leave the street now?'

'No, that's the problem. She refuses to ...' Hannah took a deep, steadying breath before continuing, 'She says the house is full of memories of my grandad. That's why she's refusing to go.'

Russ tutted. 'And what do you want me to do?'

'I just needed to talk to someone. You're the only other person who knows as much as I do. I thought perhaps you could help. Maybe if you go to the police and tell them what you know ...'

'Are you fuckin' joking? The minute I come out of hiding, I'm a dead man.'

'But won't the police protect you?'

'Get real, Hannah. This isn't some fuckin' detective series on the TV. This is life. Why would they want to protect me? They probably wouldn't even believe me. I'm a nobody and Jez is a respectable businessman as far as they're concerned.'

Hannah hung her head not knowing what to say. Although Russ had brought a lot of this on himself because of his lifestyle and the people he hung about with, she couldn't help but feel sorry for him. That feeling was reinforced when he spoke again.

'Look at the state of me, Hannah! Do you really think I can help anyone? It's taking me all my time to keep my head above water. I'm even scared to go to a fuckin' cash point to get some money in case Jez somehow gets someone to trace it. I'm well in the shit. I've not eaten for two days. If you ask me, you're in a better position to help me than I am to help you.'

Hannah could hear the anger in his words, and she felt bad once more for not bringing the things he had asked for. But how was she to have known he was in such a bad way?

'I'm sorry,' she said. 'But it was you that said we might be able to come up with something if we put our heads together and I was banking on it, to be honest. How else will I be able to put a stop to it all? The police don't seem to be doing much because there's no proof.'

'What about the fire?'

'As far as I know, nobody saw anything. The police will be investigating but there's no guarantee they'll come up with any clues. I don't know what to do, Russ. I'm shit-scared my nana will be next. I wish we had something more on Jez. Something we could prove. But there's nowt. He hasn't even put his name to the company.'

'Who did you say the directors are?' asked Russ.

'I didn't, but they're Samuel Sweeney and Thomas something.'

'No, not heard of a Samuel Sweeney. Can you remember the other guy's name?'

Hannah thought hard, trying to recall the other director she had seen listed for Pake Holdings. 'Erm, it began with an M. Malcolm, I think.'

'Malcolm?' asked Russ. 'You sure it wasn't Markham?'

'Yeah, that was it. Markham.'

'Fuckin' hell!' yelled Russ. 'I don't fuckin' believe it.'

'What?' demanded Hannah, picking up on his alarm.

She noticed how his facial expression had changed. In the space of a few seconds his shocked words were now suffused with a look of deep sadness. 'I know him,' he said, his voice low and thick with emotion.

'How? Where from?'

'You don't need to know that. But let's just say he's definitely connected to Jez. And believe me, this guy's a bad bastard. He's just as bad as Jez if not worse.'

Hannah was confused. What could this man have done to cause such a change in Russ's countenance? But she decided not to pursue the matter. He'd tell her in his own good time. Instead, she said, 'Well, I suppose that at least we're a step nearer to proving Jez is definitely connected to the developers.'

'Well, knowing and being able to prove it are two different matters.'

'I know. But there must be something we can do. Neither of us can carry on like this.'

Russ became pensive. 'I'll need time to think,' he said. 'Maybe we could meet up again.'

Hannah grinned and shook her head disapprovingly. She had a feeling Russ might be using her predicament as an excuse to see her. But what choice did she have? As she had already decided he was the only person who might be able to help her. After all, he knew more about Jez and his outfit than anyone she knew.

There was also a tiny part of her that felt something for Russ. It was sad seeing him like this, and she thought it was the least she could do to help him out. 'OK, we'll sort something,' she said. 'I'll give you a call. Can you take me back to the pub now?'

'We'll stop near to it. I don't want anyone to see me. That fuckin' Jez has eyes and ears everywhere. I've already taken a risk meeting you at the pub, but I couldn't think of a quieter place that you'd be able to find.'

They made their way back and were on the main stretch about two minutes' drive away from the pub. 'Drop me here,' she said, noticing a deserted dirt track off to the side.' I'll walk from here but wait for me. I'll be back in about half an hour.'

Russ looked at her, bemused, till she said, 'You wanted something to eat, didn't you? I noticed that pub serves food, so I'll get you something. Is there anything you don't like?'

Russ's eyes lit up at the thought of a hot meal. 'No. I'll fuckin' eat anything at the moment. I'd kill for some proper grub. So, as long as you don't turf up with a bleedin' salad, we'll be fine.'

Hannah smiled. 'I'll see what I can do.'

She rushed to the pub and scanned the menu at the bar. 'Which meal has the shortest waiting time?' she asked the waitress.

The waitress shrugged, obviously thinking it was a strange request. 'Erm, not sure. I suppose the pies have been arriving quickly.'

'OK, I'll have a steak and ale pie. And what about the chips and veg?' asked Hannah. 'Will they take long to prepare?'

'No. We've just done a batch of chips and the veg is already on the go.'

'Alright. In that case I'll have a steak and ale pie with chips, all the veg and gravy, but can you put it on a plate to take out please?'

'Oh. We don't do take outs.'

'OK, put it on one of your plates. I'll pay extra for it if I have to, but I need to take it to someone who can't get inside right now.'

Hannah knew that by being vague the girl might take pity on her, thinking that perhaps she was taking it to somebody who was disabled or incapacitated in some way.

'Right, I'll be right back,' said the waitress.

It was ten minutes later when the waitress appeared with a meal on a plate covered in cling film. She smiled widely at Hannah as she handed her the plate with a knife and fork and took her payment.

'Thanks very much,' said Hannah as she turned to go.

'It's fine. But the manager asked if you could return the plate and cutlery next time you pass.'

Hannah smiled. 'Sure. Thank you.'

Back at the car, Russ sat up in his seat as he saw her approach carrying a plate. He opened his car door, sniffing the air as she arrived. 'Ooh, that looks good.'

He practically grabbed the plate from her and eagerly tore away the cling film. 'Bloody hell, it smells delicious.'

Without a further word, he tucked into the meal. 'Keep hold of the plate and cutlery,' said Hannah, dropping two ten-pound notes on his lap before turning to walk away. 'The pub will need them back. Oh and, by the way, I'll bring you a change of clothes next time I see you.'

Russ paused momentarily from devouring the pie. 'Thanks, Hannah. You're a pal.' Then he smiled impishly. 'See you soon.'

22

While Russ tucked into the meal, he felt a brief period of contentment. He was so glad Hannah had come up trumps for him. Seeing her had lifted him, not only because he was sexually attracted to her but because she was a good, caring person who made him realise what life could have been like if he had been an honest man rather than following the wrong path in life.

As soon as he finished eating, his thoughts turned to the discussion he had had with Hannah and, in particular, to the revelation about Thomas Markham. *That bastard!* He might have known he would turn up again one day. Bad pennies like him always did.

It must have been three years or more since Russ had seen him. And their last meeting hadn't been a good one. Because that was the day Russ had accused Markham of killing his best friend.

Russ had known Bryce from school, and he was the best mate anyone could ever have. Even though Russ didn't agree with some of the activities Bryce was involved in, he didn't let it stand between them, because Bryce was a true friend. Russ felt sure that he wouldn't have dobbed him into Jez like Chris had done, no matter what Jez might have on him.

Bryce would have fronted it out and taken his punishment like a man. That's the sort of guy he was.

Bryce had confided in Russ about the problems he had been having with Thomas Markham: a disagreement over drugs, which Russ had hoped would wash over. But it hadn't. And when he hadn't been able to get hold of Bryce one day, instinct told him there was something badly wrong. Two days later, there were police reports of Bryce's body being found badly slashed and dumped on some waste ground.

Russ had known who was responsible and dashed round to the club he frequented to have it out with Markham. To hell with the consequences! Surprisingly, it had been Jez who stopped Russ from giving Markham the hiding he deserved. He'd known then that there must have been a reason for it, that Markham was useful to Jez in some way. And if Jez told you not to do something, you didn't do it. He was too powerful a force to mess with.

After that, Jez had offered Russ a job, maybe because he was handy or maybe because he wanted to keep him sweet, Russ didn't know, but he had taken it. And he hadn't seen Thomas Markham since.

Russ had assumed Markham was keeping a low profile, knowing the finger of suspicion was pointing towards him. But now he was back, and it seemed that he had got away with killing Bryce. Russ assumed the police hadn't been able to prove anything, though he strongly suspected that not only was Markham responsible, but he was also on Jez's payroll and fronting the property company that Jez was behind.

When Hannah had come to see him today, Russ hadn't believed there was anything he could do to help her. But now he knew that he must do something. He had to put a stop to Jez and his associates, not only to help Hannah and her family, but also for himself. He had to honour the memory of his best friend, and besides, he couldn't go on living like this. Somehow, he and Hannah would find a way.

Connor Davis stood on the other side of the desk from Jez inside his office at The Gilded Cage. Jez surveyed the lad who must have been no more than eighteen, if that, and was scrawny but with a look that screamed streetwise. The kid had come to him begging for work, telling him a tale about his mother who was on the verge of being turfed out of her council house and desperate for money.

It wasn't that Jez had pitied the lad, more a case of not being one to pass up on an opportunity. There was no job at the club that would suit a lad like him, and Jez had told him as much. But there was something he could do. In fact, the lad had called at the right time.

When Jez had told the lad what he wanted him to do, Connor had seemed reluctant at first. But the offer of a sum of five hundred pounds on completion had soon tempted him. In his fingers the lad clutched a piece of paper.

'Here's my mum's bank details,' he said.

Jez grinned at his boldness. He might be able to use him more regularly in the future. He took the slip of paper and scanned it quickly.

'OK. Now, are we clear on what you need to say to the police?' he asked.

'Yeah,' said Connor, repeating the instructions Jez had given him before asking, 'How much time will I serve?'

Jez laughed. This kid was older than his years. 'Not much. In fact, maybe none at all. You'll probably get community service or some shit like that. It'll be well worth it. Trust me, your mum will thank you for it.'

He watched the kid's eyes light up but before he could get too cocky, he said, 'But this stays between me and you, do you hear? If you breathe one word of it to anyone, then it won't be just the fuckin' bailiffs your mum will be worried about. So don't give me any reason to send my men round. You understand?'

'Yeah sure,' said Connor, eagerly.

Just then the phone rang. 'Go on then,' Jez said to Connor, reaching across the desk to answer it. 'And don't forget what I've said.

Jez picked up the receiver as the lad made his way out of his office. He recognised the voice on the other end of the line straightaway: DS Jones, a corrupt officer who was on his payroll.

'What have you got for me?' he demanded.

He listened to what the man had to say before responding, 'About bloody time! I thought you'd never come through.'

'It's not fuckin' easy y'know,' said Smith. 'Trying to come up with something on the quiet. I'm putting my fuckin' livelihood on the line here y'know.'

'Cut to the chase and stop fuckin' whinging. What have you got?'

'His car's been spotted. Last night.'

'Where?' asked Jez.

He listened again before saying a brief goodbye and cutting the call without saying thanks. With the phone still in his hand, he called up Joel Barton's name and dialled his number.

'Joel!' he boomed. 'Whatever you're up to today, drop it. I want you and Dom up at Werneth Low.'

'Werneth Low? Why?' asked Joel.

'Because Russ Coles has been spotted there. He was in the car park of a pub called the Fox. He was driving a dark blue Volkswagen Golf.' He quoted the registration number before adding, 'I want you and Dom on it straightaway. You need to find the bastard. And when you find him, I want you to bring him in.'

23

The black Audi sped into the car park of the Fox, almost colliding with a Peugeot 108 being driven by an elderly man.

'Fuckin' tosser!' yelled Dom as the Peugeot driver wound down his window and shouted back, 'Lunatic!' while gesturing with his hands.

'The fuckin' old cunt,' Dom shouted to no-one in particular, glaring after the man.

'Pull in over there and shut it,' ordered Joel.

'What's wrong with you?' asked Dom as he parked the car.

'You! You knobhead. The last fuckin' thing we need is the cops after us for speeding.'

'I wasn't. I would have been OK if he'd have got out of the way.'

'Is it worth the mither for some old bastard? Let's get on with what we've come for.'

Joel got out of the car and Dom followed. The car park was full, and they walked around it, looking for any signs of a dark blue Golf or of Russ Coles hiding out in another vehicle.

'Don't forget what I told you,' said Joel. 'He could have switched motors.'

Dom nodded but didn't speak, too busy carrying out his instructions.

After two minutes with no joy, they made their way inside the pub where they scanned every room in search of Russ. Once outside, Joel stated the obvious, 'Fuckin' twat's not here anymore.'

'What now then?' asked Dom.

'Get back in the car. We'll circle round and see if there's any sign of him. He might not have gone far.'

They drove for some minutes, Joel staring out of the window while Dom kept his eyes fixed on the road. They came to a small village and circled the few streets, searching for any sign of Russ or his car. When that drew a blank, Joel ordered Dom to drive back down the road towards the pub.

Joel repeated the exercise, scanning the lanes they passed, but this time his focus was on any to the left of him. He'd already checked out those on the right when they'd headed up the road in the opposite direction.

They were about two minutes from the pub when Joel thought he spotted something down a dirt track. It was narrow but had a wider passing place further up. Through the bushes, he caught a glimpse of something blue. He craned his neck to examine the spot, but it was too late; Dom had passed the track and whatever had been there was now hidden behind dense bushes.

'There!' shouted Joel. 'There was something there.'

Dom slammed on the brakes.

'No! Don't stop the fuckin' car, you dick. Turn it round. We need to go back and check it out.'

He watched in frustration as Dom completed a turn in the road. Even on this main stretch it wasn't particularly wide, and Dom's manoeuvre took several turns before the car was facing the opposite way.

Joel pointed out of the window. 'Up there. On the right. I saw summat in a layby.'

As soon as they turned into the dirt track, Joel saw the blue car well in the distance. He couldn't be sure from here that it was a blue Golf, but he was determined to check it out. He turned to Dom. 'Right,' he said. 'Now you can fuckin' speed. Step on it!'

Hannah was feeling troubled, not only because of what was happening in her nana's street but also because of the shock of seeing Russ in such a state. When she came away from their meeting, she had been dogged by guilt. All he had wanted was a hot meal and a change of clothes, and she hadn't bothered taking either, only redeeming herself at the end of their meeting by buying him a meal from the pub and leaving him what little cash she had on her.

The next day she had rung him and arranged to meet again that evening, promising to bring him the things he needed. Fortunately, her mum had agreed to look after Kai. She could tell Russ had qualms about staying in the same area for two consecutive days, but they had agreed to work out an alternative meeting place once she saw him.

Russ's reaction had made her nervous, and as she drove to their meeting place, she could feel her heart thudding in her chest. When she arrived at Werneth Low, she checked the clock on the dashboard. There were fourteen minutes to go till their pre-arranged time and she was only a few minutes away from the meeting point. That meant she would be around ten minutes early.

Not wanting to hang around for too long in a dark, secluded area waiting for Russ to show up, she decided to stop along the way. She pulled up outside a late-night store and nipped in for some chewing gum. Back in the car, she flipped a piece out of the packet and put it in her mouth. The chewing action helped to steady her nerves.

While Hannah kept a mental note of the time, she checked through the bag of things she had brought for Russ. She cringed as she looked at the underwear she had dashed out to buy that day, hoping she had got the right size and style. Then there was a clean pair of jeans and a shirt, which she hoped would fit, some baby wipes for him to clean himself, a can of anti-perspirant, two packets of sandwiches, a multipack of crisps, a bunch of bananas and a few bottles of water.

She found herself hoping that he would be happy with her purchases. Then she checked the time once more, put the bag of goodies to one side and started the engine.

While Russ waited for Hannah to arrive, he kept watching the main road, hoping to see her car turn down the dirt track. There weren't many cars making their way along the country road at this time of night so when he saw a black Audi, it alerted him.

He couldn't see properly who was inside the car, but he

could make out the outline of two men, one driving and the other sat next to him. The passenger was the smaller of the two and he had a shock of red hair. It immediately put him in mind of that night in The Bush when he had spotted Joel Barton and his sidekick, Dom, who had been sent to find him by Jez.

It might have been a coincidence; Joel wasn't the only man around with red hair who hung about with a much bigger guy. But Russ had a bad feeling, and he didn't want to take any chances. He couldn't escape via the main road because Joel and Dom might block his exit. But Russ had been touring the area for a while now, so he knew his way about.

He started the engine and set off, moving away from the main road so that he could follow a maze of dirt tracks and narrow lanes, which would eventually lead to a town miles from here.

24

It took less than a minute for Russ to become convinced that the people inside the black Audi were Joel and Dom. That realisation was reinforced when he spotted the car heading his way. Why else would they turn back from the main road and follow a dirt track other than to pursue him? And why else would they now be driving at speed?

Russ sped up, still confident he could shake them off by following the network of country lanes that covered a vast area before reaching the town. As he turned several corners, obscured by the wooded areas, they would find it impossible to guess where he had got to.

The first turn-off was coming up on his right. He had the beginnings of the route plotted inside his head. He'd take that turn-off, knowing it was followed by two left turns in close proximity. He'd then take the second left in the hope they'd opt for the first when they couldn't spot him.

His mind was so taken up with planning the route while negotiating the winding track, that he didn't notice what was happening further ahead. Then he spotted something. Another car further up the track, and it was heading towards him.

With a ditch on either side of the dirt track, Russ knew

there was no chance of passing the car, which meant he was trapped. He had a weird panicked sensation, as though his heart had plummeted into the depths of his stomach. Then instinct kicked in. He floored the accelerator while sounding his horn in the hope that the driver of the vehicle would sense danger and reverse out of the way.

Through his rear-view mirror, Russ could see that the driver of the black Audi had also sped up. Russ wasn't far from the first turn-off he had envisaged. If he could get the driver of the oncoming vehicle to reverse past that point, it would give Russ a route of escape.

But the driver carried on, relentless. *What the fuck!* Who was it? Somebody else working for Jez? Or a random member of the public? The nearer he got, the more Russ's heart sped up until, finally, Russ slammed on the brakes, narrowly missing the car in front which had also come to a stop.

Russ had a momentary image of a raging thirty-something man in a silver Volvo before he felt a thud from behind, and shot forward, feeling the pull of his seatbelt as it restrained him. The impact propelled his car, which crashed into the silver Volvo.

The Volvo driver jumped out of his car and hammered on Russ's window. 'What the fuck do you think you're playing at? Lunatics like you need teaching a lesson. Get out of the car you fuckin' idiot!'

But Russ stayed put and pressed down on his door lock. 'Get out of the fuckin' way!' he yelled. 'You're gonna get us both killed.'

His fear wasn't of the man banging on his car window but of the two men in the Audi who were also outside their car. Through his mirrors, Russ could see them clearly now. The spiteful features of Joel, and his sidekick Dom.

The man turned his attention to them. 'Are you all fuckin' mad? Have you seen what you've done to my Volvo?'

Seizing his chance while the three of them were distracted, Russ started his engine and floored the accelerator again, trying to bump the Volvo backwards so he could make his escape.

He managed to shove the other car a little till the man was out of view. He sensed movement outside and heard the man yelling. Then his anguished yells were silenced, and a spray of blood splashed onto Russ's window. He felt a dense thud against the rear door and wondered what had happened.

Russ desperately searched for a way out. Then an idea came to him. If he could push the Volvo at an angle, he might send it into the ditch, leaving the track free for him to make his escape. But he was too close to have any leverage. He slammed the gears into reverse and backed up awkwardly until he hit the Audi a second time.

Guessing that he had reversed sufficiently, Russ put the car into gear again and pressed forward, steering to the left. But in his panic, he had oversteered. Instead of hitting the Volvo with force, he merely caught the edge of it. The Volvo juddered for a moment before the momentum stopped.

Rather than sending the Volvo into the ditch, Russ was headed there himself. He hit the brakes then put the car into reverse again, but he didn't get far. The Audi was in the way. And there was something else slowing his progress. Some object or other. And he didn't know what it was.

His progress became even more cumbersome. He heard a

loud popping noise followed by another, then another, and he realised that someone was slashing his tyres. A hissing noise confirmed it. Russ glanced ahead to see Joel standing to the side of the Volvo but looking directly at him with an evil sneer on his face.

'Give it up Russ! You've got no fuckin' chance,' Joel yelled. 'Dom's already slashed your tyres. He's gonna brick your windows next, starting with the windscreen. How do you fancy a face full of glass?'

Russ was desperately trying to weigh up his options with a panicked mind.

'Come on!' Joel continued. 'Jez just wants a word. That's all. Are you gonna come back in one piece or do we have to drag you back looking like a fuckin' hedgehog 'cos of the amount of glass that'll be stickin' out of you.'

Russ wasn't keen on the analogy, but he could see Joel's point. He tried again to accelerate, but it was no good. The Volvo was hardly shifting. Feeling resigned, he killed the engine and got out of the car. He didn't believe a word of Joel's assurances, but he didn't think he had any choice other than to do as he said.

As soon as Russ stepped out of his car, he realised what had stopped him moving backwards. Behind his vehicle, he saw the battered body of the Volvo driver, which must have fallen when his car moved forward. The sight of the body pumping out blood on the ground made Russ's mouth fill with bile.

Before he could react, Dom and Joel had hold of him, quickly wrenching his arms behind his back and tying them up. They dragged him inside the Audi, dumping him on the back seat where Joel climbed in beside him. Then Dom hit the central locking, started the engine and reversed at speed back to the main road.

Hannah was surprised at how excited she was feeling at the prospect of seeing Russ. She quickly dampened it down, telling herself that her enthusiasm was because she was expecting to get more information out of him. When he caught sight of the items she had brought, he would hopefully be more amenable, and maybe she would find out why he had acted so extremely at the mention of Thomas Markham.

She passed *The Fox*, and two minutes later she turned into the dirt track and parked her car in the passing place. Surprisingly, Russ hadn't arrived yet, even though she was two minutes late by now. However, she could see a dark blue car in the distance and wondered if it was his. She was tempted to drive a bit closer, but then she'd struggle to turn her car back round, so she decided to stay where she was. If it was his car, then surely he would make his way to her once he saw her arrive.

But there was no sign of him, and this place was so eerie in the dark it was freaking her out. But she tried to keep a check on her nerves while she carried on waiting for Russ to arrive. Then she saw movement in some bushes to the side of her car and her heartbeat sped up. Hannah fixed her eyes on the scene as the bushes parted and an object slowly came into view. It wasn't until it had fully emerged from the bushes that she realised it was a fox.

Thank God! she thought, letting out a big puff of breath that she hadn't realised she had been holding.

Hannah had dismissed the blue car as a coincidence by now and she wished Russ would hurry up and arrive. The incident with the fox had freaked her out and the woodland noises were making her anxious. Her senses were on high alert and every toot, squeal or tweet was heightened in her head. But she persevered. She had to see Russ; he was the only person who could help.

After fifteen minutes, the dark blue car still hadn't moved. She wondered again if it was Russ's car and the thought unsettled her. The problem was that it was impossible to tell the model from her vantage point.

Hannah knew she couldn't go home without checking out the car first, so despite her nervousness, she got out of her own car and made her way on foot. The fear that had unsettled her inside the car now felt overwhelming. She kept her vision focused on the lane ahead, trying to ignore the peculiar night sounds coming from the bushes on either side of her.

As she drew nearer, she saw something on the ground behind the car. Was it a man? But what was he doing on the ground? And had he been here for the last quarter of an hour? An uneasy feeling enveloped her. What if it was Russ? Had he been lying there badly injured while she had been sitting in her car?

A few more steps and she could tell it wasn't Russ. It was somebody else, lying still, lifeless. And then she noticed the blood. She approached the man, her heart hammering in her chest. One look at him close up told her he wasn't alive. She didn't stop to examine him. She was so panicked by the sight of all that blood that she fled.

★

Russ recognised the centre of Manchester and knew they were headed towards The Gilded Cage. Then Joel gagged him and tied on a blindfold. Russ couldn't understand why he'd bothered with the blindfold; it was obvious where they were going. But he tried to keep his wits about him anyway. He felt the car turn to the left and assumed Dom had taken the side road that would lead them into the back entrance of The Gilded Cage.

They took him through the back door and led him down some stairs. It was a difficult descent for Russ. Unable to see and with his hands tied behind him, he had to feel his way one precarious step at a time. Russ had never been in this part of the club before, but as he took in the musty smell, he assumed he was being led into an unused cellar. He heard a door being unbolted, and then somebody pushed him inside. The temperature immediately dropped by several degrees and the mustiness became more pronounced.

Then he felt hands on his body. Searching him. Taking out his belongings. The sound of several items crashing to the floor told him Joel had found his phones.

'You won't be fuckin' needing them here, will you?' Joel hissed, and when Russ heard the sound of stamping feet and something smashing, he surmised that Joel was destroying the phones.

He was shoved again, this time with some force, which made him lose his footing and he tumbled to the ground.

He heard Joel's voice saying, 'Look at the fuckin' state of

him.' There was a pause before he added, 'Well, come on. What are we waiting for?'

Russ was shocked to feel a hard boot in his gut, sending spasms of pain through his body. Before he could find any relief, the violent kick was followed by another, which winded him. As he struggled to get his breath, he could feel his body being bombarded on both sides as unrelenting kicks and blows assailed him.

It seemed to last forever, and when it finally came to an end, he could feel rough hands pawing his face. Then the blindfold was wrenched away, and he looked up to see Joel standing a metre away now and sneering at him, his face illuminated by a single lightbulb that hung overhead. In that instant, Russ was vaguely aware of a few old chairs and boxes slung around the space. But what he noticed the most was the knife that Joel was wielding.

'Enjoy that, did you? You've been asking for that for ages. I bet you thought you were fuckin' smart getting away from us, didn't you?' Then he bent over till his face was mere centimetres from Russ's and said, 'Well you ain't so fuckin' smart now, are you?'

He spat in Russ's face before straightening up and looking across at Dom with a wide grin on his face. Dom grinned back.

'Bastard!' cursed Russ through clenched teeth.

Joel laughed and his eyes switched to the knife. '*Bastard* wants to have a bit of fun.'

Russ felt a rush of dread, knowing what was to follow, and with his wrists still bound tightly behind him, he wouldn't even be able to defend himself. As Dom looked on, Joel stepped forward, thrusting the knife. 'Let me see, where should we start?'

The cold steel blade was touching Russ's face now and he could feel his breath coming in short gasps.

'Ooh, I could easily carve you up. I'd leave a really pretty picture.' He ran the blade along Russ's cheek towards his hairline. 'How about taking your ear off? That'd be fun. You'd look a right fuckin' mug with only one ear, wouldn't you?'

He chuckled maniacally but nobody joined in his laughter. Joel looked across at Dom, a smile still on his lips then strode around to the back of Russ.

'I know,' he said excitedly. 'We'll chop your fingers off. One by one.'

He leant forward and hissed into Russ's ear again, 'You'd like that, wouldn't you? Can't do much without fingers, can you? Then maybe we'll do the face after. You're an ugly twat anyway so it won't make much difference.'

Then Russ felt a piercing cut to his right hand, and he screamed in agony. He couldn't tell which finger had been cut as all of his hand was a throbbing mass of intense pain. And it didn't stop. During his torture, he could feel Joel's rapid breath against his cheek as he chopped away at him.

Russ heard him speak. He was addressing Dom. 'Fuckin' thing won't go through the bone. We should have brought a saw or summat. Looks like I'll have to do the face after all.'

To Russ's surprise, Dom raised a hand and stepped towards Joel. 'No, don't, mate,' he said.

Russ could hear Joel's tone of incredulity as he demanded. 'Why the fuck not?'

'Well, we don't know how Jez will react, do we? He might be well pissed off if he finds out we've beaten him to it. And I for one don't wanna get on the wrong side of him.'

For a moment there was a stillness in the room, and Russ could sense Joel's hesitation. After an unbearable silence, he appeared in front, still waving the knife around. 'OK, we'll leave it for now.' Then he snarled at Russ, 'I suppose you'll have to wait till Jez gets his hands on you. And, believe me, he won't fuck about. He's gonna cut you up into little pieces and he'll enjoy every minute of it. I might ask if I can join him. I don't wanna miss all the fun.'

The two of them backed away towards the door. But before they exited, Joel ordered Dom to remove the broken phones. 'Don't want him thinking he can still use them,' he said before leaving Russ with a few parting words: 'Enjoy the hospitality.' Then he switched off the light.

They left the cellar in a cacophony of laughter. Russ heard them slide the bolt, then the sound of their footsteps becoming more distant, the laughter more diminished as they made their way up the stairs, leaving him cold, petrified and alone.

25

As Hannah raced to get away from the gruesome scene, a feeling of dread overwhelmed her. She knew it was Russ's car she had seen and there was another car behind it, a Volvo. Assuming the man was dead, she wondered how the hell he had ended up next to Russ's car.

Was Russ responsible? And if so, why had he left his car there? And what about the Volvo? Did that belong to the dead man? Was he one of Jez's men sent to get Russ? Perhaps Russ had killed the man in self-defence then fled in panic once he realised what he had done. But that still didn't explain why he would flee on foot and leave his car there. Maybe there was some other explanation. But she couldn't think what it might be.

As she drove, thoughts were racing through her head. Should she report what she had seen to the police? But what if Russ hadn't killed the man? The police would be bound to pin it on him due to the evidence. And how would she explain her presence there? If Russ was responsible, then she might be implicated because she had gone to meet him.

In the end she decided to keep it to herself. But it didn't stop her worrying, not only about what had happened to Russ but about everything else too. Hannah had been holding out hope of Russ being able to help her, and now she was at a loss as to what to do next.

When she arrived home, she'd tried ringing Russ on the last number she had had for him, but the phone just kept ringing. Was that because the police had arrested him for killing the man on Werneth Low? Or had Russ also been killed? But if that was the case, why hadn't his body been there too?

Since he had gone into hiding, Russ had been using several burner phones he'd bought previously. He had told her he was nervous of using the same one twice in case it was traced, as he was convinced that Jez had at least one police officer on the payroll. Now she had no choice but to hold fire and hope that Russ would somehow find a way to contact her. But she just prayed that he was OK.

Russ gazed around him though his sight was bleary and his eyelids already beginning to swell. It was so dark inside the cellar that it was difficult to see anything. The beating had been savage and frightening. He'd had beatings before, but this one had felt worse because he had been bound and blinded to it, so he didn't know where the next ferocious blow was coming from or when or how it was going to end.

He couldn't understand why Joel had then removed the blindfold, but Russ guessed it was so that he could see Joel's sneering face as he and Dom left Russ in agony on the hard cellar floor. But they hadn't removed the rope that bound his arms behind his back, and he struggled to get to his feet without the aid of his hands for balance.

The movement made him more aware of his injuries, and

by the time he was on his feet it felt as though his whole body was throbbing and tender. Russ felt the thick blood trickle down his chin. He couldn't even wipe it away.

The cellar was cold and deathly quiet. Russ hobbled towards the door, looking for the light switch, but it was so gloomy that he couldn't see anything, and he bumped into objects several times. It took a while until he reached the wall, and he had to feel his way along it till he found the raised area of a doorframe and then the door handle. It was a difficult procedure because Russ had to do it backwards, leaning over so that he could reach up as far as possible and feeling the strain on his upper arms and shoulders.

Russ didn't know whereabouts the light switch was. But he knew it was near to the door as Joel had flicked the switch just as he and Dom had left. Feeling disorientated, Russ tried the wall on either side of the door, recoiling as his fingers touched something moving. He tried to reassure himself that it was probably just a spider, but it still freaked him out. There was something about being in the dark that heightened all your senses and made everything seem a lot scarier.

Deciding the light must have been further away from the doorframe, Russ began the process again, trying to gauge the distance from the doorframe by using both hands. He started on the left-hand side but when he still had no joy, he moved over to the right. Nothing.

He was feeling desperate now, his throbbing muscles and feelings of inadequacy almost reducing him to tears. But he took a deep breath, gave himself a stern talking-to and carried on searching. 'Come on, Russ. It's got to be here somewhere,' he said to himself.

Eventually, he was rewarded with the feel of a light switch, and he pressed down on it. The cellar was immediately flooded with light, and he had to shut his eyes for a moment while they adjusted. When he opened them again, he took in his surroundings. The space hadn't been inhabited for some time. That was evident from the dusty concrete floor and the bare brick walls, as well as the musty smell. But it had been used.

As he looked around him, he noticed a proliferation of old furniture, not just chairs but tables as well. Most of it was either broken or with the upholstery ripped. There were also boxes full of rubbish many with spiders' webs stuck to them. He peered into the nearest one and saw a few leftover wall tiles and a part-used roll of wallpaper he recognised from the club upstairs.

This was obviously a dumping ground for old, unwanted crap, and judging by the mould patches on some of the chairs, they had been here for some time. He tried walking around, but the pain of his battered body overwhelmed him, making the process laborious.

Eventually, when the pain became too much, he sat down on a grubby old chair and tried to think. There must be some way out of this. But with his level of injuries, it was difficult to concentrate, and he felt weary. His sore and tired state gave way to despair. He just wanted to rest. Maybe later he would feel a bit better and then he'd think about what to do next.

Pat had been to see her friend Gwen. The two women had known each other for years. In fact, Gwen had moved into Rovener Street not long after Pat, and they'd been friends ever since. Gwen wasn't too keen on the retirement apartment she'd moved into. She'd told Pat she preferred things the way they used to be. For most of the evening, the two women had shared memories of the old days and some of the fun they'd had. Gwen was always good for a laugh.

As she sat on the bus during the journey home, Pat became carried away in her thoughts. She was feeling wistful. All those friends from the street she had known for years and now they were scattered far and wide. But at least she still saw some of them, even if it meant having to catch the bus rather than just popping down the street.

She soon reached her stop and got off the bus, turning into Rovener Street, which looked deserted. Her feelings turned to dread, as they always did nowadays when she was returning home at night. But she didn't let it stop her going out. She was buggered if she would let some greedy developer intimidate her.

But her feelings belied what she was really thinking. Her heart was hammering in her chest and her senses were on high alert as she rushed down the street, eager to be inside her home.

When she arrived, she put her key in the door and gave it a push. A loud bleeping sound coming from the interior made her jump, and for a moment she forgot what it was. Then she recalled the burglar alarm that had recently been installed to give her peace of mind. She quickly keyed in the numbers, but in her haste, she mistyped, and the incessant bleeping continued.

'Oh, you bloody thing!' she cursed, keying the numbers in again till the sound stopped.

She heaved a sigh, then noticed how much her hands were shaking. 'Don't be so daft,' she told herself. 'It's only an alarm.'

But she hated the damn thing. She'd only had it installed because Hannah had nagged her after she'd found out about the attacks. Still, at least she knew nobody had been inside her home while she was out because, if they had done, the alarm would have been blaring by now.

Nevertheless, she performed the same routine as she always did lately, either after an evening out or before she went to bed. She locked and bolted all the doors and windows, then double-checked them before she finally felt able to settle down for the rest of the evening to watch TV. She'd check them all again before she went to bed.

It was only a few minutes later when she heard the doorbell. Instinctively, she looked at the clock. 9 p.m. Who could be calling round at this time? Her heart pounded in her chest as she deliberated over whether to answer it. If she did, she could be leading herself into danger. But if she didn't, they'd think there was no-one at home and might take advantage. She'd heard about thieves who randomly knocked at houses on some pretext or other when they were really checking to see if anyone was at home.

In the end she decided to ignore it and hoped they'd go away. But they were persistent. She tried to focus on the TV, tempted to turn the volume up to drown out the noise of the doorbell, but doing that would let them know that she was in. Every time the doorbell rang, her fear went up a notch and she willed them to go away.

Then the phone rang. *Why won't they just bugger off and leave me alone?* she thought in desperation. She snatched up the receiver, determined to have it out with whoever was hounding her despite her fear.

'Yes!' she barked into the mouthpiece, listening intently while the person on the other end of the line responded. Then her tone altered as she acknowledged the caller. 'Oh. It's you.'

Concerns over Russ had led Hannah to thoughts of her nana. To Hannah, she was the person at the centre of all this; the one she was worried about and the one that was close to all the danger. Although Hannah knew it was late, she had decided she would make a quick visit to her nana while Kai was with her mum. In her present state of mind, she wouldn't be able to sleep until she knew Pat was alright.

Hannah had known Pat was in. The lights were on, and she could hear the faint sound of the TV humming in the background. She persisted in ringing the doorbell, but when there was no response, she had grown even more worried. Next, she rang her grandmother's landline to see if she could get any answer that way.

Hannah was surprised by the brusqueness of Pat's tone. She knew it was late, but she also knew that her nana could be a bit of a night owl who thought nothing of calling her at ten o'clock at night. And she would often stand at her door or that of one of her neighbours gossiping until the sun went down. But Hannah supposed that the situation had changed since many of them had moved out.

'Hi, Nana,' she said.

She could hear the relief in her nana's voice when she said, 'Oh. It's you', and suddenly Hannah felt guilty for calling round at this hour and worrying her unnecessarily. In the old days, it wouldn't have been a problem, but now it evidently was.

'Sorry it's late,' she responded, 'but I just thought I'd call while I was passing.'

Once she'd received her acknowledgement, Hannah cut the call and waited the few seconds it took for her to come to the door. Hannah heard Pat sliding a bolt then there was the sound of a chain rattling and then finally the key turning in the lock.

'Hello, love, come in,' Pat greeted her.

She threw her arms around Hannah, but despite her enthusiastic greeting, Hannah could feel the tension in her muscles. She parted from her nana's embrace, shutting the door behind her, and as she did so, she took in the new bolt and chain that had been fitted. Then she spotted the alarm panel in the hall.

'Wow! I'm glad you've taken my advice about the alarm. When did all this happen?' she asked.

'Oh, only recently. I'm still getting used to the bloody thing,' Pat replied.

Her nana didn't elaborate so Hannah didn't probe, not wishing to focus on the evident dangers that had come to the street. She knew Pat would only try to play it down like she usually did. However, she did notice the good measure of brandy in a glass that was standing on the coffee table. Like the heavy security, this seemed to be a recent addition to her usual behaviour.

'Sit down, I'll make you a cuppa,' said Pat. 'Unless you'd like something stronger. I thought I'd have a little tipple myself, although don't get me wrong, I don't make a habit of it.'

'No, it's OK,' said Hannah. 'I'm driving. A cuppa will be fine.'

Hannah waited while Pat busied herself in the kitchen, returning with her cup of tea and a plate of biscuits.

Once Pat was settled back in her armchair, without preamble, she said, 'They've got someone for that house fire, y'know.'

'Really?' said Hannah, sitting forward in her chair.

'Yeah, a young lad, charged with arson. Connor Davis he's called. It was in the local paper. I'm surprised you've not heard. Eighteen he is. Said he did it for a dare, but he wouldn't name whoever put him up to it. Little bugger! Anyway, they've released him, but he's got to go to court. I hope they throw the bloody book at him.'

Hannah stared back at Pat in astonishment. 'But, I thought it was the developers who had done it.'

'So did I, but it just shows how wrong you can be.'

'Well, I suppose it's peace of mind in a way. If they've caught him for it, then hopefully there'll be no recurrences.'

'Let's bloody hope so,' said Pat.

Hannah flashed her a reassuring smile, but despite her kind words, she still had her doubts.

26

Russ sat in the grubby old chair for some time with frightening thoughts occupying his mind. How long were they going to keep him here? When would Jez come to see him? And when he did come, what would he do? Russ knew too much, and he also knew this left Jez with a problem. Would he threaten Russ to shut him up, or would he dispose of him altogether?

Eventually, Russ decided to turn the light off and try to get some rest. He knew he should really try to formulate a plan of escape, but he was in too much pain. He struggled to the door again, taking a mental note of the position of the chair he had been sitting in and of the location of the light switch. Hopefully he would be able to find it more easily next time.

He made his way back to the chair and settled into it again, waiting for the pain to ease. It was pitch black in the room now and the eeriness unsettled him. Russ had no idea what time it was. With very little source of natural light, it was impossible to tell.

Russ fell asleep sat upright in the chair. His dreams were troubled ones with visions of Joel's mocking face, Jez coming at him with a knife, blood spurting out of a wound on his arm, and, amid all the violence, there was Hannah. Despite his current situation, visions of her lifted him, but he soon fell straight back down again once he was awake.

He didn't know how long he'd been asleep or even whether it was night or day. But then he realised that it must be day because it wasn't quite as dark as it had been before he fell asleep. That meant he must have been here all night. And yet there still hadn't been a visit from Jez. The thought caused a jolt of fear to run through him.

After a few minutes, Russ decided to switch the light on again. Sitting here inactive wasn't going to get him anywhere: it was time to orientate himself with his new environment. He rose unsteadily from the chair, his muscles stiff from sitting there for what was probably several hours. The trip to the light switch was still uncomfortable as well as hazardous.

He had a better awareness of its position than he had done the previous night, but it was still difficult to find his way around and complete even the simplest of tasks. He was relieved to see the room bathed in light again. He glanced around to get an idea of the scale of the place. It was big, and the boxes and old furniture that occupied the cellar took up about half of the space.

Russ guessed there was too much stuff to have accumulated after only one refurb. By the looks of it, the cellar had been used as a dumping ground for years. That meant that ordinarily it would have been visited only on rare occasions, unless Jez had previously held people captive. Russ got the feeling that he was probably the first. Surely, if other people had stayed here, he would see some evidence of it.

That thought made him aware of his full bladder. He needed to find a spot where he could relieve himself. But first, he checked out his injuries. Although he was still sore, he noted that the damage took the form of mostly bruises, except for his fingers and his face.

His throbbing nose, together with the dried blood on his top lip, told him that it had been bust too. But he couldn't find any other cuts. That was a good thing. If Jez was thinking of leaving him here for several days to sweat it out, then at least he didn't have to worry about anything getting infected apart from his finger.

Hannah had not slept well. There was too much going on inside her head, including visions of the dead man lying in a pool of blood. Since Russ's no-show, she had tried to ring him several times but hadn't been able to get hold of him. She couldn't understand what had happened to him, but surely if he was OK, he would have made some effort to contact her by now?

Russ wasn't the only thing that was bothering her. She was still thinking about the visit to her nana. Hannah wasn't convinced that an eighteen-year-old was solely responsible for the torching of one of the houses. It seemed too much of a coincidence considering everything else that had been happening.

To her mind, he had either been paid to do it by somebody else or he had been persuaded to take the rap on someone else's behalf. But there was no way of proving any of it. She wondered whether Russ might know Connor Davis and whether he had any links to Jez or Pake Holdings.

She felt frustrated at not being able to discuss the situation with him as well as concerned about his whereabouts.

Hannah was also worried about her nana. It was obvious from the enhanced security as well as the brandy that this situation was getting to Pat more than she let on. If only there was something Hannah could do to put her mind at ease.

By the afternoon Hannah was scrolling through the Internet again. With no Russ, she felt as though she was now fighting this battle alone, and she was desperate for information. Hannah couldn't find much about Jez, other than references to his legal business dealings, so she decided to carry out some research on the two named directors of Pake Holdings instead.

She started with Thomas Markham, entering his name into an Internet search engine. There were a few Thomas Markhams and Tom Markhams in the results, including an artist and an author and various people no longer alive. She checked each of them in turn except the ones who were obviously not him. It was a while until she finally found something that she felt might relate to the person she was looking for.

Having scrolled through three pages of search results, it occurred to her to check the news pages instead, and there it was, on the second page. A news article about a man being charged in Manchester for GBH. The report then went to describe the callous attack that Markham had carried out on a client who hadn't settled his drug debt. She should have been shocked at the brutality of it, but, given the few facts Russ had imparted about Thomas Markham, it was pretty much what she'd expected.

Hannah carried on scrolling through the news reports for a few more pages, but finding nothing more, she gave up. Even if she found something else relating to Markham's prison record, it wouldn't help. She really needed something connecting Jez to the Rovener Street attacks.

Becoming desperate for something, anything, she entered Samuel Sweeney's name into the Internet instead. Again, she had to scroll several pages before she found anything. Unlike Thomas Markham, Samuel Sweeney didn't appear to have a criminal record, at least not one for which she could glean any information. But then she saw something that was even more alarming, and she covered her mouth in shock.

27

Russ made his way around the cellar. He wanted to check out every inch of the place to see whether there might be any way of escape. Once he had got halfway across the room, he saw that the pile of junk was coming to an end. The part of the cellar furthest away was relatively empty, so he found a bare corner in which to urinate without the prospect of it seeping into the cardboard boxes and intensifying the stench. But then he remembered that he didn't have the use of his hands, and he didn't want to do it in his pants, so he'd have to wait.

He needed to somehow free his hands and he wondered whether there might be something of use in one of the boxes. But he drew a blank. Most of the lids were sealed, and with his hands tied behind him, he was unable to undo them. He gazed around. The walls were high but not too high that they couldn't be scaled with the aid of some old, battered furniture or storage boxes. But what would be the point of that, and how would he lift everything?

Russ made his way back to the front of the room, intending to plonk himself back on the chair. But then something occurred to him. The first box he had looked in contained tiles. If he could somehow break one of them, it would leave a sharp edge. And maybe that would enable him to cut the rope binding his arms together.

He walked over to the box again. It was stacked on top of two others and the top of it came to about chest height, giving him a view of the inside. Unfortunately, he wasn't able to put his hands into the box. So, he did the only other thing he could do. He charged at it, so that it fell over and crashed to the ground, spilling its broken wares over the floor.

Russ felt a surge of fear, knowing the tiles had shattered into several pieces. He was just about to examine them when he heard a sound from outside the door. Footsteps. And then voices. One of them was quite distinct. It was Joel. They were back.

Hannah stared at the PC screen for some minutes as she read through the news article that mentioned Samuel Sweeney. It related to a charity auction that had been organised to raise funds for a local hospice. As Samuel Sweeney was the area manager for the event's main sponsor, he had been asked to give a quotation.

The quotation itself wasn't very enlightening. It was just the standard lines about how the company was happy to be involved with such a good cause etc., etc. But the part of the article that had alarmed Hannah so much was the name of the company. Oliver Tomlinson Estate Agency. The same estate agents where her stepfather worked as a branch manager.

★

Russ used his feet to swipe at the broken tiles, trying to ensure that they were hidden behind another pile of boxes. He didn't want Joel and whoever was with him to figure out what he had been up to. Russ couldn't do anything about the upended box other than ensure that none of its contents were hanging out of it. He was sweating as he tried to conceal the tiles to the sound of the bolt sliding on the door. By the time they walked into the cellar he was several painful paces away from the box, hoping that it would draw their attention away.

'Ha! Bet you thought you'd seen the last of us, didn't you?' said Joel, sarcastically. 'Well, Jez is away on business, so you'll be pleased to know that you'll have to wait a bit longer till he sees to you.'

'When will he be back?' asked Russ.

'How the fuck do I know? Anyway, you're not really in a position to be asking questions, are you?'

Then Joel's eyes flashed to the upturned box and Russ's heartbeat sped up. 'What the fuck's happened there?'

'I tripped up. It's hard to see where you're going in the dark.'

Joel sniggered. 'Clumsy bastard!'

To Russ's relief, Joel didn't go over to the box to assess the damage. Maybe he wasn't so bothered because the cellar contained nothing but rubbish. Thank God he didn't realise that there were sharp tiles inside the box!

Instead, Joel approached him, stopping only inches away and examining his injuries. Russ could feel a rush of adrenalin as he anticipated what Joel was going to do next.

'Not bad,' Joel taunted. 'Those two black eyes are coming along nicely. How's the hand?'

'Fuck you!' spat Russ, incensed, despite his fear.

Joel whacked him across the face with the back of his hand. The blow stung and Russ let out a howl. His instinct was to raise his hand to rub his cheek, but he couldn't. The combination of pain and frustration brought tears to his eyes, which amused Joel.

'Aw, did that make you cry? Diddums,' he teased.

Russ gritted his teeth, refusing to be goaded. He didn't want to sustain any further injuries. That would only make things more difficult for him. And he needed to be on form.

Dom then approached and Russ noticed he was carrying a bottle of water. Dom stepped over to him and opened the cap, holding the bottle upside down over Russ's mouth. Russ ignored the wet feeling as the water dribbled down his face and onto his clothing. He opened his mouth wide, sucking in as much water as he could. It felt so good and helped to ease his throat, which had become parched as blood from his bust nose had dribbled down it.

'Right, that's enough!' Joel ordered after Russ had taken no more than a few sips.

For a moment Dom didn't stop, until Joel, angry that he hadn't immediately obeyed his command, slapped the bottle out of his hand. Russ watched in anguish as it catapulted across the room, landing metres away on its side, the precious liquid dribbling out onto the floor.

'Right, that's it,' said Joel. 'We'll be back tomorrow.' They made their way to the door till, finally, with a mocking tone, Joel said, 'Don't do anything I wouldn't do.'

Then they were gone once more. Russ was still thirsty, and hungry too. He wondered how long they were going to leave him here without food and just enough water to survive till Jez doled out his punishment. But Russ refused to let despair overwhelm him. The fact that Jez hadn't appeared yet was a good sign. It gave him a bit longer to try to figure out how he could get out of this place.

Feeling positive, he returned to the broken tiles and got down awkwardly onto the floor till he was sitting in front of them. Russ peered over his shoulder and grabbed at a jagged piece, his injured hand screaming in pain as he gripped it. He manoeuvred it till the sharp edge connected with the rope binding his wrists. Then he set to work.

Hannah tried not to get too carried away with her thoughts. Just because her stepdad worked at the same company as Samuel Sweeney didn't mean he knew anything about Pake Holdings. But then she had a vague recollection of her mum mentioning Pete investing money in something connected to a senior member of staff at work.

She wondered whether that member of staff was Samuel Sweeney and what exactly the investment was. No matter how much she tried not to get carried away, she kept thinking about how little she knew her stepdad. He'd come into their lives ten years ago and swept her mum off her feet.

On the surface of it, he seemed the perfect gentleman and had always treated her mother well, not to mention her and Kai. But he was very materialistic, and she wondered whether he might take unnecessary risks for financial gain or perhaps even put money before family.

When Jill had first introduced Pete, Hannah had found it difficult to accept him. It didn't feel quite right, but she hadn't been able to figure out exactly why. She'd put it down to the fact that she'd never really got over the death of her father. It was difficult to see her mother moving on, but in the end, Hannah had seen how happy Pete made her mum and had decided to at least give him a chance. But what if her initial instincts had been right?

Hannah was tempted to ring her stepdad and find out exactly how much he knew about Samuel Sweeney and his investments, but caution made her hesitate. It would be far better to speak to her mum first. Hannah knew Jill would never be involved in anything dodgy. She'd brought up Hannah to be honest and law abiding and went by the same code of conduct herself. But what if she was unaware of what Pete was involved in?

Russ didn't know how long he had spent hacking away at the rope. His hands were sore and tired, and his shoulders ached. But he pushed on, knowing it was his only chance. A fraction of the rope began to tear, and it gave him the encouragement he needed to keep at it. A quick glance over his shoulder told him he had cut through one third of the rope. There were still two thirds to go. But at least he had made progress.

After intermittent rests, Russ kept at the rope until he cut through another third and then, finally, it gave way. Tears filled his eyes once more as a feeling of relief surged through him. He stared in wonder at his hands as though a miracle had occurred. Then he wiggled his fingers and circled his shoulders. A stab of pain shot through his injured finger but, nevertheless, he enjoyed the feeling of movement as blood pumped through his cramped arms once more.

Russ rushed over to the bottle of water, which was still lying on its side where it had landed with some of the liquid remaining. He picked it up and gulped most of the water down. A half smile played on his lips. This felt almost like being human again.

Now that he could walk around the room without stumbling, he went back to the bare corner, unfastened his trousers with throbbing hands and let out a long stream of urine. His shoulders sagged with relief, and he sighed.

Next, he paid attention to his fingers. They were full of sticky red blood, which made it difficult to see the injury. He took the remaining water and dribbled it onto his hand, gritting his teeth as the water stung. He knew it was important to keep it clean and free from infection, but it would also enable him to assess the damage.

Russ could see now that the blood had come from the middle finger of his right hand, but it was a deep open cut, which went about two thirds of the way round his finger. Joel had obviously tackled it from different angles in the hope of cutting through the bone. No wonder it had felt as though his whole hand was on fire!

Russ was worried about the wound becoming infected till he thought of something. The phrase 'licking his wounds' came to him, and he recalled how dogs licked their wounds to help them heal. It was something to do with saliva having antiseptic properties. That was why cuts inside the mouth were self-healing. He remembered being told that as a teenager after a particularly gruesome visit to the dentist.

Trying to ignore the intense pain and feeling of revulsion, he put his injured finger inside his mouth and traced a path round the cut with his tongue.

Feeling a bit easier in his mind once that was over, he decided to explore the cellar in greater detail. He took it slowly, examining anything that might feel like a possible means of escape. But there were no windows and only the one door. He tried pushing against it till his bruises throbbed. But it refused to budge.

There was a keyhole, and based on the time it took Joel to enter the cellar once Russ had heard him on the stairs, he gauged that there must be at least one bolt as well as a mortice lock. It was useless. There was no way out. It looked like he was going to be stuck here till Jez decided what to do with him. And, knowing how ruthless Jez was, whatever he decided to do, it wouldn't be good.

28

It was another two days before Hannah could get chance to see her mother when Pete wasn't around. But even then, she was forced to take Kai with her. She let her son spend some time with Jill before telling her mum that she needed a word in private. They settled Kai with some toys and Hannah kept her voice low as she broached the subject.

'Mum, do you remember a while back when you told me Pete was going to invest some money into a business, something his boss at work had told him about?'

Straightaway, Hannah noticed a perplexed look on her mother's face. 'Yeah, 'course I do. We put a few thousand into it, and from what Pete tells me it's been doing well. Why? Why do you want to know?'

'Who was it that recommended the investment to him?'

'His boss at work, like you just said.'

'Who though? What's his name?'

'I don't understand why you need to know, Hannah.'

'It's important, Mum. Please can you just tell me? I'll explain later.'

Jill sighed. 'Well, it was the area manager. Erm, Mr … let me think. Oh yeah, Sweeney. It was Mr Sweeney, the area manager.'

'OK. And do you know the name of the business you invested in?'

'No. I don't think Pete said, but I know it was something to do with property. He handles all our finances. I mean, he did get me to sign some paperwork at the time and told me how many shares we'd bought, but I don't remember seeing the company's name. I didn't take much notice to be honest. I just left him to it. I trust him, Hannah. He's good at that sort of thing, and I can't really be hassled with it all. What's the problem anyway? Why do you need to know the name of the company?'

'Please can you just tell me, Mum? I can explain, I promise.'

Hannah softened her tone as she spoke the last sentence, aware that this discussion was in danger of becoming heated. When Kai paused in his play and looked across at her, she went over to him.

'Are you enjoying that, darling? You be a good boy and play with your toys while me and Grandma have a chat. Then I promise you'll get a treat later.'

Kai seemed assured by her words and resumed whatever game he had been playing with his toys, so Hannah went back over to the couch and sat beside her mother again.

As though she had been chastised, Jill lowered her voice as she asked, 'Why do you need to know the name of the company, Hannah?'

This time it was Hannah's turn to sigh. Then she replied, 'Because I think it's Pake Holdings, the same company that is trying to buy all the houses in Nana's street.'

'No! It can't be. Pete would never get involved in anything like that!'

'Well, we don't know how involved he is yet, Mum. He might have bought shares unaware of what the company was up to. And we don't definitely know yet that his shares are in Pake Holdings, do we?'

'I'll have a look through Pete's paperwork. Give me a minute.'

Jill dashed from the room as though eager to disprove Hannah's theory. She soon returned. 'You're right, Hannah. It *is* Pake Holdings. That means he's bought into the company that are trying to buy your grandma's house. What I can't understand is why he's not said anything.' She crossed to the coffee table and reached for her phone. 'I need to speak to Pete.'

'No, wait,' said Hannah, putting a restraining hand on Jill's arm. 'Let's not rush into anything, Mum. We need to think about this.'

Despite no longer having his hands bound behind him and therefore being able to walk about the cellar more easily, Russ hadn't found any other route of escape. For the past two days, Joel and Dom had repeated the same routine, coming into the cellar in the morning, giving Russ something to drink then leaving the cellar again after some sneering comment or other from Joel. If they had noticed that the bottle of water they fetched no longer contained any liquid, they didn't say. Russ surmised that they weren't vigilant enough to check.

During the visits by Joel and Dom, Russ had sat on the manky old chair with his hands behind him, the torn rope fashioned into a loose knot in case they should check. But they hadn't checked. The sight of Russ supposedly with his hands bound behind him had been enough.

Russ had been so tempted to charge at them and try to break out through the open door. But he weighed up his chances and knew that he could never fight off both of them. Dom was big and strong, and Joel was a knife-wielding lunatic, and Russ doubted that Dom would be able to talk Joel out of punishing him this time if he tried to escape and failed.

By now Russ was ravenous and desperate to find a way of escape. On the third day, something finally occurred to him. He'd been puzzling over the fact that it wasn't quite so dark in the daytime, convinced that there must be light getting in from somewhere. Then he remembered. When he'd been outside previously, he'd noticed a cellar hatch at the front of the nightclub. But if that was the case then where was it?

Russ thought hard, trying to get his bearings. When they'd brought him here, Joel and Dom had dragged him in through the back door and taken him down the steps. Russ remembered that they had soon come to the cellar steps without making any turns and then the steps ran forward towards the front of the nightclub. At the bottom of the steps, they had turned right and gone through a door.

Once he was inside the cellar, the space stretched out to either side of the doorway, meaning that the front of the club was to the left of the cellar entrance, and the back of the club was to the right. He also knew that the cellar hatch was quite a distance from the club's entrance and to the right of it.

With this clear in his mind, Russ walked in the direction where he thought the cellar hatch would have been situated.

He took it slowly, making sure he examined the whole area next to the front wall of the cellar. And then he saw it; the tiniest chink of light where the ceiling joined the outer wall. He couldn't believe he hadn't noticed it before. But then, he hadn't been looking until now.

Joel and Dom hadn't made their morning visit yet so Russ waited patiently until they had been and gone, knowing that he would have all day and night to work on his escape, if necessary. Once he could no longer hear their footsteps on the stairs, he returned to the area where he had seen the chink of light.

Further investigation of the wall told him that there were a few more chinks of light close to that one. He dragged an old table into the space and put a solid box on it to form a step. Then he climbed up and examined the area where the light streamed through. He tapped the ceiling close to it and then further along, realising that the sound was denser in parts but close to the small chinks in the plaster, the sound was tinnier.

Russ was convinced that this was the area where the hatch had been situated. He climbed back down and returned with a sharp piece of tile. Chipping at the plaster nearest the wall, he found that it soon gave way, telling him it must have been some time since the cellar hatch had been plastered over and the plaster was now crumbling.

It wasn't long before he had cut through a sizeable length next to the wall. But the crack wasn't very wide. He assumed it was because plasterboard had been fitted so he ran the tile along the crack feeling for the edge of the plasterboard. Once he had located it, he cut around the board.

It took him a long time before he had cut around the

plasterboard completely and he had to keep taking breaks and resting his arms. But eventually the board gave way and came crashing down on him, bringing with it remnants of plaster, which clung to his hair and clothes. He lowered the plasterboard to the ground and dusted himself off. Then he assessed the area that he had opened up.

Russ didn't take long to spot the underside of one of the hatch doors, and fitted into the side of it was a bolt. He felt a flutter in his stomach as his adrenalin kicked in, giving him a strange mix of excitement and nerves. With shaking hands, he drew the bolt and slowly forced up the hatch, looking around the outside street to make sure there was no-one about. Then he pulled himself up and out of the hatch.

He'd done it! He'd escaped.

29

At first, Jill didn't look convinced when Hannah told her it was best not to tell Pete straightaway. Hannah needed to convince her, and that meant she'd have to give her something that changed her viewpoint.

'Pake Holdings aren't just offering to buy people's homes, they're intimidating those that won't sell up, attacking them, and they even torched one house.'

'Well, your nana hasn't said anything about any attacks. I know she's been on edge, but I thought that was just because all her friends have been moving out and she wants to stay. And they got a young lad for that torching. It was nothing to do with the developers.'

'She confided in me. She didn't want to worry you knowing you'd persuade her to move. But she's adamant she's staying. She doesn't want to leave all her memories of Grandad.'

Jill looked put out for a moment and Hannah felt bad that she had been the one her nana had confided in. 'I wish you'd have told me,' Jill said.

'She made me promise not to. And I'm not convinced that that young lad is behind the torching. I think somebody put him up to it.'

'Bloody hell! That sounds terrible. I'm surprised Mum would want to stay with all that going on. But then, she always was stubborn.'

Hannah didn't respond to her mother's last comment. Instead, she said, 'Samuel Sweeney is a director of Pake Holdings, which is probably why he was encouraging people to invest in the company.'

'B-but, how do you know that?' asked Jill.

'I did a bit of research on the company on the Internet. And then I found out that Samuel Sweeney is also a senior manager at Pete's firm.'

'Really? I didn't know you could find out all that.'

'Yes, it's easy enough to do a search.'

'Right. So, what are you saying? That Mr Sweeney is getting someone to terrorise people out of their homes?'

'Not him directly, no. There's someone else behind it, someone who is very corrupt.'

'Who? And how do you know all this?'

'Erm, somebody in the club told me,' said Hannah, not letting on that her boss was the person behind all the intimidation because she knew her mother's immediate reaction would be to get her to jack in her job.

'But I don't get it. If Mr Sweeney is the director, then how could someone else be behind it?'

'Because his directorship is just a front for the real brains of the operation.'

'Why? You're not making any sense.'

'Well, like I said, the man behind things is corrupt, and he doesn't want to put his name to anything. He's the sort of person who gets everyone else to do his dirty work by either offering them financial incentives or putting the frighteners on them.'

'OK. So, if that's the case, Mr Sweeney could be completely innocent.'

'Not necessarily. As the director of the company, it's likely he knows about the offers to residents, and I would assume that he'll also know about the intimidation, as a minimum.'

'But that doesn't mean Pete's involved.'

'He must know something, Mum. He's invested money in the company so presumably he knows what projects it's involved in.'

'Well, *I* didn't know anything about it,'

'That's because you'd forgotten the name of the company Pete invested in. But Pete's not like you. He's very switched on financially, isn't he? Believe me, Mum, if he's invested a few thousand in a property company, he'll be following their operations to see how his investment is doing. And that means he'll know they're the company buying up Nana's street. But the strange thing is, like you said, why hasn't he mentioned it?'

'Maybe he does know they're the company developing Mum's street, but he won't know about the intimidation.'

'Can you be sure of that, Mum, when he's already kept certain things to himself?'

For a moment Hannah saw a flicker of doubt flash across her mother's face. It was soon replaced by a look of disappointment. 'He's been trying to persuade Mum to take their offer. I thought it was because, like us, he wanted what was best for her.'

It didn't surprise Hannah that Pete was trying to persuade

her nana to take the developer's offer as she recalled him vehemently telling them both that Pat would be better off in a retirement apartment. The question was, how much did he know? Was he trying to persuade Pat to protect his investment, or to protect her from the consequences of not accepting the offer from Pake Holdings? Knowing how secretive he had been, she suspected the former.

Just then Hannah's phone rang, and she looked at the screen. 'It's Nana,' she said. 'I'll ring her back in a bit. I've got to get going soon anyway. But before I do, please promise me you won't say anything to Pete. It might be that he doesn't know about the intimidation, but can you afford to take the risk?'

Hannah felt bad as she watched the changing expressions on her mother's face. Her earlier look of disappointment had now switched to a mix of shock and fear. 'But surely I could just persuade him to sell his shares if I tell him what the company's up to?'

'You're assuming that he doesn't know, Mum, but are you really sure of that?'

Jill said nothing for a minute. Finally she looked into Hannah's face and said, 'Alright. I'll keep quiet for now. But you need to be careful too, Hannah. Whoever you've been talking to at that nightclub seems to know plenty. I think you'd be better off keeping out of it.'

'Don't worry, Mum. I'll be careful. Oh, and by the way, it might be best if you don't repeat any of this to Nana either. I'd hate her to know that I'd broken her confidence.'

Her mother nodded then watched as Hannah went over to Kai and asked him to say goodbye to his grandma. When he stuck out his bottom lip, she said, 'Don't worry, you'll be coming back later when Mummy goes to work, won't you?'

'You can leave him now if you want, save you coming back later. I've got spare clothes and things for him.'

'Oh, thanks, Mum. That would be good.'

Hannah bid them both goodbye then went to the car and checked her phone. Pat had left an answerphone message, so Hannah played it back, perturbed to notice how upset she sounded. She rang her back straightaway.

'Are you alright, Nana?'

'No. I'm not. There's been another house fire. The police and fire engines are here now. One of the neighbours spotted it this morning. They think the fire started in the night.'

'Alright, try to stay calm. I'll be straight round.'

30

Hannah had deliberated over whether to tell her mum about the fire. But if she did, it would only worry her, and Pat had already asked Hannah not to say anything about the intimidation. Aside from that, her mother would insist on coming with her, which would mean bringing Kai, and she didn't really want her son to pick up on her nána's anxiety again.

She saw the flames from a few streets away and knew that this fire was much bigger than the last one. Fortunately, it wasn't too close to Pat's house, but nevertheless, Hannah could feel the heat coming from it as soon as she stepped out of the car. A small crowd had gathered as near to the fire as the police and the blaze would allow.

Before knocking at her nana's house, Hannah walked a bit nearer and did a quick scan of the crowd, but Pat wasn't standing among the onlookers. Hannah walked back and pressed Pat's doorbell. Her nana took a while to answer, but when she finally did, she looked distressed. It was clear to Hannah that she'd made a quick effort to clean up her tear-stained face, but her eyes were still red rimmed and her cheeks flushed.

She let Hannah inside without speaking, and Hannah

noticed how much her hands were shaking as she clutched the door. Hannah shut the door behind her, and they hugged. But it wasn't like their usual loving hug, it was more of a comforting gesture, and as Hannah held her nana tight, she could feel her trembling.

'Oh, Nana,' she soothed, and that was all it took for Pat to dissolve into tears again.

Hannah had never seen her like this in her whole life. Things must be bad if they had reduced her once strong nana to a quivering wreck. Hannah gave her a few moments to gather herself before she sent Pat through to the lounge and offered to make them both a cuppa.

When Hannah came through with the drinks, her nana was sitting in her armchair clutching a sopping bunch of tissues. Pat sniffed and attempted to dry her eyes then focused on her drink.

Hannah could tell she wanted to talk so she waited until she was ready.

'It happened in the night,' Pat began. 'One of the neighbours saw flames when he set off for work. But I – I can't understand why the family wouldn't have done something about it ... unless they didn't know.'

'Maybe they're on holiday.'

'No, the neighbours said they're at home. They hammered on the door but there was nothing.'

'So, what's happening now?'

'I don't know. I couldn't bear to watch.' Pat paused for a moment, gathering herself but her next words were chilling. 'Two little boys. Eli and Josiah, they were called. Very biblical I always thought. But the parents weren't religious. They were a lovely couple, only in their thirties. And them two. Ooh, they were lovely little things. Fat lot of good their religious names have done for them now though.'

Hannah couldn't fail to notice Pat's use of the past tense. 'Are you saying the family have died?'

'It looks that way.'

'But you don't know.'

'Well, it's not been confirmed yet, but I know.'

Hannah went over to her nana, knelt on the ground and took her arms in hers, staring directly into her eyes. 'We can't afford to talk like that. They might have gone to visit family. That could be the reason no-one's seen them.'

Pat shook her head solemnly, but she didn't say anything further.

'OK,' said Hannah, standing up. 'I'll go and see what I can find out. Are you OK on your own for a bit?'

Pat nodded, dabbing at her eyes once more. Then Hannah made for the door, and as she went, she heard Pat say in a weak voice, 'Please, for God's sake, bring us back some good news.'

Outside the crowd was building despite the ferocity of the fire. Within seconds Hannah felt uncomfortable in the blazing heat and the stifling fumes. There were very few people there whom she recognised as most of Pat's neighbours had now left the street. Hannah assumed that news of the incident had spread to surrounding areas and morbid fascination had drawn people in. Hannah found herself hoping that at least some of them had come in the expectation of a positive outcome.

It didn't take her long to pick up on the gossip, which confirmed what her nana had said: the family had been at home all evening and people suspected they hadn't survived the fire. Two teams of firefighters were succeeding in bringing the fire under control while the police interviewed onlookers and held the crowd back. To one side of the crowd were two ambulances on standby.

It wasn't long before the firefighters put a ladder up to the bedroom window and several of them climbed in. Minutes later, the front door, which was now clear of flames, opened and a firefighter appeared. He was dragging something, but through the density of the gathering mass Hannah couldn't see what it was. She heard a murmur ripple through the crowd of onlookers and presumed it was a body.

The action was repeated three times leading Hannah to believe that they had just carried out the family. But were they still alive? She saw the paramedics race over carrying some equipment, including stretchers. Eventually, the crowd parted to enable them to return to the waiting ambulances. Now, instead of pushing forward, the crowd was receding, and she noticed a woman walk to the back and vomit on the road.

The first of the paramedics reappeared. Hannah had a bad feeling even before she saw what he was carrying. The atmosphere had changed now; the onlookers had gone quiet and there was a distinct air of sadness. The paramedic was carrying a stretcher, his colleague at the rear. There was the outline of a body covered in a white sheet.

They moved away from the crowd and approached the ambulance, and Hannah caught the reactions of the onlookers. All were dumbstruck, some of them in tears and drawing silently away from the scene of such tragedy.

Hannah now had a clear view as the paramedics carried another body. The remaining crowd drew round the front of the house again, the feeling now one of anticipation. Then the last two of the stretchers appeared carrying first one small body and then another. Both were covered in white sheets. Hannah stepped away, weeping now at the thought of those poor children and the dread of having to tell her nana that she had been right.

It had taken Hannah some time to calm her nana down, and even then, she hadn't wanted to leave her after such a shock. Pat hadn't spoken much, and Hannah had tried to take her mind off things while they watched an old film on the TV, and she made her endless cups of tea.

Eventually, it was time for Hannah to leave for work. 'I'm sorry, Nana, but I need to go,' she said. 'Are you sure you'll be OK?'

'Yes, I'm OK. Don't worry.'

'Alright, but you really should think about telling Mum what's been happening, y'know. It's bound to be in the news.'

'I know. I've decided.'

'What? That you're going to tell her?'

'Not only that. I've decided to leave.' Then she tried to compose herself yet again before adding, 'I've had enough. I can't take any more.'

31

Hannah was tempted to skip work that night. Thoughts of that poor family kept going around inside her head and every time she thought of the children, an intense sadness came over her. Kai wasn't much younger, and she dreaded to think how she'd feel if something happened to him.

But she knew how impractical it would be to take the night off work every time she was feeling stressed. A part of her also felt that it was even more important now to remain in the same vicinity as Jez so she could gain some insight into what he was up to.

There had been so many worrying incidents lately, least of all her concerns over her nana. She hoped Pat's decision to move wasn't just a knee-jerk reaction and that she'd go through with it. As sad as it was for Pat to have to leave her beloved home, Hannah knew it would be the best thing for her.

Inside the club there was the usual mix of customers: dodgy types, gangster types, girls and lads out on the pull, and others just out for a good time. The music blared as it did every night when she worked the bar, the customers trying to compete with the pulsating beat as they chatted at full volume. Normally she hardly noticed but tonight it was making her head throb.

Hannah knew it was because she was distressed by what had happened to that young family in Rovener Street. She tried to take her mind off it by focusing on work, putting on a smile while she chatted to the customers and other members of staff. But even that was difficult, and where she would normally flirt with the attractive male customers, now their attempts at chatting her up were just getting on her nerves and making her overly conscious of the gap left by Russ.

Then she spotted Jez heading towards her, and her fake smile faded. To her dismay he didn't stop until he had reached the bar, where he placed his hands before addressing the staff.

'How are things tonight? Everything running smoothly, I hope.'

Most of the staff let out reassuring murmurs to which Jez replied, 'Good, let's keep it that way, shall we? But let me know if you have any problems.'

Hannah carried on serving a customer, trying to block Jez's presence out of her mind. She turned her back to him while she approached the optics, taking her time in the hope that he would be gone by the time she'd poured a large gin. Then she swung round, his eyes watching her the whole time as she placed the gin and tonic on the bar then poured a pint.

Jez waited until she had finished serving the customer before he said, 'Hannah, could I have a word in my office please?'

Two of the other staff gave her curious gazes to which

Hannah shrugged, attempting to appear blasé while inside she was quaking. What the hell did he want with her? She wondered whether it might be connected to her nana. Although Pat had intimated that she would be selling up, Jez wouldn't know that yet. Maybe he was going to try to get Hannah to persuade her to sell to them.

All these thoughts were going through her mind as she made her way to Jez's office. He had already gone ahead of her, leaving her to follow behind. He was now out of view and at one time she would have rushed to keep up with him. But she took her time, determined not to let him intimidate her.

The door was shut when she reached the office. Convinced it was another ploy by Jez to display his authority, she knocked loudly and confidently. She waited a few seconds until she heard him say, 'Come in,' then she turned the doorknob and walked inside.

Jez was studying something on his desk, 'Sit down,' he said without looking up.

Again, he made her wait until he pushed the piece of paper to one side and finally looked across the desk at her. Hannah was feeling very uncomfortable by now but, knowing that that had been his intention, she tried not to show it.

'I believe you're a friend of Russ Coles,' he began, his eyes boring into her.

Hannah blushed. It was as though he knew they had history. 'No more than any of the other barmaids,' she replied defensively. 'We used to chat a bit at the bar, that's all, same as I do with a lot of the customers.'

Jez's eyes remained fixed on her, and she almost squirmed

in her seat, but she fought the urge. Hannah wondered if she'd said too much. Was her lengthy explanation making her appear guilty?

'I don't know if you're aware, but he was an employee of mine,' said Jez. 'He used to do a few odd jobs connected with my other businesses; driving, that sort of thing,' he continued. 'I'm a little concerned. You see, he's been missing for a few days, and nobody seems to know where he is. I don't suppose you happen to know where he is, do you?'

Hannah shook her head, trying to keep the tremble out of her voice as she answered, 'No, I've no idea.'

'You sure?' asked Jez and Hannah felt herself blush again. 'Look, I'm not interested in any personal connections between my employees. What you do in your private life is your business. What I am concerned about is the welfare of my staff, and I've received information that suggests Russ Coles might be in a spot of bother.'

Hannah didn't have to try to look shocked; she was! She had been convinced that Jez and his men were connected with Russ's disappearance, but now here was Jez telling her otherwise. But she wasn't foolish enough to admit that she had arranged to meet him at around the time he had gone missing.

'I – I don't know anything,' she said. Then, remembering to act the part, she added, 'But if you find out where he is, please will you let me know? I'd hate to think that anything bad might have happened to him.'

'Certainly. I think you and I share the same concerns,' Jez replied, but his voice held no warmth.

***

As she worked the bar that night, Hannah found it difficult to take her mind off the discussion she had had with Jez. He had played the concerned employer, but his whole demeanour had seemed disingenuous. Not only had his tone lacked compassion, but he had seemed more intent on watching her reactions rather than worrying about Russ.

Hannah felt sure the meeting was intended to find out just how much she knew. His attitude had angered her, but it had unsettled her too. How had Jez found out about her connection to Russ? Maybe somebody connected to Jez had spotted her leaving the pub with Russ on the night when she'd stayed at his flat.

That in itself wasn't too much of a problem. Just because she'd had a one-night stand with Russ, it didn't necessarily mean she knew anything about his private affairs. But what if Jez had guessed she knew more? Did he suspect that she and Russ had been working together to try to find evidence against him?

She tried to brush it off. How could he possibly know that? But what if he knew that her nana was a resident of Rovener Street? They might not have shared a surname, but perhaps he'd found out about the connection through another source. According to Russ, Jez had eyes and ears everywhere. And if he found out about the connection, then maybe he would surmise that she and Russ were working together.

Hannah hoped that none of this would come back on her or her family. It made her determined to make sure her nana kept to her word about moving out. But as for Russ, there was nothing she could do but wait and pray he was alright wherever he was.

*

The following day when Hannah went to pick up Kai from her mum's house, she found her nana and Pete there too. They were all seated in the living room wearing glum expressions.

'Mum's told us everything,' Jill announced. 'Apparently you knew.'

Hannah knew her mum was trying to act as though the intimidation was news to her because Pat didn't know Hannah had already told her. Not only that but Jill wouldn't want Pete to twig that she had made the connection between him and Pake Holdings.

'Nana told me not to say anything; she didn't want to worry you,' Hannah replied, going along with the pretence.

Hannah wished she had been there when Pat told her mother and stepdad everything. She would have liked to have seen Pete's reaction. Would he have been shocked at the intimidation or was he already aware of what Jez and his cohorts got up to? And what about Samuel Sweeney, the man Pete had entrusted with his investment? Did he know the full story?

'Anyway, I'm selling up,' said Pat. 'Me and your mum are going to look at some retirement apartments.'

'That's brilliant,' said Hannah. 'I'd love to come too if I can.'

''Course you can,' Pat and Jill chorused.

Then Hannah said, 'Look, Nana, I know it will be difficult leaving your home but at least you'll have peace of mind.'

'I know,' said Pat. 'I realise that now and I can't bloody

wait so let's just hope things don't take too long to go through.'

'Do we know that it's definitely the developers who are intimidating people?' asked Pete.

'It's pretty bloody obvious,' said Hannah. 'One minute they're offering everyone money to sell their houses to them and the next minute people are getting beaten up, threatened and having their houses set on fire.'

Pete held up his hands in a placatory gesture. 'Sorry, I didn't mean to upset you. I know it can't have been easy for your nana these past few weeks.'

Although Hannah's mum and stepdad now knew all about the intimidation, the one thing Jill still didn't know was that Hannah's boss, Jez, was at the heart of it all. And there was no way Hannah was going to tell either her mum or Pete. It wasn't only because it would worry her mum, but it was also because of Pete. It might be dangerous to admit to him that she knew all about Jez and his corrupt ways.

To Hannah, Pete had seemed genuinely sympathetic towards Pat but there was no way of really knowing. Was he in denial because he'd just found out what the firm he'd invested in got up to? Perhaps he was having trouble coming to terms with it. But if that was the case, then, surely, he'd be sharing his concerns with his wife at least? Alternatively, was he trying to deflect because he'd known about the intimidation all along? She really didn't know what to believe.

32

Since Russ had escaped from the cellar, he had managed to lie low, but it was obvious from the heated conversation he could hear that he now had a problem. The sound of his old mate, James and his wife, Lydia, carried to the room where Russ was staying. In fact, the volume was getting louder till it became clear they were having a full-on row.

'A few days you said,' came Lydia's strident tones. 'And it's been bloody weeks.'

'Shush,' said James, his tone softer. 'He'll be able to hear us.'

'I don't give a shit!' she bellowed. 'He's overstayed his welcome.'

'OK, OK, I'll have a word.'

'That's what you said last time. And where did that get us? The whole situation stinks. The way he turned up here with all those bruises and cuts and some cock and bull story about getting jumped. Well, you might be daft enough to believe that, but I'm not.'

'Alright, I'll sort it,' said James.

But Lydia wasn't so easily pacified. 'And what about his family?' she demanded. 'Why couldn't he have stayed with them? I'm telling you, James, there's something not right about his whole situation.' She lowered her voice then as though suddenly wary of being overheard but Russ could still make out most of what she was saying.

'Those cuts on his finger … not a mugging … something fishy … never goes out … hiding from.' Then her voice rose again, 'And he's not given us a penny since he's been here. I'm telling you, James, it's not on. Either you tell him to go, or I will.'

Russ knew that living with James and his wife had been a long shot. When he'd first escaped from the cellar, he hadn't really had a plan. All he knew was that he had to get away and fast. He no longer had a car so that option wasn't open to him. And it hadn't exactly paid dividends last time he'd chosen to hide out in his car. No, he'd needed to go somewhere nobody would think to look.

James was an old friend whom he'd known from school. Russ and he had kept in touch for a few years until it became apparent that their lifestyles were completely different. For a while Russ had kept his life secret from James and carried on meeting up with him for the odd night out. But when it had become increasingly difficult to hide his activities, their meet-ups had gradually ceased.

James lived several miles away from the city centre and, in his desperation, Russ had concluded that staying with him would be a good way of keeping hidden for a while. After spending hours making the trip on foot, Russ had turned up hungry and exhausted.

He'd come up with a story about splitting up with his psycho girlfriend who had caused him to fall out with his family and lose his job because he'd taken so much time off with the stress of the relationship. Then he'd followed that up with another tall tale about having been mugged, which was why he wasn't carrying any cash or a phone.

James seemed to have believed him, or if he didn't, he was too much of a good guy to tell him so. But his wife, Lydia, was a different story altogether. She'd made it obvious from the start that she was only tolerating his presence for James's sake. And now it had finally come to a head.

Not only did Lydia not want him there, but she was also suspicious of him. She'd already commented that his finger looked as though somebody had tried to chop it off, and Russ had lied that the muggers had done it to prise his wallet away from him. But now she sounded like she had reached breaking point. And that worried him because what was to stop her reporting her suspicions to the police? If she did that, they'd all be in a fix because of Jez's connection to them.

James was a good guy, and Russ felt bad for putting him in this situation. Not only was he endangering his marriage, but he could be endangering his family too. Jez wouldn't react too kindly to someone who had been harbouring him. And that wouldn't only mean James and Lydia would be at risk, because they also had two young children. And they'd suffered already, having to share a bedroom to accommodate Russ, then living in a tense environment.

Russ got up from the bed where he had been lying and knocked on James and Lydia's bedroom door. He heard muted tones and could tell they were troubled by him visiting their bedroom; something he didn't usually do.

'Yeah?' shouted James, tentatively.

'I need a word,' said Russ.

There was more whispering before James came to the

door. 'What is it?' he asked, looking embarrassed that they might have been overheard.

'I need to speak to both of you,' said Russ. 'We can go downstairs if you like.'

James swung the door open wide. 'No, it's OK. Come in.'

Russ clapped eyes on Lydia's startled expression as he followed James into their bedroom, but James quickly explained. 'He needs a word with both of us.'

Her expression changed on seeing that Russ's demeanour was placatory, and he was quick to offer further assurance. 'I've decided to leave,' he began. 'I overheard some of what you were saying, and I realise I've put on you enough.'

Neither of the couple spoke. Even James didn't try to contradict what he was saying. They all knew that it was true. 'Before I go, I want to thank you for putting me up. It was a really decent thing to do, and I know it can't have been easy on you and the kids.' Then he looked directly at James. 'Can I just ask you one little favour before I go, mate?'

'Yeah sure,' said James.

'Can you spare a sleeping bag?'

James appeared contrite at the mention of a sleeping bag, perhaps assuming that Russ would be sleeping on the streets. He was about to say something, but Lydia quickly grabbed his arm to get his attention then shook her head.

'It's OK,' said Russ. 'I'm not trying to guilt trip you. I just need one.'

By way of reply, Lydia addressed James rather than Russ. 'OK, he can have the navy blue one.'

'Thanks,' said Russ. 'Like I say, I really appreciate everything you've done for me, and I hope I can repay the favour one day.

*

Lydia had relented slightly and let him stay till the following morning. When James went with him to the door to see him off, she made herself scarce, taking the children with her. Russ was glad, not only because it would have been awkward but also because he had one last favour to ask James, and he didn't think Lydia would approve.

'I'm sorry to ask you this, mate, but can you spare any cash? I promise I'll get it back to you once I'm back on my feet.'

James tutted. It seemed that even he was losing patience now, but being the good guy he was, he said, 'Hang on a minute. I'll see what I can do.'

He was soon back, and he pressed a wad of notes into Russ's hand. 'Here. There's one twenty there. It's all the cash I've got on me.'

Russ thanked him profusely then gave him a massive hug before walking away. Good old James. He'd really come up trumps; he'd housed him and fed him till Russ was feeling much better and his injuries had faded. But now that his time at James's was finished, Russ had a dilemma.

He had been troubling over this moment ever since he'd moved in with James. Russ had known that he couldn't stay there forever, that one day he'd have to move out and take his chances. But he'd already decided his next move. He couldn't stay in hiding forever; he needed to get his life back. And now that he was feeling much stronger, it was time to act.

33

Hannah and her mum accompanied Pat on her visit to Beech Retirement Village. Pat had already visited three retirement apartments, but she told them this retirement village was the one she was most interested in because it was where two of her old friends lived. Between Pat dragging her feet, then the retirement village saying they couldn't accommodate her viewing request straightaway due to staff holidays, it was now four weeks since she had told her family she would move.

Beech Retirement Village was set in beautiful, landscaped gardens with a secure entry system and residents' car park. Once they had been buzzed inside the grounds, Pat marched straight to the front door. She'd been here before to visit her friends, so she knew her way around.

A friendly middle-aged lady dressed in a smart suit met them at the door and introduced herself as Bev before she gave them a tour of the development. Hannah was amazed at how lovely the place was and the range of facilities including a communal lounge, hairdresser's, restaurant and laundry room. She and her mother kept passing comment about how impressed they were. They needn't have bothered as Pat was already interested.

Their last stop was at the communal lounge where Pat found her friends, Gwen and Brenda. She was so busy chatting to them that Jill had to bring her attention back to Bev who wanted to have a discussion in her office.

'See you in a bit,' said Pat to Gwen and Brenda as Bev led them away.

Inside the office, Bev sat down and invited them to take a seat. 'Can I ask which type of apartment you're interested in?' she asked.

'Oh, the one-bedroomed,' Pat replied.

'I'm afraid that could be a bit of a problem,' said Bev. 'We seem to have had a rush on them lately and it might be a while before one becomes free. We do have a two-bedroomed apartment available. It would give you lots more room, but it is an extra fifty thousand.'

'Can't afford it,' said Pat.

'Oh, well in that case, I'm sorry but you might have a bit of a wait.'

'How long are we talking?' asked Jill.

'It's impossible to say. But, obviously, given the age of some of the residents, the position could change at any time.'

None of them responded to this statement, each of them dwelling on the implicit meaning. They had to wait for somebody to die before an apartment became available, and it wasn't a cheery thought.

'Are you OK, Nana?' asked Hannah once they were outside.

'Yeah, why wouldn't I be?'

'Well, it was just that you seemed disappointed.'

'No, I'm fine. It'll take as long as it takes, and in the meantime, the bloody developers will just have to wait.

It took Russ hours to walk to Manchester, but he had decided to keep hold of as much of his money as he could because he needed it. One of the things he had to buy was a phone because Joel had taken away all of his belongings when they captured him. So, Russ had stopped at a phone shop on the way and acquired the cheapest throwaway phone he could find. He'd keep it switched off for now to save power until he had to use it.

When he finally arrived about a mile outside the city centre, he was exhausted and trepidatious. He decided to kip down in a park that was known for being frequented by the homeless. That way he wouldn't risk being spotted by anyone he knew. He found a bench then spread the sleeping bag out and climbed inside. It was still only afternoon, but he had nothing else to do so he figured he might as well get some rest while he could.

Within minutes of getting inside the sleeping bag, Russ was approached by a youth wearing stained trackie bottoms, scuffed trainers and a tatty hoody.

'Are you new?' he demanded.

Russ looked up to see a face that was battle weary. The lad's nose and one cheek were grazed and there was a scar running across his chin. Russ shuddered thinking of Joel with the knife. Had somebody done something similar to this poor kid?

'Yeah, that's right,' he said.

'Got any gear?' was the lad's next question.

'No.'

'What about cigs?'

'No.'

'Booze?'

'No.'

'What the fuck are you on then?'

'Nowt yet.'

The lad laughed. 'You fuckin' soon will be.' Then he disappeared.

Russ tried to sleep again, but it wasn't long till he was interrupted a second time. A similar conversation took place and Russ was relieved that he wouldn't be on the streets permanently as he wasn't winning any friends. He had another plan in mind, but he had to wait until the early hours to carry it out.

Deciding he'd be less conspicuous if he wasn't lying on a park bench in a sleeping bag, he rolled it up, put it inside the plastic bag he'd been carrying and changed benches to one nearer the main road.

That seemed to do the trick because Russ was left alone until darkness drew in. He sat watching the activity on the main road: cars passing and the odd couple or group of youngsters making their way into Manchester dressed for a night on the town. He was bored and wanted to continue his own journey into Manchester, but he couldn't risk it yet.

Russ saw a few of the homeless move into the park and curl up on a bench in a sleeping bag as he had done. One of them even erected a tent on the green, but nobody bothered Russ. He supposed that now he must look more like somebody suspicious rather than a homeless person.

It was frustrating not even being able to have a kip but the more people he saw enter the park, the less inclined he was to go to sleep. A lot of them were intoxicated. Whether from drugs or drink, he couldn't tell but one or two of them were even arguing among themselves. Russ was tempted to change location now but knew he'd have to be patient until it was time.

34

Pat looked with fondness at the onyx ashtray as she packed it away. She didn't smoke but Harry used to. She remembered how much he loved that ashtray when she'd bought it for him, and she couldn't bear to part with it. She'd also packed the lovely vase they'd received as a wedding present. At least she could hold onto her memories by taking her prized possessions with her.

Since she'd visited Beech Retirement Village earlier that day, Pat was coming round to the idea of living there more and more. It would be good to live near to Gwen and Brenda again. It might not be quite the same as having their own houses in the street they knew so well, but the place had changed anyway. In fact, after the events of the last few months, she couldn't wait to put this whole horrid situation behind her, and she found herself actually looking forward to the next phase of her life.

Pat had also been thinking about the other advantages. Everything was on hand at the retirement village, and she'd only have a small property to take care of instead of managing a house. She had to admit to herself that she wasn't getting any younger, and it was becoming more difficult to look after the place on her own.

She'd had to let a lot of her things go though, such as the toby jugs Harry used to collect. It had saddened her, but she'd tried to console herself by thinking of the money they had fetched at a second-hand shop. Two hundred and thirty pounds wasn't bad for a load of old jugs. Maybe her Harry had been onto something after all.

While she was putting some picture frames inside a box, she heard the doorbell ring, so she went to answer it. She found Hannah standing on the doorstep wearing a wide smile.

'Oh, hello, love,' said Pat. 'I wasn't expecting you. Is Kai not with you?'

'No, I've just dropped him off at Mum's. I thought I'd just pop in to see how you are before I go to work.'

'I'm not so bad. I've just been doing a bit of packing.'

'What, already? But I thought they said it might be a while yet?'

'Oh, I know what they said but I've got a lot to pack and, well, you never know, do you? From what the manager told us, we're waiting for someone to die. A few of the residents in that lounge looked on their last legs to me so it might happen sooner than we think.'

Hannah giggled. 'Nana, what are you like?'

Pat joined in her laughter. 'Well, it's true, isn't it?'

Recovering herself, Hannah then asked, 'Have you told the developers?'

'Told them what? There's nothing to tell them yet.'

'Just that it might be a while yet. I wouldn't want them to think you're stalling.'

'It'll be fine. They've been OK with me since I agreed to sell to them. Surely they must realise that these things can take time.'

Hannah shrugged. 'OK, as long as you're sure.'

The night had dragged for Russ, and he was glad when he found out from a homeless guy that it had reached 4.30 a.m. It should be much safer for him to go into Manchester at this time. He'd still keep his wits about him though, in case he came across anyone he knew.

Staying in the park had been a daunting experience. He'd been on constant alert in case somebody might want to rob his money or phone. But now, the fear factor had gone up a notch. The nearer he drew to the city centre, the more his adrenalin pulsed through his body until, finally, he arrived outside The Gilded Cage nightclub.

Russ checked all around him to make sure there was nobody about even though he was pretty sure the club would be empty at this time of the morning. Even Jez, who sometimes stayed after closing time, never remained until later than three, three-thirty.

Now that the club was shut, it would also be alarmed. Russ had seen the alarm panel in Jez's office when he'd gone to have meetings with him, and he knew Jez wasn't daft enough not to set it. He had too many enemies who might want to take advantage. But Russ knew from experience that the cellar wasn't alarmed.

He approached the cellar hatch, checking around him once more. Then he pushed his hand inside the plastic bag containing his sleeping bag and withdrew the chisel he had taken from James's house before he left. Again, he felt bad about it, but he promised himself he'd return it one day.

Russ knew roughly the positioning of the bolt that

secured the cellar hatch in place, so he also knew where the best place to apply pressure would be. He slid the chisel down the slight gap between the two metal doors and began to work them. As he worked, he kept checking that no-one was watching. All was quiet for a while but then he saw someone heading towards him.

He moved away from the hatch doors, spread out his sleeping bag on the steps of the recessed entrance and jumped inside, hiding the chisel next to his body. Russ discreetly watched the man approach, and as he watched, he could tell the man was either drunk or drugged. His progress was slow, and his feet seemed to drag behind him as he tried to walk.

Once the man reached The Gilded Cage, Russ shut his eyes and pretended to be asleep in the hope that he would go away. He could tell the man was getting nearer because of the strong smell of cannabis that permeated the air. Wary of what the man was going to do next, Russ quickly opened his eyes again and sat up in the sleeping bag.

'Alright, mate?' the man asked, his speech slow and slurred.

He was scruffy and looked pasty. From his appearance and the way he was speaking, Russ had him pegged for a Spice Head.

'Sure,' said Russ, staring at the man, his senses on high alert.

'This your spot?' he struggled to ask as he leant against the wall of the recess for balance.

Russ nodded and the man stared at him for several seconds. It felt unnerving but Russ maintained his gaze, awaiting the man's next move, the chisel now lodged firmly in his hand in case he needed it. To Russ's relief, the Spice Head then levered himself clumsily away from the wall and carried on his way, muttering as he did so. Russ caught a few words, something about his tent and his mates sorting him out, but Russ wasn't really interested. He just wanted him to go away.

Once the coast was clear, Russ got back to work on the metal doors, trying to prise them open. It took a while and he still had to keep looking round to make sure there was nobody else around, but as he worked, he could feel them start to loosen. Eventually, he was rewarded with the sound of the doors giving way and then something dropping to the ground inside the cellar.

Assuming it was the bolt, he eased open the hatch and dropped down onto the cellar floor. Inside it was just as cold and musty as he remembered. He found the bolt with the catch plate still clinging to it. Some of the screws were poking out of the holes but others had dropped separately onto the ground. Russ collected them then fashioned a step up to the cellar hatch as he had done previously. Using the chisel and a great deal of ingenuity, he managed to secure the bolt back in place.

The doorway out of the cellar was still locked but Russ had no intentions of trying to break it down. Entering the nightclub wasn't his aim, especially as it would set off the alarm and alert people to his presence. For the moment he had achieved his objective, which was to spend tonight and perhaps several others in the place where Jez would least expect to find him: the cellar of his own nightclub.

Russ spread his sleeping bag down on the floor and prepared to settle in for the night. Having spent time here previously, he knew that hardly anyone ever came down into the cellar of The Gilded Cage, and since he had escaped, they no longer had a reason to visit. But staying close to the enemy was handy while he planned his next move.

35

'Have you seen much of Nana since we visited the retirement home?' Hannah asked her mother.

They were in Hannah's lounge drinking coffee while Kai watched children's TV.

'I saw her this morning. What about you?'

'I've not seen her since the evening after we went to visit Beech Retirement Village, two days ago,' said Hannah. 'How does she seem to you?'

'Fine. I think she's looking forward to moving to the retirement home now.'

'Yes, I thought that. She'd already started packing when I called round and, if you ask me, it can't come soon enough after everything that's happened.'

'Hear, hear,' said Jill.

Thoughts of the innocent family who had lost their lives must have triggered a memory for Jill because she then said, 'I knew there was something I meant to tell you. According to your nana that young lad, Connor Davis, didn't start the second fire.'

'What? How did they reach that conclusion?'

'Apparently, he was at home with his mother. She vouched for him.'

'Really?' said Hannah. 'What about the first fire?'

'Oh, that was definitely him. There's going to be a court case.'

Hannah nodded without commenting further. She still wasn't convinced that Connor had started the first fire, or if he had, she believed that somebody connected to Pake Holdings had put him up to it. But she wasn't going to share those thoughts with her mother just yet. Instead, she deflected.

'How has Pete been since he found out about Nana?'

'Just the same.'

'In what way?'

'Well, he seems as shocked as me about what Mum's been going through, to be honest.'

'But hasn't he said anything about the shares in Pake Holdings?'

'Not a dickybird.'

'Do you think it's because he's known all along what's been going on?'

Jill sighed. 'I really don't know, Hannah. I'm so tempted to have it out with him.'

'No, don't do that!' Hannah hastily cut in. 'If he already knows everything then he's hardly innocent, is he? And letting on that you know what he's been up to could put you in danger.'

'I just can't see him investing money in something like that,' Jill said but it came across as more of a plea.

'But, Mum, if he didn't know, he would have told you about his concerns, maybe offered to sell the shares back to Pake Holdings. But he hasn't done that, has he?'

'No, but that doesn't necessarily mean he's involved.'

'Well, the only other reason I can think of for staying schtum is because he doesn't want to miss out on a financial opportunity even though he now knows how Pake are making their money.'

Jill shuffled uncomfortably but didn't respond, so Hannah spoke again. 'Just keep quiet for now, Mum. Hopefully the police will find out who's at the bottom of the intimidation, and then it will all come to a head.'

At this point Jill looked on the verge of tears, so Hannah crossed the room and put a comforting arm around her. 'It'll work out, Mum. I promise.'

Despite her reassuring words, Hannah didn't hold out much hope of the police getting to the bottom of things, but she'd had to tell her mum something to make her feel better. Hannah's biggest hope up to now had been that she and Russ would be able to expose Jez. But now that Russ was missing, she despaired of ever putting a stop to Jez. She consoled herself with the fact that at least her nana would be moving soon and would therefore be out of the danger zone.

It was evening and Pat was watching TV when the phone rang. Pausing an episode of *The One Show*, she got up to answer it. She was shocked to hear the voice of the same nasty man who had called her weeks previously telling her he wanted her out. That time she had cut the call before he had chance to detail the repercussions that would follow if she didn't move out. But now all she could do was stare at the phone in shock. She couldn't believe he was still hassling her.

'Pat Bennett,' he began. 'I believe you've agreed a sale on your property to Pake Holdings?'

Recovering slightly, she said, 'Yes, that's right. But why do you want to know? Who are you?'

Despite her bravado, her voice dropped as she asked the last question, her nerves getting to her.

'Never mind who I am, what I want to know is why it's taking so fuckin' long!'

Pat could hear the venom in his voice and that, together with his aggressive bad language, made her tremble with fear. 'I'm waiting for an apartment to become available in the retirement home. They haven't got any vacancies at the moment.'

'Well find another fuckin' retirement home then! We haven't got forever to wait while you piss about. Get on with it and fast, otherwise you'll be fuckin' sorry.'

When he cut the call, Pat found it impossible to hold back her tears. She had thought all the intimidation was over, at least for her, anyway, although she knew some of the other remaining residents were still having problems. Only yesterday one of her neighbours had received another nasty letter and a man was threatened in the street the week previously.

But now it seemed like it wasn't over at all. And she was terrified of what might happen to her if Beech Retirement Village didn't find her an apartment soon.

36

R uss had now spent two nights back in the cellar of The Gilded Cage. It was cold and boring and, at times, terrifying. He was hypervigilant, especially when the sound of the nightclub music didn't drown everything out and every little noise made him think his hiding place had been found: outside chatter, people walking over the metal doors and people straying too close to the main cellar entrance.

After that first night he had slipped out in the early hours, walking a good distance from the city centre in the direction of Salford where he'd found an all-night petrol station. The food there was expensive and not particularly fresh, but at least he could get something to eat before he snuck back to the cellar and spent the rest of the night snoozing.

But on the second night, he came across somebody he wasn't expecting. Not wishing to use his phone too much, he had gauged the approximate time by judging how long seemed to have elapsed since the music coming from upstairs had stopped.

Russ surmised that it must have been at least four o'clock when he pulled away the bolt that had been temporarily put back in place, then pushed open the hatch doors. He heaved himself up onto the pavement, secured the doors back into place and hid the chisel inside his clothes. Once that was done, Russ jumped to his feet ready to head towards Salford. But then the front door of the nightclub opened and there on the steps was Joel.

They locked eyes at the same time. Russ's reaction was instant. He took to his heels and headed down an alleyway that led to the back of the club. He turned several times, following a series of minor roads and alleyways in the hope of losing Joel. But the sound of footsteps closing in told him that Joel was gaining.

Russ took a quick look round and saw to his unease that as well as Joel there was another larger man, possibly Dom, in the distance, but he seemed to have come to a stop. Then Russ heard him shout.

'I'll head him off the other way.'

Panic gripped Russ at the realisation that Dom intended to trap him. It was a long alleyway with no spurs off it, so the only way out was either straight ahead or back the way he had come. But Joel was blocking his way and gaining on him. Russ knew he'd stand a better chance with Joel than with Dom, so he stopped, turned around and waited for Joel to catch up.

There was a look of astonishment on Joel's face as he skidded to a stop and faced Russ. 'Oh, you fancy your fuckin' chances, do you?' he taunted, pulling the knife out of his pocket. 'Come on then, let's have it.'

Then Joel rushed him. But Russ was ready. He dodged Joel then pulled out the chisel and faced him again. He could see that Joel was shocked at the sight of the chisel. Capitalising on that, Russ didn't wait for Joel to come at him again. He plunged forward with the chisel, then struck

Joel's hand, the blow so fierce that it caused Joel to lose his grip on the knife.

Adrenalin was coursing through Russ's body producing a combined effect: fear but also anger. Joel's proximity was a clear reminder of the terror and pain he had suffered at his hands when he'd tortured him in the cellar. Fortunately, the finger was no longer painful, but he would always have a scar.

Driven by rage, he ran at Joel again, plunging the chisel deep into his gut. Joel's hands clutched his stomach, instinctively trying to halt the crimson tide that gushed from a deep wound. They stared at each other, and for a moment all was still and silent except for the strange gurgling noise Joel made as though he was trying to speak.

Russ no longer saw the usual menace or mockery in Joel's face. They had been replaced by bewilderment and then, finally, resignation as Joel fell to the ground and lay in his own blood.

For a few seconds Russ was immobile, crippled by the horror of what he had just done. A sound from further up the alleyway brought him to his senses and he looked up to find Dom approaching. Acting on instinct, he reached for the chisel, forcefully removing it from Joel's torso while gagging at the sight of the gash and the blood that still pumped from it.

He turned to Dom, ready to defend himself once more but terrified by the prospect. The guy was huge, and Russ was convinced he'd come off worse if Dom was tooled up. Then Russ remembered about Joel's knife and grabbed it quick. He stood waiting for Dom to reach him; chisel in one hand, knife in the other.

'Fuckin' hell! You've killed him,' said Dom.

He stood with his mouth agape but made no attempt to attack Russ. 'I don't fuckin' believe it!' he said, making it obvious to Russ that it was his first experience of murder.

Russ didn't speak. There was no point trying to verbally defend himself against an enemy whose sole purpose was to destroy him. For a second, he thought about making a run for it. Judging by Dom's stunned reaction, he might have a chance to escape. But then Dom spoke again.

'We don't have to do this y'know?'

'What do you mean?' asked Russ, confused.

'I mean, I didn't fuckin' sign up for any of this. When I started working for Jez, I thought it was just a way to earn a bit of easy money, but I had no idea what he was like, what either of them were like. Joel was a fuckin' sick bastard. Some of the stuff he's done, I tell you ...'

He paused for a moment and Russ could tell he was struggling with the memories.

'To be honest, the world's better off without him,' Dom continued. 'I had no choice but to be a part of it. If I'd have walked away, him or Jez would have killed me. I'm still in the shit now but nobody needs to know about this apart from you and me. Walk away. Get rid of the fuckin' blades and we'll let Jez and the cops worry over who killed him. Fuck knows, he's got enough enemies.'

'I – I won't tell anyone,' said Russ, still in a state of shock. 'But what about CCTV?'

'It'll be OK. It was a smart move to stick to the back alleys,' Dom gazed around as if to reinforce his words. 'There's fuck all here.'

'What about outside the club?'

'Oh, that one only covers the entrance. It won't stretch as far as the cellar hatch so all they'll see is Joel chasing after someone or something. They won't know it was you.'

'What about you?' asked Russ. 'Won't you be on the CCTV?'

'Yeah, but I came out after Joel, and it was only when I saw him running down the alleyway that I ran after him. I was probably out of camera range by then. I'll make summat up, don't worry, tell them I went straight home or summat and make out I didn't even see Joel going down the alley.

'We'll have to be careful now as well,' he added. 'If the CCTV anywhere gets a shot of us, it'll be a dead fuckin' giveaway that we had summat to do with this.'

Russ was grateful for the advice. In his panic he hadn't considered that.

While he was still thinking about his next move, Dom spoke again, 'Whatever you do, don't tell a soul about this. I know nowt, and if you tell anyone I do, I'll fuckin' come for you myself.'

Despite the threat, Russ wanted to thank him, but it didn't seem appropriate under the circumstances. So, instead, he walked away from the scene of devastation, his head bowed low and tears clouding his eyes.

37

The phone call the previous evening had left Pat shaken. She hadn't slept well that night, and although she'd kicked the habit of turning to brandy every night to help her sleep, she found once again that it was the only thing that worked.

When Pat got up the next day, she had that familiar morning after feeling of dry mouth and pounding head, but her stomach was also upset, and as she tried to make herself a cuppa and some breakfast her hands were trembling. Plonking herself in front of the TV while she ate her breakfast, she couldn't concentrate. All she could think about was the danger she was in and the fear of what that nasty man might do if she didn't carry out his instructions.

Pat found it hard to believe that she was still in this position after she had already agreed to move out and say goodbye to her lovely home. As she looked around her tidy living room, her eyes filled with tears to think of the sacrifices she was making only to have the developers still intimidating her.

She put her half-empty plate to one side of the sink and went up to take a shower. By the time she had got dressed and tidied her hair, she had made a decision. She was through with worrying her family. If she rang Jill or Hannah, they would only tell her to move in with them till her apartment was available. But she didn't want to put on them: she wanted her independence.

Pat knew she couldn't sit by and wait to see what would happen, so she took matters into her own hands. She rang Beech Retirement Village, explained that she needed to move as soon as possible and asked if any apartments were free yet. She didn't care even if it was a two-bedroomed apartment as long as it was available. She'd find the extra money somehow.

The manageress explained that since her visit to the retirement village, even the two-bedroomed apartments had been taken. Unfortunately, she couldn't tell Pat how long it would be until any others became available.

Trying to hold it together, Pat cut the call and put down her phone. Some of her old determination came back to her. Just because Beech couldn't help her, it didn't mean she was powerless. There were other things she could do, other apartments. A few phone calls should sort things out. She picked up the phone again and prepared herself for a busy morning.

Russ had been lying low ever since he had killed Joel two days previously. Terrified of being caught, he had spent his time in the cellar of The Gilded Cage with nothing to do but chase the troubled thoughts that were going round and round inside his head.

He didn't feel bad about killing Joel because, like Dom had said, the world was better off without him. But he felt bad for taking a life, any life. It was a disturbing feeling to know that he was a killer capable of such a brutal act, and he couldn't stop thinking about the blood and the strange gurgling noise Joel had made when he went down.

Russ was glad he had already stocked up with food, so he didn't have to risk going out and being picked up on CCTV. He had no doubt the police were swarming the area once the body was discovered, and they would soon connect Joel's death to The Gilded Cage.

He had hedged his bets, worried at first that the police might search the building including the cellar. But then he consoled himself with the thought that Joel's body was found several streets away, so there should be no reason to search the cellar. And Russ had decided that the risk of being seen outside far outweighed the risk of being found inside.

He was also anxious about Dom. What if he went back on his word, especially if Jez started piling on the pressure and demanding to be told if Dom knew anything? Dom didn't owe Russ any loyalty. He could easily tell Jez that Russ had escaped from him after killing Joel.

And on top of all that, Russ was concerned about how long he could last in the cellar. He didn't have enough food to last more than a few days, so sooner or later he would have to venture out and take his chances. But for now, he would stay put.

'You're doing what?' asked Jill, surprised.

'You heard. I'm moving to Armeria Gardens.'

'When?'

'A week.'

'A week?' asked Hannah. 'That's quick, isn't it? What's caused your change of heart? I thought you were dead set on moving to Beech Retirement Village.'

Hannah and her mother had called round to see Pat and were surprised to see how many full boxes were stacked in Pat's living room. It seemed she had been working hard and was keen to move. But Hannah had a bad feeling about this. To start with, her nana had been adamant she wasn't going to move at all, then she had decided to move to the place where two of her friends lived after she had been intimidated. And now, she was in a rush to move to one of the developments that she had initially rejected.

'I could be waiting forever for an apartment at Beech, so I'm going to Armeria instead. I've found a nice little apartment I'm going to rent till something becomes available at Beech.'

'But I thought you didn't like it there,' said Jill.

'Yes. And why would you want to rent when you could buy your own home?' asked Hannah.

Before Pat had chance to respond, Hannah stared directly at her and said, 'You haven't received any more letters, have you?'

Her nana looked sheepish as she replied. 'I had another phone call.' Pat's voice was low as though she didn't really want to tell them.

'What did they say?' asked Jill, affronted.

'The usual thing. They want me out. So now I'm going. I've had enough of it.'

'But it will mean having to move twice,' said Hannah. 'And you'll have to fork out for rent.'

'I know, I've thought of all that. Don't worry. I'll have it all sorted.'

'But you could stay with us,' said Jill.

'No, no. I wouldn't hear of it. You don't really want to put up with an old fuddy duddy living with you any more than I want to litter somebody else's home. Besides, I've only got a week to wait before I can move to Armeria. The removal van's already booked. It'll soon fly by.'

'Bloody hell! You have been working hard,' said Hannah. 'Are you sure you'll be alright, Nana?'

'Yeah, 'course I will. If that nasty man rings again, I'll just give him my moving date. That'll keep them developers off my back.'

'It's a pity you can't have the apartment you really wanted,' Jill chipped in. 'You should be able to stay here till it's available. It's terrible what that development company are doing to you. They want stringing up.'

'I don't care anymore,' said Pat, and both Hannah and her mother were surprised at the ferocity of her tone. 'I just want to get away. I don't bloody care what I have to do anymore as long as I'm away from this street and all the bad memories.'

Hannah cast her mind back to the sickening feeling she'd had when the paramedics had pulled the bodies from that house fire, and suddenly, despite the unfairness of it all, she understood just what her nana meant.

38

Russ waited two more days before he ventured outside. He had run out of food earlier that day and was ravenous. Still wary of being captured on CCTV, he had fashioned a hood and scarf out of a pair of old curtains he had found in a box in the cellar.

Keeping his head low, he headed in the direction of Salford towards the late-night garage he had used previously. He knew that his choice of headgear alone could single him out, but at this time in the morning there was hardly anyone about. Those that were still about were mainly the homeless or the inebriated who wouldn't recognise him anyway.

When he arrived at the garage, he put away his headgear. In the time that he had visited the garage, he had become familiar to the staff, who were bound to ask questions if he was wearing the hood and scarf. It was better to appear as normal, and he felt sure that he was far enough away from the city centre to be safe from detection.

He noticed the odd look on the cashier's face as she flared her nostrils, and he realised that he must stink. He hadn't had a shower for days or changed his clothes. Fortunately, she was too polite to pass comment.

Outside, Russ checked his money, perturbed to notice

that it would all be gone in a matter of days. He walked the streets of Salford devouring two bags of crisps. Then it was time to cover his face again and make his way back to The Gilded Cage, his heart hammering as he drew nearer.

Russ was relieved when he arrived safely and hid down in the cellar once again. But he knew this situation couldn't last forever. His money was running out and he felt that it was only a matter of time before his luck did too.

When Pat went to bed that night, she was feeling content. For the first time in a long while she felt positive about the future. She'd come to terms with the fact that she was leaving her home, and now she was looking forward to the move in just a few days' time. It would be nice to be away from this deserted street and among people her own age again.

Armeria Gardens wasn't her ultimate destination, but it would be OK for the time being, and at least she'd be able to sleep easy at night. She also planned to put all those little knick-knacks that reminded her of Harry in a prominent place so it wouldn't feel as though she'd forsaken his memory.

As she lay in bed, she mentally ticked off a list of jobs in her head. As well as arranging the removal van, she'd contacted the utility company, the insurance company and her Internet provider, and she'd also arranged to have her post redirected.

While she was going through this mental check list, she remembered she hadn't got in touch with the developers. She needed to chase the money from the sale of the house to make sure it was in her bank account ready if an apartment at Beech should become available. It also wouldn't do any harm to let them know she had a moving date. She'd make sure she did it in the morning.

Eventually, Pat drifted off with thoughts of the move dominating her mind. Then something broke her sleep. She wasn't sure what it was at first and she stared around the bedroom in confusion, catching sight of the bedside clock, which showed 3.03 a.m. She'd normally wake around this time to go to the loo but, although her bladder was full, that wasn't what had disturbed her.

The sound was unfamiliar, so it took her a while to realise that it was, in fact, the burglar alarm that she'd had fitted. Immediately she was gripped by fear. Did that mean somebody was in her home?

When she'd had the alarm fitted, it had given her peace of mind, knowing that if someone had broken into her home while she was out and about, she would be warned about it. But she had never contemplated how she would feel if the alarm went off in the middle of the night.

Pat sat up in bed clutching her chest, her breath coming in short gasps and the whole of her body shaking. Convinced she was having a panic attack, she tried to bring her breathing under control. But the fear wouldn't go away. Neither would this alien feeling that seemed to have taken over her body.

She knew she should go downstairs and investigate. But she was terrified of doing so. Her mind flipped to thoughts of neighbours she could ring, but then she remembered that the people she could trust were no longer nearby. And if she rang her family, it might be too late by the time they arrived.

Realising there was nobody she could turn to, Pat decided she would have to tackle this alone. She started by jumping out of bed, deliberately landing heavily in the hope that the sound would scare them off. She now became aware of the urgent need to empty her bladder. Perhaps if she flushed the loo, it would alert them to the fact that there was somebody in the house and they might go away.

Pat was on the toilet when she heard what she thought was the front door slamming followed by the sound of voices outside. Once she had finished in the bathroom, she went to the front bedroom window and looked out, but she couldn't see anyone about; it was just the same abandoned street with most of the windows boarded up. She tried her own bedroom window too, which was located at the back of the house. Again, there was no sign of anyone around.

Feeling reassured that it was either a fault with the alarm or that whoever it was had now gone, Pat made her way down the stairs. Her heart was still pounding in her chest and her breathing remained shallow no matter how much she tried to take slow deep breaths. But she needed to see for herself what had caused the alarm to go off. She couldn't risk wasting police time by ringing them if it turned out to be nothing.

Her stairway led straight onto the hallway and Pat could see even before she'd reached the bottom that the front door was unlocked. The security chain was no longer in place and the door was slightly ajar. It was only as she got closer that she noticed the living room door was also ajar. She was certain she'd shut it last night as she did every night before she went to bed.

Instinctively, she pushed the front door to, and the lock

clicked into place. Pat felt clammy and faint and her knees felt weak as she approached the living room, standing back and pushing the door fully open before she went further. On trembling limbs, she walked across the hall and peered inside the room. Pat was horrified at what she saw.

The room had been completely trashed, her stacked boxes tipped over and her sofa slit so that the stuffing was hanging out. The few ornaments that she hadn't yet put away were strewn around the room, many of them smashed into pieces. But the most alarming sight that met her was the message that was emblazoned across the opposite wall in vivid red letters. *Your time is up. Get out NOW!*

Hannah thought she'd pay a surprise visit to her nana and check if she needed any help with the remaining packing. As the time for Pat to move out was drawing nearer, Hannah knew she'd be feeling sad despite her attempts to put on a brave face. Maybe a visit from Hannah and Kai would be just the tonic she needed.

As Hannah drove down Rovener Street with Kai in the child seat, she caught sight of the two burnt-out houses and couldn't help but recall that dreadful day not so long ago when the bodies of that poor family had been carried out. Thank God it was all coming to an end, for her nana at least.

When Hannah left her car and walked up to Pat's house, she was perturbed to find the curtains still drawn. That wasn't like her, especially as it was now eleven o'clock in the morning. A chill went through Hannah, a visceral feeling that something wasn't right. And when Pat didn't answer the door after the third ring of the doorbell, that feeling of dread intensified. Hannah rang the landline, and from out on the street she could hear it ring, but that also went unanswered.

For a moment Hannah deliberated over what to do. She had a spare key, but she also had Kai with her, and her instinct was to summon help rather than go inside as she didn't know what she might find. But help with what? She didn't even know what had happened and from this side of the door she wasn't likely to find out.

Once she'd rung the bell a couple of times and received no answer, Hannah knocked on the window too and shouted through the letterbox. 'Nana, are you alright?' She was tempted to go round the back of the house and do the same there, but one look at the deserted street was enough to make her lose her nerve. The back alleyway would be even more desolate.

'Where Nana?' asked Kai.

'I'm not sure. Maybe she's still asleep,' Hannah replied, forcing a weak smile.

Unsure what to do, Hannah finally decided to ring her mum to get a second opinion.

'Mum, there's something not right at Nana's. She's not answering the door and the curtains are shut.'

Hannah could hear the shock in her mother's tone as she said, 'Oh my God! That's not like her. I wonder what could have happened.'

The words 'what could have happened' struck Hannah with force. Her mother could have said 'I wonder where she is', but they both knew that Pat would never go out and leave her curtains shut.

'Have you got your spare key with you?' Jill asked.

'Yeah, but I don't like to use it, not when Kai's with me.'

Jill read her meaning straightaway. 'OK, wait in the car. Me and Pete will be straight there. Oh, and ring the emergency services while you're waiting. There's definitely something not right.'

Hannah did as her mother advised and rang the emergency services who didn't sound convinced that there was something amiss till Hannah told them about all the suspicious incidents that had taken place in Rovener Street recently. She didn't really like the idea of Pete being involved, but it might be handy to have a man around if the emergency services didn't turn up straightaway. It would also mean one of them could stay in the car with Kai until they found out what was awaiting them inside Pat's house.

39

Hannah was singing nursery rhymes to Kai, helping to pass the time for both of them, when she saw Pete's BMW zoom down the street before parking in the space behind hers. He and her mum dashed out of the car, and she met them on the pavement.

She could tell by her mum's pale face and stress lines that she was assuming the worst and was feeling the strain already. Jill was clutching her own spare key as she said to Hannah, 'Come on, let's see what's the matter.'

'No,' said Pete, holding up his hand. 'Best leave this to me.'

Hannah could tell he was trying to protect her mum from any potential shocks. Considerate of him, she thought, playing the supportive family man. *Who would have thought he had the potential to be involved in such a ruthless money-making scheme?* But she kept her thoughts to herself. Like Pete, she was concerned about her mother.

'Pete's right,' she said. 'We don't know what we might find. Why don't you stay here with Kai, Mum, and I'll go inside with Pete?'

Hannah was also dreading what might be awaiting them indoors, but she didn't think it was appropriate for Pete to be the only one going inside. She no longer trusted him and felt that a member of Pat's family should also be present.

Pete took Jill's key, and they entered the house, Pete leading the way. Hannah's dread intensified as she followed him into the living room. As she hesitated nervously by the door, Pete ran across the room.

Hannah's eyes took in a scene of devastation and the vitriolic words on the wall. But she didn't notice her nana at first. Pete was blocking her view till he dropped to his knees. There, spread out on the floor, Hannah could see her nana, and she let out a horrified gasp.

'Fuck!' Pete cursed, grabbing Pat's wrist and feeling for a pulse.

Then his head was on her chest, his ear pressed up close as he checked for a heartbeat. After a few seconds he cursed again. 'Shit!'

'Is she dead?' shrieked Hannah.

'I don't know. I think I can hear summat, but it's only faint. Go and make sure your mum and Kai don't come in. They can't fuckin' see her like this.'

For a moment Hannah was indecisive, but then Pete began doing heart compressions and something about that desperate act spurred her into action. She fought back tears as she came out of the house. Her mother looked at her pleadingly and Hannah didn't know what to say.

In the same split second, Hannah noticed the ambulance that had stopped across the street and the two paramedics who emerged from it. 'Over here,' she shouted, waving them across the street then focusing on her mother again as the paramedics went inside.

Jill had opened the door of the BMW by now and Kai was scrambling to get outside. 'No, stay there with grandma,' said Hannah.

'Wh-what's happened?' asked Jill.

Hannah looked at Kai and shrugged, searching for what to tell her mother but also wary of letting her son overhear anything. 'We don't know yet but there's been a break-in and she's erm ...'

'Just say it, for Christ's sake!' yelled Jill. 'Is she ... is she ...'

She didn't finish the sentence. Hannah didn't know whether it was because she couldn't bear to utter the word *dead* or whether she was conscious of the effect it might have on Kai.

'We don't know yet,' said Hannah. 'Pete tried to listen. He wasn't sure if he could hear a beat or not,' she said, choosing her words carefully so Kai wouldn't understand. 'I think the paramedics must be working on her now. I'll go and see.'

Then she dashed back inside the house, knowing her mother wouldn't follow while she had Kai with her. When Hannah reached the living room door it was closed. She edged it open to see the two paramedics leaning on the ground over Pat. One of them was using a defibrillator while Pete watched from a metre away, his features taut.

The sight made Hannah tearful, and she found it impossible to watch. For a few seconds she stood in the hall trying to calm herself before she went to join her mum and Kai in the car.

'They're still working on her,' she uttered.

'Oh my God!'

Jill tried to get up out of her seat, but Hannah stopped her. 'It's best to stay here, Mum. It isn't nice.' Then she noticed Kai's look of confusion. 'Why don't the three of us stop in the car together. I tell you what, why don't we have a game of I-spy?'

She forced a smile for her son's benefit and tried to derive some joy when he chuckled in response. Hannah had to admire her mother's bravery as she joined in with the game, both of them willing the paramedics or Pete to come out with some good news.

It seemed an age before Pete appeared at the door and walked over to the BMW to deliver the news. 'Hannah, I need to have a word with your Mum. Do you want to take Kai home? He shouldn't be here for this.'

Both Hannah and her mother knew from those few words that Pat was dead. They didn't need him to say it. Her mother jumped out of the car and into Pete's arms and began sobbing.

'Ganmar crying,' said Kai, the bewilderment evident in his tiny voice.

As he held Jill, Pete said, 'They're bringing her out in a minute.'

His words were aimed at Hannah rather than her mother and she knew she'd have to put her sorrow on hold. She needed to get her son away quickly. And if she was honest with herself, she didn't want to hang around either. It was upsetting enough seeing the bodies of the young family being carried out, but she knew that if she was to witness the same for her nana, there was no way she could hold herself together.

She dashed to her own car, started the engine and made her way down the road, blinking away the tears as she tried to focus on her driving and her confused three-year-old son.

It had been a particularly difficult day for Hannah. Not only had she lost her nana under dubious circumstances, but she'd also had to hold it together for the sake of her son. Throughout the day all she had felt like doing was breaking down, but she couldn't let her son see her like that.

When she had driven away from Pat's house, she had addressed Kai's confusion by telling him Nana was poorly. She'd do the 'up in heaven' talk another day when she felt more up to it. Then she had distracted him by asking him how many dogs and cats he could spot on the way home.

Now he was in bed, and it was finally time for Hannah to deal with her pent-up emotions. After a good cry, she pulled herself together and gave her mum a call. Unfortunately, the sound of her mum's voice reduced her to tears again, and it was a while before either of them could get any words out.

Eventually, Hannah said, 'I'm sorry I dashed off, Mum. I didn't want Kai to see us all upset.'

'You don't have to explain, love. I understand. I'm just sorry for your sake that you had to dash away. We should be together at a time like this.'

'I know, I promise tomorrow I'll see if I can get a friend to look after Kai so that I can help you with the funeral arrangements.'

The word 'funeral' brought back the reality of what they were dealing with, and they both began sobbing again.

Once they were both calm enough, Hannah asked, 'Did the paramedics say what it was?'

'Yeah, they told Pete it was a heart attack probably brought on by shock. It's no wonder considering the state of her house. Pete said somebody had trashed the place.'

'That's right, Mum. Did he tell you what they had scrawled on the wall too?'

'No, he didn't mention that.'

Hannah thought it was strange for Pete not to mention it, so she filled her mother in on what had been written on the wall.

'It's that bloody development company, isn't it?' asked Jill, her voice breaking.

'It looks that way, Mum. I just hope they can catch up with them after this.'

'Well, the paramedics got the police involved, and I got a call from them today. They're coming to see us tomorrow. They asked me for your address too and said they'll be calling at yours as well.'

'OK, thanks,' said Hannah, determined to tell the police all she knew. 'I'm going to get going, but let me know when you want me to come round to sort everything so I can arrange a babysitter. I hope you'll be OK, Mum.'

'I'll be alright, love, and at least I've got Pete here with me. He's been a Godsend. You take care.'

'I will do,' said Hannah.

She cut the call without telling Jill what she was thinking about Pete; her mother was upset enough without her adding to her grief. Pete might have been playing the supportive husband now, but it didn't alter the fact that he had invested in the company responsible for killing her nana. He might have even known what type of people they were when he put the money up. And Hannah couldn't help but wonder whether he was playing the doting husband to ease his guilt.

40

Russ was back at the all-night garage in Salford. He was down to his last ten pounds and was terrified of spending it and ending up skint. But he needed food. He had already removed his makeshift hood and scarf, and as he approached the glass door of the garage's shop entrance, he caught sight of his reflection. He hardly recognised himself now he had a small beard, but his greasy locks, tatty clothes and soiled face also gave him a shock.

That might explain the change in the lady who regularly worked nights at the garage. She had been very friendly at first, but on the past couple of occasions he had noticed a wariness in her eyes every time he entered the shop.

Russ waited till the shop was empty of other customers then approached the counter, conscious of his dishevelled appearance and the malodourous air of sweat, dust and neglect. She smiled, but Russ could tell she felt uncomfortable.

'I erm, I was wondering if you could help me,' he began.

Her eyes flashed with alarm, but she didn't respond so he continued.

'You see, I've fallen on hard times. I'm homeless and, to be honest, I don't know where my next meal is coming from. Please could you spare something? Anything. Even if it's just a bag of crisps.'

Instead of reacting negatively, there was a look of recognition on her face as if, by speaking the unspoken and explaining his predicament, he had actually put her at ease. Russ decided to capitalise on her perceived change of heart.

'I hate to ask,' he said. 'But I'm desperate.'

'Is there no-one you can turn to for help?' she asked.

'No, there's no-one,' he said sadly.

It was the truth. His parents were no longer around, and his only sibling lived in France. She had married well and had never had much time for her younger tearaway brother. Eventually they'd drifted apart, and now he never saw her. Of course, he didn't mention that he could no longer call on friends because he didn't know who he could trust anymore.

The cashier smiled at him and said, 'You'll get me shot, you will. Go on, grab a couple of bags of crisps but be careful no-one sees you.'

'Thank you so much,' said Russ dashing to the crisp stand.

Keeping his back to the cashier, he grabbed four bags, figuring that he might as well make it worth his while. He tucked two of them inside his clothing then left the shop, waving to the cashier as he did so.

Hannah was on the way back from the funeral director's with her mum and Pete. Her friend, Taylor, had readily agreed to look after Kai once Hannah told her what had happened. She was a good friend whom Hannah trusted.

The police had been to visit Hannah the day after Pat's death and Hannah had told them everything she knew, including her suspicions about Jez. She had asked to remain anonymous in case of any comeback. Hannah had also asked them whether they were any nearer to finding proof relating to the intimidation, but they were unable to give her any information.

The only thing she hadn't told the police was about Pete buying shares in the company. It didn't prove any involvement with the intimidation. He might have been one of many people who had innocently invested in the business. So, Hannah decided to keep schtum, mainly because she was cautious about upsetting her mother who already had enough to deal with.

Now though, she was having second thoughts about having told the police what she knew about Jez and his dealings. What if it came back on her? Was there any point in putting herself at risk when there was nothing to gain anymore? Her nana was gone, and nothing she did or said was going to bring her back. But a part of Hannah remained angry at the injustice of it all, not only for her nana but for all the other people who had suffered.

Once the three of them were back at Jill and Pete's and were going over some of the details surrounding the funeral and other matters, Pete took them by surprise when he asked, 'What about the house? Is the sale still going through?'

'You what?' asked Hannah, incensed despite her decision not to challenge him.

'Are we still selling to Pake?' he reiterated. 'I mean, it *is* a good offer, and we'll have no chance of selling to anyone else, not when the street's being redeveloped. People will know something's amiss as soon as they see all the empty houses.'

Suddenly, all the sorrow and rage Hannah had been holding inside now came to a head. 'Are you fuckin' serious? My nana has just died, and all you can think about is making money?'

Witnessing Hannah's anger, he backtracked. 'I'm just being practical, that's all.' Then he spotted the stupefied expression on Jill's face, and said, 'I'll understand if you prefer not to discuss it yet. It's just that, these developers won't wait forever, you know.'

'Oh yeah, and you'd know about that, wouldn't you?' said Hannah.

Before he could respond, Jill jumped in. 'Now, Hannah, let's calm things down. This isn't the time or the place. Let's talk about this more when we're all feeling a bit less upset.'

Hannah's eyes flashed from one to the other of them, wondering what was going on here. Why was her mother trying to protect him? But then, she was the one who had asked her mum not to say anything about his involvement with Pake Holdings.

'OK,' said Hannah. 'I'm going home. I'll give you a call.'

She addressed her last comment to her mum, not even looking at Pete in case she lost it altogether and said something she might regret.

Jill trailed behind her into the hall and in a hushed voice said, 'I'll speak to him, love.'

Hannah followed her mother's cue and also lowered her voice. 'I think you need to, Mum. But be careful. Like I told you before, if he's involved it could put us both in danger.'

'Don't worry,' said Jill. 'He's my husband, and it's about time I dealt with this in my own way.'

Hannah knew a rebuff when she heard one, and she decided not to upset her mother any further. 'Alright,' she said, 'But call me straightaway if you have any problems.'

Hannah left her mum's house feeling very confused. Was she right to have left her mum alone with him? What if she told him about their suspicions? How would he react? But then, Jill had seemed confident she wouldn't come to any harm. Was that because she trusted her husband? Or could there be another reason? Could Hannah's mum be in it as deep as him? No, that was ridiculous! But was it? Hannah wasn't sure. She didn't know who she could trust anymore.

41

'Hannah's right,' said Jill, staring into her husband's eyes. 'It's inappropriate to be asking about the house sale when Mum's only just died, and we've just come back from the funeral director's.'

'I was being practical, that's all.'

'Yeah, you said, but did it not occur to you that me and Hannah would be upset?'

'No, yeah, I suppose so. Sorry, I mean, I didn't think. I didn't mean to upset you, love.'

He went to put his arm around her, but Jill shrugged him off. 'We know,' she said.

'Know what?'

'We know about you buying shares in Pake Holdings.'

'Yeah, 'course you do. I told you at the time. Why's that a problem?'

'You told me you'd bought shares in a property development company, but you didn't tell me which one. It seems strange that you've been pushing for the sale of Mum's house to the company you happen to own shares in.'

'You signed the bloody paperwork! Look, I'm sorry if I upset you, it was just an error of judgement. I was being practical and ...'

Jill cut in, not wanting to listen to the same excuse over and over. 'It was the developers that trashed Mum's house and wrote that message on her wall.'

He gazed at her with a look of confusion.

'Yes, I knew about that,' Jill said. 'Hannah told me.'

'It just slipped my mind to mention the writing. I told you about the place being trashed but I thought it was some hooligans who had done it.'

'No, it's Pake. Well, I mean, it might be some hooligans, but it's Pake that's put them up to it.'

'Ridiculous! Why would they want to go around trashing your mother's house?'

'For the same reason they've been intimidating the other residents in the street. To force her out, that's why. Mum didn't want to leave, did she? But she's been intimidated. She's had nasty letters and phone calls.'

'But what makes you think they're from Pake?'

'Because the horrible man who rang and frightened the living daylights out of her said so. For God's sake, Pete! You already know about people being intimidated in the street. What made you think they would treat Mum any differently? Not only that, but the words on the wall were a bit of a giveaway, weren't they? "Your time is up. Get out now." Why would anybody other than the developers write that?'

'Hang on a minute,' he said, throwing her off her stride. 'You don't trust me, do you? I bought shares in Pake Holdings, so you therefore think I'm the enemy, is that it?'

'I didn't say that,' Jill muttered.

Pete sighed. 'Do you honestly think I'd have bought

shares in the company if I'd have known how they were going to behave?'

'I just wanted to be sure,' Jill said. 'Anyway, you know now, so I think you should relinquish your shares.'

Pete puffed up his chest. 'Well, we'll lose a lot of money, y'know.'

'I don't care about the bloody money, Pete. The company is corrupt. How can we have shares in a business that is forcing people out of their homes? Did you know they even set a house on fire? All the occupants died. The parents and two young children.'

'Oh my God! I heard about that on the news. I didn't realise it was all part of the intimidation. In fact, I didn't know that fire was in your mother's street.'

'Well, it was.'

Pete held up his hands in surrender. 'OK, I'll sell the bloody shares if it makes you happy.'

'It's not about making me happy, Pete. It's about doing what's right. People's lives are more important than money.'

'I know. I agree. But give me a break, will you? I didn't know Pake had forced your mother out. I've hardly had a chance to get my head around it.'

'Right, well I'm glad you agree. I'll forgive you, but on one condition.'

'What's that?' he asked warily.

'That we let Hannah have the proceeds of sale once mum's house is sold. That way she won't have to pay rent and it'll give her a chance to get on her feet until Kai's in school. Then she can go back to the job she loves.'

'Well, I think that's a bit drastic—'

Jill cut in. 'Why? You did agree that people's lives are more important than money and we've got more than enough.'

She looked at the resigned expression on her husband's face and knew she had him.

Russ was soon ravenous again. He figured it was high time he did something about the predicament he had found himself in although he wasn't sure what. Wearing his usual disguise, he made his way through the city centre and found himself in the same park where he had spent time before breaking back into the cellar.

It made sense to be in a place that was frequented by the homeless. After all, he was one of them now, so maybe he would learn how they managed to survive on the streets. He couldn't hide out in the cellar forever; someone was bound to find him sooner or later, and he had nowhere else to go. There were still some people he could have called but he didn't want to put them in danger. He already felt bad enough for the ill feeling he had caused between James and his wife.

As he had done previously, Russ stretched out his sleeping bag on a bench and climbed inside. He was pestered again by many of the homeless, but after assuring them several times that he had neither money nor drugs to give them, they eventually left him alone, and he lay there staring at the stars, thinking about what an enormous fuck-up he had made of his life.

Russ hadn't realised he'd fallen asleep until he was awoken by a feeling of movement close to his body. In his semi-conscious state, he saw someone running away. Then he became aware of the fact that the zipper of his sleeping bag had been pulled down and instinct told him that the feeling of movement was probably somebody trying to steal something.

'Shit!' he cursed, reaching inside the bag to check his money and phone.

To his dismay the money was gone. 'Shit!' he repeated, frantically continuing the search for his phone.

His hands touched on the shiny surround, and he heaved a sigh of relief. He also checked for the chisel, reassured when he felt the cold metal. He had decided to keep it despite Dom's advice, although he had got rid of the knife. Russ pulled the phone out of his pocket, and for a moment, he stared at it, deliberating over whether to make a call. He was tired of this life on the run. He needed help.

Before he could make a decision, Russ was disturbed by someone approaching. He looked up to see a face he recognised, which immediately put him on his guard until he realised where he knew him from. It was the homeless man who had passed him after he'd been trying to break into the cellar of The Gilded Cage, except he was in a more sober state than the last time Russ had seen him.

'Hi, mate, you alright?' he asked Russ.

That day outside The Gilded Cage, Russ hadn't taken too much notice of the man's appearance. He just knew that he was scruffy, off his head and reeked of cannabis, and Russ had therefore assumed he was homeless. The smell was still the same, but as Russ gazed at him in detail, he could see that he was a young man of perhaps early twenties, and he had kind eyes.

Replying to his question, Russ said, 'Nah, someone's nicked my money. It was my last tenner. I don't know what the fuck I'm gonna do now.'

To his embarrassment there was a tremble in his voice as he spoke, and he had to fight to hold back tears.

'I saw him running off,' said the man. 'I'd have grabbed him, but he was too fuckin' quick. I know who he is though. The guy's a fuckin' snake. He's always doing it. He had me when I was first homeless.'

'Any idea where I can find him?' asked Russ, thinking that the chisel might come in handy after all.

'Yeah, he hangs out at a few different places. I can show you but not tonight. I need to get some kip.' Then, after a pause, he added, 'I've not seen you about much. Are you new to this?'

'Yeah, pretty much.'

The man stuck out his hand, 'My name's Luke.'

'I'm Russ.'

They shook hands and Luke said, 'OK, stick around. I'll show you the ropes. You're definitely better off here than in the doorway of that nightclub. The guy that owns it is a bit of a twat from what I've been told. He gets his bouncers to chuck water over us if they find us dossing in his doorway.'

Despite his plight, Russ couldn't resist a snigger. That sounded exactly the type of thing Jez would do.

42

Hannah had been eager to ring her mum ever since she had left her house. She was worried but tried to console herself that her mum knew Pete better than she did, and in the ten years they had been together, he had never harmed her. Despite this, she was relieved when her mother finally rang her the next day.

'Mum, are you alright?'

'Yeah, 'course I am. I'm just ringing to tell you what I've agreed with Pete.'

'OK.'

'Right, well, for a kick-off, I've told him I know about the shares. He seemed genuinely sorry, Hannah. I know he found out about the intimidation, but I don't think he knew anything about the sort of company Pake was when he invested in it. I think he's perhaps been in denial since Mum told us about them a few weeks ago, and to be honest, a part of him was probably reluctant to sell because of the money. Anyway, he's now agreed to sell back the shares.'

'OK, that's good.'

'Yes, and not only that, once Mum's house is sold, we're going to give you the money so you can buy a home of your own.'

Hannah was touched by her mother's words, and her eyes grew misty as she said, 'Aw, Mum, thank you, but you didn't have to do that, honestly.'

'It's what I want,' said Jill, before quickly correcting herself, 'it's what we both want. It'll set you back on your feet.'

'Thank you so much. I don't know what to say.'

'You don't have to say anything, love. You're my daughter, aren't you? And Mum would have wanted you to have it anyway. You know how much she thought of you and Kai.'

Once Hannah had come off the phone, she couldn't help but shed a tear. She was overwhelmed by everything and so grateful to her mother for letting her have the proceeds from the house. When she set up her new home, she would always be reminded of Nana Pat. As for Pete, she wondered whether her mother was right; maybe he hadn't been aware initially of the type of company he was dealing with.

The fact that he had agreed to sell back his shares made her view things differently. Maybe she should ease up on him. After all, he had never given her reason to question him in the past. And, currently, she was too besieged by grief to pursue things any further by questioning him herself. So, maybe it was best to leave things alone and concentrate on getting through the forthcoming funeral and then carrying on with her life even though her lovely nana was no longer a part of it.

When Russ woke up the next day, he quickly checked his sleeping bag. He was relieved to find the zip fastened and his phone and chisel still tucked inside. He sat up, pulling the zip down slightly to free his hands then rubbing the sleep out of his eyes. One of the first things he noticed, as he did every morning, was the sour taste in his mouth. Russ couldn't remember the last time he'd brushed his teeth and knew his breath must reek.

Looking around, he saw that many of the homeless were still asleep but a few of them had left the park. For a few minutes he sat there wondering what to do next. He was curious about what had happened to his new friend, Luke. Then, as if in answer to his thoughts, Luke appeared.

'Hi, mate, how was your first night in the park?' he asked with a big grin lighting up his sallow features.

'Shit!' said Russ, returning a sardonic grin but neglecting to mention that he'd stayed in the park once before.

'You'll get used to it.' There was a pause, before he said, 'Come on, we'll go and find Twister, get you some cash.'

'Twister?' asked Russ.

'Yeah, the guy that nicked your money. I don't know why they call him that. Probably because he's a twisted little fucker, who nicks off people who are in just as much shit as he is.'

Russ undid the sleeping bag fully, packed his things away and stood up to join Luke.

'You wanna bung your stuff somewhere?' asked Luke.

Russ stared at him for a moment. The only stuff he owned was the clothes he was wearing, the chisel, phone and sleeping bag. He was reluctant to give up the chisel and phone, but he could see the sleeping bag becoming a bit of a hindrance.

'Where?' he asked.

Luke was in deep thought for a while before he said,

'There's a place where I stash my gear but don't fuckin' tell anyone.'

Russ knew Luke's thoughts had revolved around whether he could be trusted and he was quick to reassure him. 'Eh, I wouldn't do that to a mate even if it is a mate I've only just met.'

Luke smiled and Russ noticed how good looking he was despite the pallid complexion and tatty hair. 'Come on then,' he said, and Russ followed him.

It soon became clear to Russ that they were heading towards a group of boulders that were in one corner of the green. They had obviously been put there for decoration at some point but now they were weather worn and full of moss and graffiti. As they walked, Luke kept checking around him; Russ presumed it was to make sure nobody had noticed where they were heading.

Once they reached their destination, Luke walked around to the other side. There was a small gap between the boulders and Luke pointed to it.

'You see that hole?'

'Yeah.'

'Well, it only looks small, but it opens up inside. You can shove your gear in there. Nobody else knows about it, only me, so if any of my stuff goes missing, I'll fuckin' know who's had it, and I swear we'll be after you. I know a lot of handy people.'

Russ guessed that the lad's claim was probably a lie to scare him, but he took pains to reassure him again that he could be trusted before he pushed his sleeping bag through the hole, a bit at a time until none of it was visible. By the time he stood back up, Luke had already set off and Russ rushed to catch up with him.

'Why are you helping me anyway?' he asked.

'Because I was in the same boat as you. I know what it's like. You'll find that a lot of the people on the streets are alright with you. They're not all criminals like everyone else seems to think. They're just having a bad time. We look after each other, well, most of us anyway.'

Curious now, Russ asked, 'So, what happened to you? That's if you don't mind me asking.'

'Sure, no sweat, mate,' said Luke. Then he seemed to take a deep breath before he continued. 'I was at Manchester Uni but still living at home. One of the other students gave me some weed on a night out. It seemed like a lot of them were into it, so I had some. Then one thing led to another and before I knew it, I was into fuckin' coke too.

'Anyway, I got kicked off my course when I turned up to a lecture late and stoned. The professor got me to empty my pockets. He was fuckin' fuming, mate, I tell ya, especially when he saw what was in them.

'I didn't tell my mum and dad at first even though they kept asking why I wasn't going to lectures. In the end, they were so pissed off with me hanging about the house, nicking their money and getting in late most nights that they rang the uni to find out what was going on. My dad went fuckin' apeshit when he found out and then he chucked me out.'

He shrugged as though it was no big deal, but Russ could tell it was.

'Won't they take you back if you get off the gear?'

'I doubt it. They were that pissed off with me. They already knew about their money going missing but when they kept that hidden, I started selling stuff from the house. Finding out I'd been kicked off my course was the last straw for my dad. Besides, I doubt I'd be able to kick it now anyway.'

'Aren't there places that can help you?'

'It's not that fuckin' easy mate. When you're on the street, you'll take anything you can get your hands on. A bit of wacky baccy and coke aren't the only gear I take. But I never nick owt from mates. I've learnt my lesson. I still feel bad about my mum and dad.'

Russ could hear the emotion in Luke's voice, but when he stared directly into his face, Luke turned away as though the facts were hard to deal with.

'What happened to you?' asked Luke, shifting the focus away from himself.

Russ gave him a diluted version of events, telling him he didn't have any family so when he lost his job and subsequently his home, he had nowhere else to go. He knew better than to mention the other events relating to Jez and Pake Holdings.

'Are you not taking owt?'

'No, never touch the stuff. A few drinks now and again, that's all.'

They walked for a while, stopping at various points in the city centre while Luke said hello to his friends, introduced Russ and asked if anybody knew of Twister's whereabouts. Russ became aware of the risk he was taking in being exposed, and wished he hadn't given Luke his own name. But then he reasoned to himself that Luke's friends were unlikely to have contact with anyone connected to Jez.

Apart from that, after that night when he'd spotted his appearance in the garage window, Russ was aware of just how much it had changed. He knew that his body odour alone would make most people want to avoid him rather than check him out.

Suddenly, Luke started running. 'That's the fuckin' scrote,' he yelled.

Russ ran behind in pursuit of a small, slight man with dark hair. Despite Twister's speed, Luke was gaining on him, and Russ felt the first flush of enthusiasm he'd had in days at the prospect of getting his money back.

Luke caught up with Twister, and by the time Russ had joined them, Luke had slapped him up against an old semi-dilapidated wall in a back alleyway. Up close, Russ saw that Twister was somewhere in his thirties and was currently rubbing the back of his head and whimpering. He was thin with a dull pallor and a twitchiness that told Russ he was probably a regular cocaine user.

'Right, get your fuckin' hands in your pockets and show us what you've got,' said Luke.

'You've hurt my fuckin' head.'

'I don't give it a shit! You fuckin' deserved it. Now give us what you've got.'

Twister was reluctant until Luke got hold of him by the scruff of the neck and rammed his head into the wall again. There was a crushing sound and a loud yell coming from Twister.

'Alright, alright,' he pleaded. 'Give me a chance.'

Russ could see fear in the man's tear-filled eyes as he

pulled some change out of the pocket of his trackies. But Russ didn't have any sympathy for a man who had robbed him while he was asleep.

'And the rest,' said Luke, examining the money. 'I want to see the inside of your fuckin' pockets!'

The man put his hands inside his pockets again, pulling out more cash as well as a small, lidded container, which Russ guessed was coke. Without preamble, Luke snatched the lot from him.

'Right, you can fuck off now!'

'Eh, come on mate. I only had a tenner off him.'

'I don't give a shit,' said Luke, turning away. 'And I'm not your fuckin' mate!'

Russ flashed a glance at the man and saw his facial expression change, his sad eyes entreating him to challenge Luke. Russ turned away too and fell in step with Luke as he made his way back out of the alleyway. There was no way he was going to undermine Luke in front of this little shit.

'Let's find somewhere we can split this lot,' said Luke.

They sat down on a bench near Saint Anne's square and Luke counted the money. 'That's £47.72. There you go,' he said, handing Russ some notes and coins. 'It's £23.86 each. I'll keep the pot if it's what I think it is.'

'I only want my tenner back,' said Russ, staring at the money in his hand.

Luke looked at him and grinned. 'Don't be daft. You don't need to feel bad about it. That little snake will soon fuckin' earn it back. He goes begging as well as robbing people. In fact, most of that cash is probably what he fuckin' nicked anyway.' Then he stood up and took a step away, leaving Russ no choice but to take all the cash. 'Come on. We need to go somewhere quieter. I want to check out this pot of stuff.'

Again, Russ fell in step with Luke. He had nowhere else he needed to be and no-one else to rely on. Luke might have been a ruthless operator, but he seemed to be on his side, so he'd stick with him for now. And at least, because of Luke, Russ now had cash in his pocket. He was already dreaming of what he would buy with it. Maybe a nice hot pie and a cuppa. He was going to enjoy it while it lasted, because once it was gone, he didn't know what he would do for food.

43

It was two weeks since Pat's death. It had been a tough time. Hannah missed her nana terribly, and the circumstances of her death didn't help to alleviate Hannah's feelings of loss and despair.

For months she had been trying to find evidence against Jez and Pake Holdings so she could put an end to the intimidation. But her attempts had amounted to naught. Neither she nor anybody else could prove anything, and it made her feel as though she had failed her much-loved nana as well as the other residents of Rovener Street.

It had been difficult to carry on working in the place owned by Jez while at the same time making funeral arrangements with her mother and looking after her son. But the money at the club was good. She had regulars who always tipped well, and cash always came in useful with a three-year-old child.

Hannah had managed to get her hands on a book that explained death to young children. After she'd read it to Kai, he had cried at first but then seemed to accept what had happened.

Since then, Hannah had been putting on a brave face while she awaited the funeral with dread. She had to stay upbeat for the sake of her son and her mother, and she figured that if Kai could come to terms with Pat's death, then she, as an adult, should be able to as well. Keeping busy had also helped to take her mind off what had happened.

It was evening, mid-week. Hannah had put Kai to bed half an hour ago and was settling down to watch some TV when her mobile rang. Thinking it would be her mother, who had been in regular contact over the funeral arrangements and other matters concerning Pat's belongings, Hannah picked up her phone. She didn't recognise the number on the screen, but curiosity made her take the call anyway.

She was shocked to recognise the voice at the other end of the line. 'Russ! Where the bloody hell have you been? And why wouldn't you take my calls? I thought you were dead for fuck's sake!'

'I know, I know, I'm sorry. I was captured by Jez's men. They had me in the cellar of The Gilded Cage. I couldn't ring you 'cos they'd taken my phone.'

'Well, what about the man? The one at Werneth Low. Was he one of Jez's men? Did you kill him?'

'No, I didn't kill him!' She could hear from his tone of voice that he sounded affronted. 'It was Joel, one of Jez's henchmen,' he explained. 'The poor bastard was just in the wrong place at the wrong time.'

'Oh my God!' said Hannah as memories of that night engulfed her. Then a thought occurred to her. 'How the hell have you managed to ring me now if they took your phone?'

Hannah could feel her temper rising. Russ was the one person who could have helped her, and she wasn't totally convinced by what he was saying.

'I memorised your number,' he replied. 'I knew there was

a good chance they'd get to me, so I memorised it just in case.'

'Well, if they captured you, then why the hell was Jez asking me where you were?'

'Jez? You're joking, aren't you? When was this?'

'Ages ago. A couple of days after you were supposed to meet me.'

'The bastard! That must have been around the time that I escaped.'

'Oh yeah,' she said cynically. 'And where have you been in the weeks since then?'

'I stayed with an old mate from school. He doesn't know anyone connected with the club. He lives out of town. In fact, I hadn't seen him for years till then. I knew it was a long shot and, in the end, his wife got suspicious, and I had to get out.'

'Oh, I get it. You've got nowhere else to go so you thought you'd give me a ring and see how I'm fixed. Is that it?'

'No, it's not like that, Hannah. If you must know, I was trying to keep you out of things to protect you. Why are you being like this? I thought we were on the same side. Besides, I just needed a bit of time to get my head together, especially after what Jez's men did to me and to that poor bastard at Werneth Low. I was shitting myself, knowing that Jez was going to kill me as soon as he got his hands on me. But he was away. He left his men to do his dirty work for him. They did me over good and proper, nearly took my fuckin' finger off!'

The distress in his voice told Hannah he was probably telling the truth and for a moment she didn't know what to say.

Russ broke the silence. 'Jez obviously knows you've got some connection to me if he pulled you in the office to ask questions. Hannah, you need to be careful! Jez is a nasty bastard, and if he thinks he can get to me through you then you might be in danger.'

'I doubt it. Surely if he thought that, he'd have done something by now.'

'Not necessarily. They might have been watching you thinking you could lead them to me. You need to be careful who you're talking to about the intimidation. But don't worry, I'll make sure they can't trace you through me.'

'Look, why are you ringing me, Russ, when you're supposedly trying to protect me?'

'Alright, I'll give it to you straight, Hannah; because I don't know what else to do.

'My fuckin' life's on hold. I daren't come out into the open in case they find me so until I get evidence against Jez, I'm stuck. I thought you wanted the same anyway, to put a stop to all the intimidation.

'No, I'm done with it.'

'What? I don't understand. Don't you wanna help your grandma?'

'It's a bit fuckin' late for that!' she raged. 'She died over two weeks ago.'

'Hannah, I'm so sorry. I didn't know.'

'Well, you know now! There's no point in me trying to fight what Jez is doing, Russ. It's too late. My nana's gone. There's nothing left to fight for. Don't you understand?'

She could feel her voice breaking as she spoke and knew Russ had been taken aback by her emotional rant.

'OK, OK. I get you,' he said. 'But Hannah, please, take a

note of my number. I'll keep hold of this phone, and if you ever need to get in touch with me, just give me a ring.

But instead of replying, Hannah cut the call. Getting involved with Russ was the last thing she needed. It was taking her all her time to get through each day.

After she'd had a good cry, she felt guilty about how she'd treated Russ. It wasn't his fault her grandmother had died, and he'd suffered at Jez's hands too. She supposed she had taken it out on him because he was a link to Jez. But she wasn't going to ring him back and apologise. It was best if she kept him out of her life and tried to carry on as best she could.

Nevertheless, she decided to store his number in her phone. She couldn't reason why she did it. Maybe it was for old time's sake or maybe it was just a visceral feeling that one day she might well need him.

44

Six Months Later

Hannah was running late. She pulled up outside her mother's home and checked the time. *Shit!* Only twenty minutes till she was due at work, and the trip could take anything from twenty minutes upwards depending on the traffic. Jill must have been watching out for her because she appeared at the front door before Hannah had even reached it.

'You look frazzled,' she said.

'Oh, Mum, he's been a little monster. He fought me all the way when I tried to put his coat and shoes on, and the minute my back was turned, he pulled one of his shoes back off again. He's tired. He fell asleep in the car on the way but woke up again as soon as we got here.'

'Don't worry, I'll soon settle him down again.'

Hannah smiled and stared into her mother's eyes, which were perpetually sad since Pat had passed away. 'Thanks, Mum. I've got everything he needs in my bag.'

She handed the bag over to Jill then followed her into the house, leading Kai by the hand. As soon as Hannah let go of Kai's hand, he ran to his grandma.

'Ganmar!' he squealed.

'Oh dear! It looks like it might take you longer than you

thought to settle him down,' said Hannah, picking up on his excitement. 'Anyway, I must dash, or I'll be late for work.'

She had noticed Pete sitting on a chair in the lounge but hadn't yet acknowledged his presence. Ever since the loss of her nana, she had found it difficult to remain on friendly terms with him, sharing only an occasional hello or goodbye for the sake of her mum who seemed to have sorted things out with him.

She gave Kai a quick peck on the cheek and the same for her mother before saying her farewells and turning to go.

'Don't you worry,' Pete chirped up. 'We'll soon have the little fella settled.'

Hannah forced a smile and headed for the door. *Damn Pete!* She still couldn't forgive him for his involvement with Pake Holdings, but she hoped for her mother's sake that in time she would learn to live with it.

Half an hour later Hannah was behind the bar of The Gilded Cage. She was serving a customer when she caught sight of Jez several metres away. He was chatting to a much younger woman dressed in a bra top and long skirt with a side split up to the thigh.

From what Hannah could see at this distance, she was a pretty young woman with long dark hair and the height and figure of a model. She stood a few inches taller than Jez but that didn't seem to deter him as he stared up at the girl, his weaselly features and minute frame taking on an ingratiating demeanour.

As Hannah watched, his hand slid onto the small of the girl's back, and he led her towards the bar. Realising they were headed her way, Hannah went to serve the next customer.

For a few minutes she busied herself, trying not to look at Jez who was now sitting on a stool with the young woman beside him. Every now and again his voice carried, which irritated her. She caught snippets of the conversation, which basically consisted of Jez bragging and trying to impress his quarry who giggled coquettishly and hung onto his every word.

To Hannah, there was no way this girl could possibly be physically attracted to Jez, and she wondered if his allure was more about money and power. She wished there was a way of warning the girl what she was getting herself into. Jez was more than a rich and powerful man; he was evil.

There came a point when Hannah had to serve a customer near to Jez. She was giving the customer his drinks when Jez raised his hand dramatically, allowing his shirt sleeve to slip down so that his expensive branded watch was on display.

'Erm, here when you've finished,' he demanded.

Hannah bristled at the lack of manners, but she tried not to let it show as she served him a double malt and a cocktail for his female friend. She was relieved once they left the public area and went through the staff entrance. She could only imagine what was going on in his upstairs office while his wife was unaware. But that wasn't her concern.

Jez could do what he liked in his private life as far as she was concerned but his attitude had rattled her. He was so smug and superior, and she hated the thought that his smart, fancy clothes and expensive watch had been paid for through the misery of others.

Hannah had been tracking the progress of the Rovener Street development in the news. There was only one remaining end-terraced house now occupied, and building work had begun at the opposite end of the street. A spokesman for Pake had commented that their offer to the remaining occupant had been accepted and they were confident that the sale would now go ahead. Then he had gone on to boast about how the development was set to bring prosperity to the area.

Now that she was no longer in the early throes of grief where the slightest thing could have her in floods of tears, Hannah's feelings were dominated by anger. She hated what Jez and his cohorts had done and she spent an interminable amount of time dwelling on the death of her poor nana and the other people who had suffered at their hands. She often awoke with her mind occupied by images of the dead family being carried from a burnt-out wreckage that had formerly been their home.

She had also read in the news about the forthcoming trial of the young lad arrested for the first fire in Rovener Street. She had no doubt that Jez was behind it, and it saddened her to think that the culprit might be another victim of Jez's warped ambition.

Despite her feelings, Hannah still wouldn't give up her job at The Gilded Cage. Those desperate times when she had been too grief-stricken to contemplate a change in job had now passed. Instead, there was a strange new feeling that she couldn't quite define. It was as though she wanted to keep tabs on Jez even though the sight of him infuriated her.

*

When Hannah went to collect Kai from her mother's house the next day, she was pleased to find that Pete wasn't there. It would give her and her mum a chance to chat.

After she'd fussed over Kai and they'd settled down on the sofa, she asked, 'Did you know it's the trial of that young lad next week?'

'What young lad?'

'Connor Davis, the lad who started the first fire in Nana's street.'

She saw her mother's face cloud over with sadness and felt bad for a moment. 'Oh,' was all Jill said.

'I was wondering if you might want to come to the trial?'

'What? The trial of that young lad? Why would I want to do that?' asked Jill.

'Well, it was Nana's street, wasn't it? I thought it might give us some kind of closure.'

'I doubt it. It's not going to bring Mum back, is it?'

'I know. But I just feel as though we owe it to the residents.'

Hannah saw a moment of indecision flash across her mother's features. 'What day is it on?'

'Wednesday.'

'Oh right. Well, I don't know whether I can get the time off.'

'Will you try though, for me?'

'What about Kai?' Jill asked.

'It's OK. Taylor will mind him.'

Jill stared hard at her daughter and this time it was sympathy that Hannah saw in her eyes. That and a shared grief. 'You really miss your nana, don't you?'

Hannah nodded and she could feel her eyes misting over. It still got to her when she least expected.

'Alright,' said her mother. 'I'll see what I can do. But I can't promise.'

45

Hannah and her mum entered the public gallery at Manchester Crown Court. As usual, Hannah was running late so they'd only just made it in time, and she followed her mother as they filed into the second row.

Straightaway Hannah noticed somebody familiar. She was tempted to walk out before he spotted her. But it was too late. Her mother was already sitting down and as Hannah took the seat beside her, the man turned round. He must have seen her walk in. It was her boss. Jez.

'Oh hello, Hannah,' he said, his voice loud and confident. 'What brings you here?'

Hannah was flummoxed, but before she had a chance to speak the officials walked in and the judge requested order in court. As the first witnesses were interviewed about the fire they had discovered, Hannah's mind was on other things and she was full of trepidation, her hands and face sweating.

What the hell was Jez doing in court? If he had put the lad up to the crime then surely it would be better to keep a low profile. But it seemed that he wanted to make sure the kid went down for the crime he'd carried out on his behalf. Perhaps he was so cocksure of himself that he thought no-one would suspect him when he appeared in the public gallery.

By the time there was a recess, Hannah had a ready reply for Jez when he approached her. 'My mum comes here regularly,' she said. 'It's a hobby of hers. She keeps telling me about juicy cases, so I thought I'd come along and find out for myself what it was all about.'

She could tell Jez wasn't convinced when he flashed a look across to Hannah's mother, who appeared confused. But Jill knew better than to contradict Hannah in front of him. 'I'm off to get a coffee,' he said, without waiting for an introduction to Jill.

'Come on, Mum. We'll go to that coffee shop nearby. I don't want to sit in the restaurant while he's there.'

'Who is he? And why did you tell him a lie?'

Hannah sighed. 'He's my boss from work, but I also think he's the man behind Pake Holdings.'

'So why the hell is he here?' asked Jill.

'That's what I've been asking myself.'

'But more to the point, Hannah, why are we here? And don't give me any of that nonsense about wanting closure. I wasn't born yesterday.'

For a moment Hannah deliberated over what to tell her mother. Then she said, 'OK, OK, I was curious. I don't believe the lad did it off his own bat, so I wanted to find out for myself.'

'But surely if your boss is the man behind Pake Holdings then it's not a good idea to let him see you at court.'

'I didn't know he would be there, did I?'

'Well, if he's been terrorising the residents of Rovener Street then I don't think you should be working for him.'

'I've got no choice, Mum. I need the money. Anyway, I'm hardly going to come to any harm just because I've turned up at the same trial as Jez, am I? He doesn't know I suspect him of being behind Pake. But just to be on the safe side, please don't tell Pete about the connection.'

Jill tutted. 'As long as you're not getting any further involved, Hannah. I've already lost my mother and I don't want you putting yourself in danger too.'

'Don't worry, Mum, I'll be fine.'

Jill swallowed the lie, but Hannah was already mulling things over. Because, for her, Jez's presence at court was even more reason to suspect his involvement in the intimidation that had resulted in her nana's death.

Later that day, the prosecuting barrister examined Connor Davis. Hannah watched as Connor walked across the court then took his place on the stand. He had the cocky strut of a streetwise kid, but it looked as though he had tried to tone it down. As she took in his appearance, Hannah noticed how scrawny and young he was, making him appear vulnerable in the courtroom setting. Connor was dressed in formal trousers with a shirt that was too big for him and a tie tucked into his trousers.

As he waited to be examined, Connor looked around the court, his demeanour nervous but at the same time shifty. His eyes looked pleadingly at a couple on the first row who Hannah assumed must be his parents. Although they were seated next to each other, their body language told Hannah they were no longer a couple, and at recess, she had noticed they took different directions without talking. They had stood out to her because of how they were dressed: the man in tatty faded jeans and a worn leather jacket and the woman in an unflatteringly tight polyester dress, which clung to her backside after she'd stood up.

Then Connor's gaze settled momentarily on Jez, taking in Hannah who was on the row behind. As Connor's laser stare cut through her, all his vulnerability was gone, and Hannah understood how he could be capable of such a reckless crime. But she knew the object of Connor's hostile attention was Jez, and she wished she could have seen her boss's reaction.

When the prosecuting barrister began questioning him, Connor's eyes shifted towards him as he paid attention to what was being said. The prosecutor began with the evidence that had been given that morning from two witnesses who claimed they had seen him in the area prior to the fire and had recognised him when the police had shown them a photograph. This resulted in a swift denial from Connor who claimed he had been at home and hadn't ventured near Rovener Street.

As the evidence against him grew more damning, Connor's denials became more desperate, his voice taking on an anguished tone. Apart from the two witnesses, Connor had been spotted on CCTV a few streets away, not long before the estimated time that the fire had started. But the most crucial evidence was yet to come, and by the time it was presented, Connor was almost on the verge of tears.

The vital evidence that cinched the case related to a container that crime scene investigators had recovered from a nearby dustbin. Examinations by police forensics teams had shown the remains of accelerant in the container as well as trace fingerprints that matched those of Connor Davis.

When the prosecutor described the police findings, there was a collective gasp from the public gallery. Jill nudged Hannah and flashed her a knowing look. But then Hannah's attention was drawn back to the witness box as Connor spoke up.

His words came out as an exasperated yell. 'It was *his* fault! He told me to do it.' As he spoke, he pointed at Jez, his arm and finger unwavering so that nobody was in any doubt as to whom he referred. 'It's not my fault. I needed the dosh. My mum got behind with the rent. We were gonna get kicked out!'

There was now an excited rumbling from the public gallery as well as the jury. A tremor of anticipation ran through Hannah, and she saw Jez's shoulders stiffen. *I bet he wasn't expecting this*, she thought.

Just when it was getting interesting, the judge called for calm. Then he explained that the case to answer was against the defendant, nobody else. The reason for Connor Davis's crime was irrelevant, and if there was anybody else involved in the crime then that would have to be investigated and tried separately.

The trial continued until all the evidence had been read, the prosecution and defence had completed their summing up and the jury had retired to reach a verdict.

'Come on, Mum,' said Hannah. 'I need a drink.'

'Bloody hell!' said Jill once they were seated in the pub and she had checked none of the courtroom attendants were in the vicinity. 'That was a turn up for the books, wasn't it? Do you think they'll investigate your boss now?'

'I dunno. But even if they do, it's his word against Connor's, isn't it? And he has a lot more influence than Connor, believe me.'

Although it had been a revelation, and Hannah was glad that the lad had outed Jez in court, she was still wary of getting too excited. Knowing Jez, he'd worm his way out of this just like he did with everything else. In fact, she wouldn't be surprised if he was getting in touch with one of his contacts now and ordering them to wipe any CCTV that might produce evidence of Connor entering the club in the lead up to the arson attack, assuming he kept it that long.

46

A few days had passed since the trial, but Hannah was still feeling upset. She couldn't stop thinking about the way Connor had behaved in court. She was certain of Jez's guilt, but it was so frustrating not being able to prove any of it. She'd seen him at work since the trial and he had acted as though nothing had happened, reverting to his usual smarmy, superior manner. It was as though he was confident that nobody could make anything stick against him.

As for Connor, he'd been found guilty because, as the judge had said, he'd still committed the crime, no matter what the circumstances. Hannah could still picture the smug look on Jez's face as he had left the courtroom. And that look was going through her mind, over and over, taunting her. Making her feel tense and irate. She had to do something! She might not be able to bring her grandmother back, but Jez couldn't be allowed to get away with it any longer.

In her mind she recapped what she knew up to now. It was all a jumbled mess, and the more she thought about it the more her head ached. So, she decided to write it all down:

– *Jez mentioned Rovener Street on the phone at around the time that Pake Holdings were trying to buy up the houses.*

– *Jez told Russ he wanted him out of the Rovener Street shop.*

– *According to Russ, Jez owns the three shops in the street.*

– *Connor Davis pointed Jez out in court as the man who put him up to the first arson attack.*

– *Jez is involved in some shady dealings and has tried to get Russ to intimidate people.*

– *Russ was captured and tortured for non-cooperation and the fact that he knew too much.*

God! Seeing it all down on paper highlighted all the facts. There was no way Jez was innocent in all this. One thing many of these facts had in common was that they were all things Russ had told her. And, according to Russ, Jez probably had a high-ranking police officer on his payroll. So, he was protected. If only there was a way to prove Jez's guilt.

That evening Hannah was sitting at home with her phone in her hand, flicking through banal posts on social media.

She should switch the TV on or get out a book, but she was too preoccupied to focus on anything.

Hannah knew she was only delaying the inevitable. There was only one way to confront the troubled thoughts that raced through her mind every morning and every night. She knew what she was going to do as soon as she had picked her phone up. So, she brought up her list of contacts and found Russ's number.

The more she had thought about it, the more she had convinced herself that Russ would be the key to gaining evidence against Jez. After all, he had worked for Jez so he must know plenty about his illegal practices. She hoped he had kept the phone as he had promised all those months ago. Because Hannah knew that if she wanted to see justice done, then Russ was the only person who could help her.

Russ was in a squat Luke had found for them. It was an old, abandoned theatre just outside the city centre, which was now occupied by dozens of homeless people. It suited Russ for now only because it was warmer and more comfortable than sleeping on the streets.

But it was loud. There were always discussions taking place, some of them heated, or people being noisy simply because they were high on something. Then there was the music people played on their phones, often more than one at a time. Mostly they played the throbbing rap that was popular. And because of the acoustics, every little sound carried.

When they'd first entered the squat, Russ had been

surprised to find that most of the seats remained in the main auditorium. The curtains were there too; heavy velour drapes that were torn in places and full of dust. A musty smell permeated everything: the seats, curtains and threadbare carpets. But it was also suffused with the heavy, putrid aroma of cannabis and unwashed bodies.

Russ had stayed clear of drugs even though temptation was all around him. At times it would have been good to have something to help him sleep or to pass the time. But he'd resisted, knowing that the world of the homeless was a volatile one and it helped to have his wits about him.

Russ's bed for the night was a row of seats on the bottom tier where he spread his sleeping bag. He'd got used to the gaps in between and the chair arms that dug into his body whenever he turned over.

One thing he'd learnt about being homeless was that, aside from the worry and fear, it was fuckin' boring. The highlight of Russ's day was when he was lifting fruit and veg from the markets or snacks from newsagents. Occasionally he got lucky and managed to get hold of booze or cigs that he could flog cheaply to one of the homeless people he knew. The problem was the shops and stalls soon got wise to him so he had to find new places where he could go shoplifting.

Luke had proved to be good company and a loyal friend, even though he could be a nightmare when he was stoned. This evening, he was out trying to score while Russ had stayed inside the relative warmth of the theatre.

He regularly checked his mobile now for messages since he had obtained a charger and Luke had shown him places like coffee shops where they could charge their phones up for free. Since he had spoken to Hannah all those months ago, Russ still held out hope that one day she would contact him. In fact, it was his only hope, because she was the one person who could help him to nail Jez. And he'd thought of an idea that just might work.

But, as with every other day, there was no record of any calls or messages. He was about to switch off his phone when he heard a disturbance coming from the back of the auditorium. Two guys were having a heated discussion, about drugs, he guessed from the few words he could pick up. The argument turned to violence when one of them landed a right-hander in the other one's face.

Russ sat up, taking it all in now that things had turned nasty. One of the guys was unknown to him. He hadn't seen him about previously. But the guy who had taken a punch was a friend Russ had met on the streets called Scott. He'd always been alright with him, and Russ knew he couldn't just stand by and watch the lad get a pasting. But Scott was up for the fight. As his nose pumped blood, he jumped onto the other guy, his flailing fists whacking him around the head.

The other guy soon recovered. He was bigger and stronger than Scott, and as Russ took in the scene, the man rushed at Scott, overpowering him till he lost his footing. Scott's body was now dangling across the seating, and Russ got up quick and dragged off his sleeping bag so he could race to Scott's rescue.

But before he got chance, the other guy took hold of Scott and launched him over the seats. The auditorium was steep, the seats packed tightly together, and Scott rolled over several rows before his momentum ceased and he landed with a thud on the floor.

Russ bounded up the steps, taking them two at a time till he reached Scott who appeared to be badly injured. He looked dazed, and when Russ flicked his fingers in front of his face, Scott was slow to respond. A quick check of his pulse told Russ that he was still alive, but he had landed on his head, which might have left him concussed.

He looked up at the guy who had attacked Scott. Their eyes locked. The guy was looking panicked now, and he made a dash for the steps on the opposite side. But two other mates of Russ's stopped him, and Russ soon blocked him from behind while a group of girls went to help Scott.

Between Russ and his two mates, they laid into the guy with kicks and punches till he was just as dazed as Scott. Some of the girls were screaming now at the level of violence as the guy's blood spurted around him. There was a lot of noise, and it took Russ a while to pick up on what they were saying. At that moment his phone rang, but he didn't hear it above the cacophony.

Russ signalled at the other guys to stop when he could see the lad had had enough. It wasn't out of pity because he deserved all he got. The reason for stopping was that another death on his hands could cause problems.

'Let's get the cunt out of here,' he ordered.

They dragged him through the theatre and to the back door, kicking him out into the rain-soaked night.

'And don't you ever fuckin' dare come back!' shouted Russ, giving him one last kick before he went back inside to see how Scott was.

Thankfully Scott was coming round now. 'What was all that about?' Russ demanded.

'The twat took my whizz,' Scott complained. 'And when I tried to get it back, he smacked me one.'

Russ wasn't worried about the drugs, knowing Scott would soon find a way to get hold of some more. He was more concerned that this guy had come into their squat throwing his weight around. Hopefully, they had scared him off, and he wouldn't bother coming back for more.

Knowing Scott was OK, Russ went back to his improvised bed ready to settle in for the night. He remembered that he hadn't switched his phone off, something he was in the habit of doing at night so that the power lasted longer. When he picked it out of his pocket, he was surprised to find he had a missed call. He checked the caller ID and was even more surprised to find it was from Hannah. A surge of excitement ran through him, and he wasted no time in pressing the number then hitting the call return button. Then he waited.

47

When Hannah heard her mobile ring, she knew it would be Russ returning her call. She eagerly pressed the reply button and answered, 'Hello.'

Russ's voice was low and cautious when he replied. 'Hannah. I thought I'd never hear from you again.'

On hearing his voice, all her old feelings for him came flooding back, but she also felt bad on recalling how she had treated him last time they'd been in touch. 'I er, yeah, I know. Look, I'm sorry I was offhand with you the last time we spoke, but I was dealing with a lot. Where have you been for the last few months anyway?'

There was a moment's hesitation before he said, 'I'm staying in a squat. That's all I can tell you. I need to keep my whereabouts secret.'

'Oh, Russ, I'm so sorry. I'd let you stay here but there's no room. My son …'

'It's OK,' Russ cut in. 'I wouldn't expect you to put me up. It might put you in danger and I wouldn't want that. It's best that I stay hidden. Anyway, don't worry, I'm fine where I am. At least I'm not out on the streets. And, by the way, I'm sorry too. It must have been horrible losing your grandma.'

'It was and the bad thing was, there was bugger all I could do about it.'

'Why? What happened if you don't mind me asking?'

Hannah let out a puff of air, preparing herself to relive all the painful details. 'Well, you already knew she was being intimidated, didn't you? And unfortunately, it got worse.'

She took a breath again, trying to hold back the tears but she couldn't stop the tremble in her voice as she uttered, 'She had a flat lined up. She was going to rent it till one she really wanted became available. My nana was that desperate to get out, she didn't want to stay there any longer. But they got fed up with waiting and before she had chance to move out, they broke into her property. I found her, Russ.'

By this time, she couldn't stop the tears, and she paused for a moment to calm herself down before continuing. 'She had a heart attack. It was because of the shock of seeing her ransacked living room and the nasty message they'd scrawled across the wall saying her time was up. And as if all that wasn't bad enough, I also found out that my stepdad, Pete, bought shares in Pake Holdings.'

'Why would he do that?'

'I don't know. He bought them ages ago and he says he didn't know what type of people he was dealing with.'

'And you believe him?'

'Not really, no. But my mum's taken his word for it, so I guess I'll just have to go along with it.'

'I'm sorry about your grandma, Hannah. She was a nice lady. I wish we could have stopped them before that happened.'

'So do I,' she sobbed. Then, after taking another breath,

she said, 'I still want to get Jez. I couldn't handle it before, but now I'm ready. I want justice.'

She then went on to tell him what had happened in the court case against Connor Davis before adding, 'Jez is still fuckin' walking about as though nothing's happened, Russ. I can't stand how cocky he is! Why don't you go to the police and tell them what you know? Surely that, together with what Connor said, will be enough for the police to charge him?'

'No, Hannah, it's not enough. I've told you before, he's got someone in the force on his payroll. We'd have to make sure everything was watertight before we could even think of going to the police. As it stands at the moment, we can't even prove he's connected to Pake.'

'What *can* we do then?'

'Well, I've been thinking, there is something, but it's risky, and I don't want you getting involved if you're not sure about it.'

'Run it by me, let me decide.'

'OK, well, do you have any access to Jez's office?'

'Kind of. I walk past it to get to the staff cloakroom, but I don't really go in there.'

'OK, well I'm sure I saw some documents with Pake Holdings on them a while back, when I went to see him in his office one day. I didn't think much of it at the time because I didn't know what I know now. But, now I come to think about it, he covered them up straightaway as though he didn't want me to see them. If you could find any of those documents that show he's connected to Pake, that could nail it. But, like I say, don't be taking any risks if you're not happy with it.'

Hannah thought for a moment before she said, 'OK, I'll do it, but on one condition. Once I've got what we need, I want you to go to the police and tell them what you know.'

'OK,' said Russ. 'I will. But be careful, Hannah. If you're gonna go searching his office, then make sure you don't get caught.

Jill turned over in bed, put down her book and switched off the bedside light. Next to her, Pete was still reading.

'Oh, sorry, love,' she heard him say. 'I didn't realise you were ready for bed. Let me just finish this page.'

Not long after she felt his body move closer to hers then he leant over, gave her a kiss on the cheek and said good night. She heard the flick of the switch on his side of the bed then it went dark.

As she lay there with her eyes shut, she knew that sleep would evade her as it had done on many nights since her mother had passed away. There were too many negative thoughts going on inside her head.

Why was Pete being so obsequious? Normally he would have kept on reading knowing that she had no problem drifting off in the half-light, but now it seemed he was unusually eager to please. It was the same with other things: letting her have her way with the television, helping her with jobs where he normally wouldn't bother and lots more.

At first, she had thought his attentiveness was because she was grieving. But when it had continued, it made her question whether there might be another reason. The more she thought about it, the more it seemed that the change in him had come about ever since she had faced him about his involvement with Pake Holdings.

Although she had accepted his explanation when he told her he had unwittingly bought the shares in Pake, his current behaviour was making her doubt herself. Was he really that innocent? And, if he was, then why was he still behaving this way?

It was putting their relationship under strain. Jill felt like she was living a lie. They had been pretending everything was OK when, in reality, his involvement with the company connected to her mother's death was like a barrier between them. But she didn't know what to do about it. Because it was hard to admit, even to herself, that she no longer trusted her own husband.

48

It was Hannah's first night at work since her telephone conversation with Russ. His suggestion had made sense, and she couldn't believe she hadn't thought of it before. If she could find something tying Jez to Pake then that would back up Russ's evidence together with what Connor Davis had said in court. She was already thinking of approaching Connor's mother to see if they could wangle a prison visit and persuade the lad to give evidence against Jez.

But first, she needed to infiltrate Jez's office. She knew he was in the club tonight as she'd seen him earlier circulating with the crowds, which meant there was a good chance his office would be unlocked. But it had been too early at that point. She couldn't leave a packed bar on some pretext when she had only been in work for twenty minutes.

As she served the customers, Hannah observed the crowds surrounding the dance floor to see if she could spot Jez. An hour passed before she caught sight of him. Another member of staff had recently arrived to help with the later influx of customers, but at this point it wasn't any busier than earlier. Hannah decided it would be a great opportunity to sneak off.

She had soon entered the door marked 'PRIVATE' and she

listened for any signs of people around before she made her way down the corridor. Jez's office was the first room along. The makeshift staffroom-come-cloakroom was further down the corridor. She couldn't believe her luck when she noticed Jez had left his office unlocked.

It was quiet, apart from the steady thrum of music, which carried from the club. Nevertheless, Hannah looked over her shoulder before she slipped inside Jez's office, unnoticed. She could feel her heart throbbing as she approached the desk and began wading through the paperwork. By the time she was halfway through a sizeable pile, she had found nothing.

Hannah had a moment of doubt. If Jez should return now, she would be rumbled. There was no convincing excuse she could think of for her presence in Jez's office. She was still working her way through the pile, checking letter headings for the names of companies, when she heard something. She froze. Her ears pricked up. The sound of footsteps. *Shit!*

Russ was worried. He knew Hannah would be in work tonight so there was a good chance she would try to get hold of the proof they needed. But he felt bad for having put her up to it. He knew when he asked her that he had more to gain from it than her. No amount of proof would bring her nana back, but for him, it could make a massive difference.

He was desperate to get his life back; to not have to stay hidden, disguised as a homeless man and living in a squat among unpredictable junkies. The only way to do that was if Jez was out of the picture. He had thought about taking him out, but he couldn't do it. With Joel it was different; he had left him no choice. But the thought of premeditated murder gave Russ a cold shiver.

He had come to the conclusion that the only way to take care of Jez was to get sufficient evidence to put him behind bars, and Hannah was in a better position to do that than he was. Sure, he could have waited till the club was shut then broken in through the cellar. He knew Luke would help him get hold of some tools to enable him to break down the door that connected the cellar to the club.

The problem with that scenario was that the alarm would go off the minute he set foot inside the main nightclub building. At least Hannah was already inside the club, and he trusted her, so she was the obvious choice. But if anything happened to her, he would never forgive himself.

Hannah ducked behind the desk, praying it wasn't Jez she could hear. She didn't like to think what the outcome would be if he found her snooping around in his office. As her heart hammered even faster, she listened to the footsteps echoing loudly on the stone floor. Whoever it was, they were getting nearer. She held her breath as the unknown person seemed to stop for a moment outside Jez's office.

But then the footsteps faded, and Hannah exhaled sharply. She heard a door being opened but it wasn't the door to Jez's office; that was already open, and the sound was further away. It was only when the door shut again that Hannah realised, they weren't coming into the corridor but going out of it.

They must have come from the staffroom, perhaps

somebody who worked behind the other bar whom she hadn't noticed leave the main area of the nightclub. But the incident had freaked her out and she still didn't want to risk anyone returning, especially Jez.

Hannah leapt up out of her hiding place and, in her panic, grabbed a handful of documents from the bottom of the pile she had been searching. Then she rushed to the staffroom and stuffed the papers into her handbag. With a bit of luck Jez wouldn't notice they were missing until after she had gone. Once Hannah had left for the night, she could browse the documents in the safety of her own home. She only hoped she would find something useful that would incriminate Jez.

The rest of that night seemed to drag, and Hannah was on edge the whole time. She kept alert for any signs of a problem, and every time Jez came near to the bar, she dreaded what he was going to say.

When the end of the night finally arrived, Hannah had an eerie feeling as she entered the staff corridor. She was expecting someone to tap her on the shoulder at any moment and voice their suspicions or maybe announce that the staff were going to be searched for the missing papers before they were allowed home.

Maybe Jez hadn't returned to his office, in which case he wouldn't be aware of the missing documents yet. Hannah went into the staffroom, relieved that there seemed to be nothing amiss. She grabbed her handbag, noticing the bulge that wasn't normally there and trying to hide it under her arm as she walked back out on shaky legs and headed towards the exit. Even her voice sounded shaky as she bid goodbye to her workmates.

Still no sign of Jez. Good. Outside all seemed normal too. She shoved the key in the lock of her car and sped down the road. She was so eager to check the documents that she was tempted to pull over and riffle through them. But it was too risky. Besides, she'd soon be home and then she could give them her full attention.

49

The next day, Hannah was shattered. She'd stayed up very late reading in detail through the documents she'd snatched in the hope of finding out something she could use against Jez. But it was already late when she got home from the club and her concentration was waning. All her nervous energy of the night had left her sapped, so she finally gave in to her tiredness and went to bed determined to read the documents the following day.

· Hannah was still in bed when she heard somebody at the door. She ignored it at first, knowing she wasn't expecting anyone and not wanting to answer the door in her nightwear. Then she heard somebody talking and it seemed to be coming from inside her home. Her stomach churned and her breathing sped up as she prepared to face whatever was waiting for her.

She heard her mum shout, 'It's only me, love!'

Hannah was relieved till she remembered she had left the documents sprawled out on the sofa. *Shit!* She didn't want her mum to see them. It wasn't that she didn't trust her mother, but it would be awkward trying to explain what she was doing with the documents. So, she tumbled out of bed, snatched up her dressing gown and put it on as she fled to the door.

Hannah met Jill in the hall, and her eyes shot to Kai standing beside her mother. As soon as he saw her, Kai let go of his grandma's hand and rushed to Hannah, squealing, 'Mummy, mummy.' He eagerly shared what he had been up to during the time he'd been away, in the broken English spoken by toddlers.

They waited till he had finished babbling, then Jill smiled and said to Hannah, 'We were going shopping, so we thought we'd drop Kai off here and save you the job of coming to ours.'

Hannah stared at her mother, nonplussed. 'We?' she asked. 'Who's the "we"?'

Hannah realised which other person the 'we' referred to even before her mother said it. *Pete!* Did that mean he was already in the flat? In the living room? The rustle of papers confirmed her worst suspicions.

She wanted to get in there now. To move the papers out of his way. To check whether he had seen them. But her mother continued chatting about her plans for the day.

Eventually, Hannah drew her attention by asking, 'Have you got time for a quick cuppa while you're here.'

Jill looked at her watch. 'Ooh, is it that time already? No, sorry, love, I think we'd better get going.' Then she shouted Pete, and he came out of the living room, his eyes locking with Hannah's for a brief spell before he nodded by way of a greeting then quickly turned away.

'Come on,' said Jill. 'We need to be off.'

As soon as they were out of the door, Hannah went into

the living room with Kai in tow. She walked over to the papers and, noticing they had been disturbed, she scooped them up, putting them somewhere out of view. She'd have to go through them once Kai was asleep. If she was lucky, he might have an afternoon nap.

It was evening before Russ received a call from Hannah. He'd been on edge all day and had been tempted to ring her several times. But he knew she'd probably be busy with her son and would ring as soon as she had any news for him.

'Wait a sec,' he said when he took the call. 'I need to find somewhere quiet.'

He was in the auditorium at the squat, so he took himself off to the stage area. He heard someone groaning in the wings and peered through the gloom of the old theatre, realising too late that it was a couple having sex. It was just one of the drawbacks of living in a place with minimal privacy. Russ made his way further backstage and sat down on a disused box. It was even darker here but at least there was nobody around, so not only would he be able to hear her better, but he would also be able to talk in privacy too.

'OK, what have you got?' he asked.

'Sod all! I've gone through the papers with a fine-tooth comb: letters from suppliers, invoices and utility bills. I've read them all but there's no mention of Pake Holdings anywhere. They all seem to relate to either the nightclub or one of his other businesses.'

'Fuck! What do we do now?' he asked, the question aimed at himself as much as Hannah.

'There's only one thing we can do,' said Hannah, her

voice full of determination. 'We keep digging until we find something. But I'm not in work again till next weekend. There's probably documents for Pake locked up in the cabinet. I need to find the key—'

'No!' said Russ before she could finish what she was saying. 'I don't want you taking any more risks. I feel bad enough for getting you to do it the first time.'

'Russ, you didn't force me. I wanted it as much as you.'

'I know but, you've got to understand, Hannah. Jez is a bad bastard! I'm worried about what he'll do to you if he finds you in his office.'

'I'll just have to make sure he doesn't find me then, won't I?'

'Hannah, no. Don't do it.'

'Well, what's the alternative?' she asked.

'I dunno. Leave it with me. I'll think of something. In fact, I've already got an idea in mind. Just give me a bit of time and I'll come back to you. But you've got to promise me that in the meantime you won't do anything stupid.'

'OK, OK, I won't do anything till I hear from you,' she said.

Her words sounded convincing, but the problem was, Russ didn't believe her. She wasn't the only one lying. He hadn't yet thought of any other way to get the evidence despite telling her he had an idea in mind. Russ knew he had to come up with something and quick because not only would it help him, but it might also save Hannah's life.

50

'By the way, I'll be late home tonight. I forgot to tell you I'm meeting an old friend after work,' said Pete, bending to kiss Jill who was finishing the last of her breakfast.

Jill noticed the obsequiousness again. Lately he'd taken to kissing her before he went to work, which he hadn't done since the early days of living together. To her it was another sign that he was hiding something, but she wasn't easily fooled.

'Who's that?' she asked.

'Rob. Remember him?'

Jill thought for a moment then said. 'Isn't that the one you went to school with?'

'Yeah, that's right. Rob Dooley.'

'But you haven't seen him for years, have you?'

'Exactly, which is even more reason why we need a good catch up. We've left it far too long.'

'Oh, alright,' said Jill, hesitantly.

'Is there a problem?' he asked.

'No, no, it's just that it's a bit last minute, that's all. I was planning a nice tea for us.'

'Oh, I'm sorry. I should have told you before now but,

like I said, it just slipped my mind. Anyway, I must dash. I don't want to be late for work.'

Then he rushed off. Jill sighed and drained the last dregs of her coffee then tidied the dishes away before she too went to get ready for work.

But something was niggling her. She cast her mind back to the last time Pete had mentioned Rob Dooley. It must have been at least two years ago. From what she could recall, Pete had said something about the man having become a bit of a bore.

As Jill drove to work, it was still on her mind. Hadn't Rob been the one who Pete used to see only occasionally when he wouldn't take no for an answer? She remembered that after their last outing, Pete had managed to avoid another meeting. Why then would he have arranged to meet him now? And why the short notice?

In all the time she had known Pete, he had always been organised, usually telling her his arrangements well in advance. It didn't do anything to alleviate the doubts that had been clouding her mind recently. She didn't believe he was meeting Rob at all. But, if not, who was he meeting? And why?

Pete waited till he got to work before taking out his mobile phone and making the call he had been desperate to make since Sunday morning. He hadn't had a chance before now as Jill had been with him all Sunday. They'd gone shopping first and then for a meal later, and he'd been unable to think of a convincing excuse to either leave her shopping alone or slip out after tea.

In the end he decided it would be better to tell her he had to meet someone after work. Why he'd decided on Rob's name, he didn't know. He supposed he just hadn't expected Jill to ask for a name. It wasn't like her. He just hoped she couldn't remember how much the guy had irritated him.

'Oh, hi,' he said when the call was answered. 'We need to talk.'

'OK, fire away,' said the voice on the other end of the line.

'No, not now. I've got a meeting in five minutes. Meet me tonight after work. It won't take long.'

Then he quickly arranged a time and a place.

Russ had been troubled ever since he'd spoken to Hannah yesterday. He knew she'd go against his wishes and try to get information from Jez's office again because she was so strong-willed. He doubted that anything he said would stop her so that meant he had four days till Friday's shift in which to come up with something.

He'd now decided on his first step but in order to carry it out he'd need a little help and the best person to advise him would be his friend, Luke. He knew a lot of people and was bound to be able to put Russ in touch with someone who could provide what he needed.

Luke hadn't been back to the squat last night. Often, when he was high on spice, he would lie down in whichever doorway was nearest and crash out for the night. Figuring it could be hours before he came back to the squat, Russ set off in search of him.

He knew it was risky walking around the city centre

in case he was recognised, but he hoped his change in appearance would be a good disguise. His hair was longer now, and so was his beard. He'd also taken to keeping his head low as he passed people in the street.

It took Russ almost two hours but after quizzing some of the homeless people he knew, he eventually found Luke slumped in a back alleyway with his head lolling to one side. Russ noticed he was wearing an old overcoat he hadn't seen before and there was vomit smeared down it. *Jesus!* he thought. *He must have been well caning it last night.*

Russ took hold of Luke's shoulder and shook it, worried when he didn't wake up. His shakes became more vigorous as panic set in until he was rewarded by the sight of one eye partially open. Luke quickly shut it again.

'Aw, man!' Luke drawled. 'What the fuck you doing?'

'Trying to wake you up. What do you think? Fuckin' hell, Luke. You must have taken some stuff last night. Look at the state of you!'

'Fuck off, Dad.'

Russ was used to the insult Luke always threw at him when he tried to chastise him for his lifestyle. But he wasn't going anywhere. He needed Luke's help, and he wasn't going to let up just because Luke had got himself in a state again.

'Do I have to throw water over you like last time?' he asked.

Luke's eyes were now fully open. 'Why don't you fuck off? I just need to sleep it off, that's all.'

'Why? So you can go straight back on it as soon as you're awake? No chance! You need to fuckin' ease up, Luke, or you're gonna kill yourself.'

'Oh yeah, 'cos I've got so much to live for, haven't I?'

'You've got friends, Luke, that care about you.'

Without listening to any more arguments, Russ got him up off his feet. 'Come on, we'll go and get a coffee somewhere quiet. Then there's something I need you to help me with.'

'Only if I can have a reefer.'

Russ knew that Luke's level of addiction was too much to expect him to function on nothing after a heavy night, so he complied with his wishes. 'OK, just the one, for now. But try to stay off the other stuff tonight, for fuck's sake!'

'Alright, alright,' grumbled Luke. 'What's so fuckin' important that you had to come looking for me anyway?'

'Let's get you sorted first, then I'll tell you.'

51

Pete was sitting in a pub not far from his place of work waiting for his contact to arrive. As he held his pint of lager shandy in one hand, he tapped nervously on the table with the other. He knew he shouldn't be doing this. Jill would go mad if she knew. But the way he saw it, he had no choice.

When his contact arrived, Pete watched him swagger across the pub carrying his usual pint with a whisky chaser. Samuel Sweeney. Unstoppable. Ambitious. Area manager for Oliver Tomlinson estate agents at just thirty-eight years of age. And one of the directors of Pake Holdings Ltd.

'Fuck's sake, Pete!' he said, putting his drinks on the table and pulling out a seat. 'What's with all the cloak and dagger? What have you got to tell me that you couldn't say on the phone?'

'It's about Pake,' said Pete. 'I saw a load of papers in my stepdaughter's house.'

'Yeah, and?'

'They looked like Jez's business documents. You know she works at The Gilded Cage, don't you?'

'No, I didn't. Fuck!' said Sweeney, furrowing his brow. 'Don't tell me it was her that took them out of Jez's office?'

'Looks that way, yeah,' said Pete, his tone low.

'Fuckin' hell. Jez has been going ballistic. He knows they're gone. What the fuck is she doing with them?. Ah ... hang on, Jez did say someone overheard him mention Rovener Street on the phone, ages ago – it must have been her he was talking about. He was worried she might realise he's involved with Pake. But why would she want documents?'

Pete hesitated, as he felt a fleeting pang of guilt for grassing up his stepdaughter. But then he remembered whose side he was on. 'I think it might be because of her nana dying. You know about her being one of the residents, don't you?'

'I didn't but, go on ...'

'Well, Hannah was really angry about the intimidation after her nana died. So, maybe she was looking for something tying Jez to what's been going on in the street.'

'Shit! OK. Well, sorry about the old woman, mate. But we didn't think she'd die. We thought it would just shit her up and she'd leave.'

'I know. Me and Jill even tried to get her to live with us, but she was stubborn. Jill's not like that. She's easy going, but Hannah's like her fuckin' grandma. I wouldn't put it past her to start meddling. She's like a dog with a fuckin' bone.'

'Alright. Well, cheers for telling me, mate.' Samuel raised a glass and took a slurp before adding, 'We'll deal with it.'

'OK, but I trust that you'll just give her a bit of a scare, won't you?'

'Yeah, don't worry, leave it with me, mate.'

But Pete was worried. It was one thing having them put

the frighteners on Hannah, but if they did anything to harm her, he wouldn't be able to live with himself.

Hannah was playing with Kai in the living room when she heard the doorbell. Curious, she made her way to the door to see what it was. She was surprised to find a man on the doorstep carrying a parcel, which he handed over. Hannah scanned the label to make sure it was addressed correctly as she wasn't expecting anything. Satisfied that the parcel was for her, she walked inside.

Too intrigued to wait, she began tearing away at the package while she was still in the hall. Once she had opened the outer box, she found a note tucked inside among some tissue paper. It read, 'To be opened in private'.

Now Hannah was more than intrigued, she was nervous. She felt around the packaging and held it to her ear but couldn't feel or hear anything that might give her a clue. Aware that she'd left her son playing in the living room, she went through to the kitchen and pulled the tissue paper away until she found another, smaller box.

Hannah lifted it out and looked at it, as if its size and shape might indicate what the contents might be. But it didn't so she ripped open the parcel tape covering it until she was able to lift the lid of the box. What she saw made her gasp.

'Oh my God!' she uttered when she spotted a small handgun nestled underneath some folded sheets of paper, which showed a faint trace of writing on the underside.

She took the paper out first. Then she popped the gun on

top of a kitchen surface while she opened the note to see what it said. There were two pages and the message on the top one read:

I know you're gonna do it anyway, so I want to make sure you've got protection. Take this with you. It'll come in handy. I've included some instructions on how to use it.

The message was a bit cryptic, but Hannah knew exactly what it meant. It must have come from Russ because he knew she'd search Jez's office again even though she'd told him she wouldn't.

She was horrified. What on earth made Russ think that she would want to use a gun? She'd never used a weapon in her life! She took a peep at the other sheet of paper. It was the instructions he had referred to. Well, she wouldn't be needing them. She had no intentions of making use of the gun.

It shook her when she heard Kai shouting 'Mummy' from the other room.

Knowing she mustn't let him see the gun, she called back, 'Hang on, love. I'll be there in a minute.'

She shoved the gun and accompanying notes back into the box and put them inside the larger box. Then she flicked her eyes over the kitchen, desperately looking for a place where she could keep the gun for now so that it was out of Kai's reach. There was a small gap between the tops of her cupboards and the ceiling, so she stashed it there.

'Mummy's coming!' she called to Kai.

Then she ran back into the living room, prepared to put on an act of normality. She'd think about how to get shut of the gun later once Kai was in bed. And she'd also get Russ on the phone and tell him what a fuckin' idiot he was!

52

Russ was currently waiting outside a Manchester nightclub called *Juicy Fruits*. He'd been trying to find Dom since the start of the week. Although he had sent Hannah the gun, he preferred to prevent her searching Jez's office if he could, so now he was pinning his hopes on Dom. He remembered how amenable Dom had been when he had killed Joel and figured it was worth speaking to him.

But Dom was proving difficult to locate. It was Thursday now, and Russ was getting desperate knowing Hannah would be in work tomorrow night. He had tried all the other pubs and clubs Dom was likely to frequent, but it didn't help that he had to hang about outside waiting to catch sight of him. Going inside wasn't an option. Even if nobody recognised him, he doubted they'd allow him inside in his current state.

It was past closing time and Russ watched from a distance as the club started emptying. He recognised a few of the faces, all members of the criminal fraternity who tended to hang out at the same places. That was why he thought he might find Dom there.

At last, he noticed him leaving the club. Dom looked worse for wear as he staggered up the road, which meant he'd probably be catching a cab home. *Good!* Russ hoped he could head him off before he reached the taxi rank. But he'd have to wait until they were a distance from the club.

Russ followed Dom, keeping to the other side of the road so he was less likely to be spotted. Eventually, they reached Peter Square, and Russ guessed Dom would be heading to Albert Square where the taxi rank was situated. He noted the arcade at the town hall extension with its small arches and decided it would be a good place to approach Dom.

The arcade was popular with the homeless because it provided shelter and, although the arches were open, the surrounding brickwork and arcade ceiling shrouded the area in darkness. That meant they could stay out of view from the main square.

Russ quickened his pace, eager to catch up with Dom before he reached the end of the arcade. Feeling breathless, he fell into step with him and glancing across, he said, 'Quick, in there. I need a word.'

At first Dom looked alarmed at this approach from a homeless man, but then recognition flashed in his eyes. 'Shit! It's you.'

Russ took hold of his arm and guided him into the arcade. 'Quick. We don't want to be seen.'

'Fuckin' hell! You reek,' complained Dom.

'Cheers, mate. I love you too.'

'What the fuck do you want?' asked Dom. 'I didn't expect to see you again after, after—'

'I need your help,' Russ cut in before Dom had chance to mention what had happened to Joel.

He led Dom to the back wall, so they were well out of

view of the CCTV or anyone who happened to be passing. 'I'm having to disguise myself,' said Russ, 'because of Jez.'

'Oh yeah,' said Dom. 'He's still after your guts.'

'I guessed he would be. But the thing is, mate, I can't go on living like this. Look at me; I'm a fuckin' mess.'

'Eh, don't "mate" me,' said Dom. 'I ain't no-one's mate. It's taking me all my fuckin' time to look after number one.'

'But the thing is,' Russ cajoled. 'Between us, we could nail him; then we won't have to worry about the tosser anymore, and we can both get on with our lives.'

'No fuckin' chance!' said Dom. 'If I go up against him, I'm a dead man.'

'You wouldn't be on your own. I've got plenty on him, but I can't do it on my own. It'd be my word against his. But with two of us, the cops would take us more seriously. And I don't know if you've heard about that kid who did the torching. He named him in court. We might be able to get him to testify.'

'No! No way. Jez has got cops on the payroll. He'll get off with it. And where will that fuckin' leave me?'

'Look, Dom, I wouldn't ask but I'm fuckin' desperate. It's not just for me. It's for Hannah.'

Russ had deliberated about how much to tell Dom. He still wasn't sure whether he could fully trust him. But he was saved the decision when Dom asked, 'You mean the girl that works behind the bar in The Gilded Cage?'

'Yeah, that's right.'

'Fuckin' hell! She's well in the shit. I heard that Jez is onto her. She's been lifting some papers from his office.'

'Shit!' cursed Russ. 'How did he know?'

'It came from a guy called Samuel Sweeney from what I've been told. Jez has been spending a lot of time with him, summat to do with that development at Rovener Street.'

'But how the fuck did Sweeney know?' Russ demanded.

'Some guy called Pete who works for him, no-one I've heard of.'

Russ shook his head. He wasn't familiar with the name either.

'Look, I haven't told you this,' said Dom, 'But she'd be better off sacking the job and keeping a low profile. If Jez catches her sniffing round his office, he'll fuckin' kill her. He was raging from what I've been told.'

'Who told you all this?' asked Russ.

Dom tapped his nose. 'News travels fast in the criminal world, Russ. You should know that as much as me. But I prefer not to name them. I've fuckin' told you too much as it is.'

He made to move away, and Russ knew he'd get no more out of him tonight. Despite the size of him, it was obvious that Dom was terrified of Jez and his cohorts.

'Thanks, mate,' said Russ. 'I really appreciate it.'

He waited till Dom was well away then walked back to the squat with his head bent low. He was feeling more dejected and desperate than ever.

53

Russ needed to get hold of Hannah. He had to warn her about Jez before she went into work the following night. Despite the late hour, he tried ringing her when he reached the squat. But there was no reply. He checked the time on his phone. 2.39 a.m. She was probably asleep as it wasn't a work night, but he wasn't prepared to give in straightaway, so he tried again several times until he finally submitted to sleep himself.

As soon as Russ woke up, he checked the time on his phone. Twelve o'clock. *Shit!* Had he slept that long? But then, he realised that he hadn't stopped ringing Hannah till turned six in the morning, so it made sense that he should sleep so late. He consoled himself with the thought that there were still a few hours to go before Hannah started work. He just hoped nobody got to her before then.

Hannah was at her mum's when she heard the phone ring. Jill had taken a day off work, and they were going to take Kai out for the afternoon to a nice country park then stop off somewhere for a meal before Hannah went to work that evening. She looked at the screen and saw Russ's number.

She knew what it would be about. He was worried she might search Jez's office again. She'd rung him Monday evening after she'd received the gun and told him exactly what she thought of him sending a gun to her home when she had a child. Then she'd assured him she wasn't going to go anywhere near Jez's office, so he had no need to worry.

She'd lied.

Now it was obvious that he was ringing her to warn her off again. She didn't need the hassle and she certainly wasn't going to answer the phone in front of her mother. It would only cause Jill undue stress if she knew everything.

'Come on, come on, answer the fuckin' phone!' cursed Russ after ringing Hannah for the third time.

She wasn't answering, and to make matters even worse, he was now out of power. He'd have to make his way to a coffee shop so he could charge his phone up. It wasn't as if he even wanted a fuckin' coffee! And he'd have to make sure there was nobody inside the coffee shop that recognised him because he still couldn't afford to blow his cover.

'Are we ready to go?' asked Jill.

Kai jumped up and down excitedly, squealing. 'Yes, Ganmar.'

At that moment, Hannah's phone rang again.

'Who is it?' asked her mum. 'That's three times they've rung you now.'

'Oh, no-one important,' said Hannah. 'Just someone cold calling. I'll get rid of them.'

But rather than deleting the number of an unknown caller as Jill suspected she was doing, Hannah switched her phone off. That would stop Russ from pestering her for now. She could ring him back later once she was on her way to work.

It took Russ an age till he walked to the coffee shop three miles out of the city centre and charged up his phone. As soon as he left, he rang Hannah again, but he was perturbed when the call went straight to voicemail.

'Shit!' he muttered to himself. 'I can't believe she's fuckin' switched it off.'

He'd just have to try again later and keep ringing in the hope that he could reach her in time.

'Thanks for today, Mum,' said Hannah. 'Kai loved it, and so did I, especially that lovely meal you treated us to.'

'Thank you,' said Jill. 'And this little fella here,' she added, tickling Kai. 'I enjoyed it.'

They were back at Jill's house, and Hannah had walked in to find Pete sitting on the sofa watching TV. As per usual, they made polite chit-chat, but Hannah still found it difficult to be civil to the man.

'Ah well,' said Hannah, looking at the clock on the mantelpiece. 'It's time I was getting ready for work.'

'Ooh, that time already?' asked Jill.

Hannah smiled and gave her mum and Kai a kiss and a hug before bidding them all goodbye. Then she left for home where she would grab a quick shower and change of clothes before heading off for work.

Two hours later, Hannah was on the way to The Gilded Cage. She had been too busy that day to give her imminent night shift much consideration. But now her head was full of thoughts of the task in hand. She was determined to find the information she needed no matter what she had told Russ. It was the only way she would get justice for her grandmother's death.

She arrived at work in time to grab a quick cuppa before taking her place behind the bar. The coffee should help her to get through the night. Then it was time to get started. In fact, she'd been so busy chatting to the other staff that she was actually a few minutes late.

Hannah dashed to the staffroom where she left her bag before she started work. She hoped Jez wouldn't notice her tardiness. The last thing she wanted to do was draw attention to herself on tonight of all nights. As she hung her handbag up on a peg, she reached in to grab her phone as she did every night.

Although they weren't allowed to chat on their phones while they were behind the bar, she usually kept it tucked into the waistband of her jeans in case she might receive an urgent call from her mother about Kai. Unfortunately, in her haste, she forgot that the phone was still switched off.

54

Jez was watching Hannah from some distance away, but she was totally unaware as she took orders for drinks and flirted with the customers. At one time he had thought her an attractive girl and one he might possibly make a play for when the time was right. But in light of what he now knew, her behaviour irritated him. *Slag!*

When he had been told she was the one who had been snooping around in his office, he was fuming. How dare she! At first, he couldn't understand why until Samuel had told him about the connection to Pat Bennett of Rovener Street. And he'd wondered how she would know about his involvement with Pake, unless she'd assumed it when she'd heard him mention Rovener Street. But the more likely reason would be that Russ Coles had told her. And he might even have got her to search through his paperwork.

So now it all made sense, but it also meant that he might have more to worry about than he had initially suspected. To be searching through his private papers, she must already know plenty. Maybe she had even figured out that he was behind her grandmother's death. The silly cow must be on some kind of revenge mission.

He could have taken her out at any point since he'd

found out about her meddling. He knew where she and her family lived. It would have been easy to send one or two of his men round to dispose of her. But that would have spoilt the fun. Jez much preferred to do it himself. She needed to be taught a lesson and needed to know that he wasn't to be messed with.

If she had searched his office once, then she would do it again. He already had her figured out. She was a feisty one, the type who would stop at nothing until she'd completed what she set out to achieve. And he was confident that she would make her move tonight.

It had been a busy night for Hannah with hardly a break. The one break she did have had been cut short when she'd accidently knocked over a punter's drink. Then, once she'd finished clearing it up and rushing away, one of the other girls had insisted on spending her break with her.

But Hannah wasn't giving up on her mission to get information on Jez. She decided the best time to do it would be after work. She'd hang around the bar, taking her time to clear up, until all the bar staff had gone. At that time of night, usually the bouncers and management were the only staff still in the building. And Jez was normally making his way around the club checking everything was in order.

By the time she reached the end of shift, she was perspiring profusely with nervous anticipation. Her palms were clammy, and she could feel a cold trickle of sweat running down her back. She bid goodbye to the other staff, telling them she didn't mind clearing away the last of the glasses. Then she watched Jez to see if he was tied up.

To Hannah's horror, he crossed the nightclub and made his way towards her. 'Everything alright?' he asked.

'Yeah, I'm just clearing up these last few glasses and wiping the counter down then I'll be off home.'

'OK, no rush. We're still seeing a few punters off the premises, so we won't be locking up for a while yet.'

Then he made his way towards the club foyer and Hannah breathed a sigh of relief. Hopefully he'd be tied up for some time chatting to the bouncers as they watched the last of the customers leave. It was time to make her move. She flung the dishcloth she'd been using into the sink and made her way towards the door marked 'PRIVATE'.

Jez greeted his bouncers and watched the last of the customers leave.

'Is that it?' asked one of his bouncers, John Macy.

'More or less. There's one of my guys in the men's and that's about it.'

'You staying for a drink?' asked John.

Jez had got into the habit of having a few drinks with his bouncers after work unless he wanted to get off straightaway. He surmised that when he wasn't there, they helped themselves to a few anyway. Normally he didn't mind. It was useful to keep them sweet and what were a few drinks compared to a night's takings? But tonight, he wanted them gone.

'No, I need the bar area keeping clean,' he said. 'So, if you guys don't mind making your way home? Oh, and make sure that guy in the toilets goes out with you too.'

The disappointed look on the two guy's faces told Jez

they had understood him. The back door had a spring latch so he knew it would lock behind them. Then, when he was ready to go, he'd lock the mortice lock too. But before that he had something to attend to.

Jez went through to the main area of the nightclub, noticing that Hannah was no longer behind the bar. Suspecting she would be searching his office, he was heading towards the private staff area when he was stopped by another of his bouncers who wanted a word. Apparently, his wife had booked him a surprise holiday for the following week, and he wanted to book some time off at short notice.

'It's a fine bloody time of night to bring this up,' Jez complained, knowing that the longer the bouncer kept him occupied, the less chance there would be of catching Hannah in the act.

'Sorry, boss, but I forgot to tell you earlier on.'

Jez tutted and took out his phone so he could put it on his calendar, all the time aware of the need to get to his office as soon as possible.

Russ was standing in a doorway in the alley at the back of The Gilded Cage. He was so worried about Hannah that he'd risked breaking his cover. As he stood there, he kept taking surreptitious glances at the club's back entrance. He'd seen most of the staff leave. A few of them had passed him, and he'd had to adopt his usual disguise, quickly slumping down in the doorway with his head bowed so nobody would recognise him.

As he waited anxiously, he checked the time on his watch again. 2.40 a.m. There was still no sign of Hannah, and he was getting seriously worried. She was normally out well before now. And the fact that there were no longer any members of staff leaving the club told him that she and Jez were possibly the only two people remaining inside, unless a few of the bouncers or members of Jez's crew had stayed.

Shit! He'd have to do something. He approached the door and heaved against it, trying to force it open. But it didn't budge. He grimaced in despair. Then he dashed round to the front of the building. Maybe there was a slight chance the bouncers were late in getting rid of a few of the punters in which case he'd steamroller his way through them and dash through the club in search of Hannah and Jez.

But the front of the club was quiet, and all the doors were locked. He wondered how difficult it would be to break through the glass. But, even if there was a brick handy, which there wasn't, the glass would be reinforced. Then it dawned on him. The cellar. He'd done it before so he could do it again.

He prayed no-one had secured the hatch since the last time he'd been down there. If not, then it should be easy enough to get in. The trouble was, he'd also have to break through the locked door that separated the cellar from the rest of the club. It would be difficult, but he'd try. His hand touched on the chisel that he still carried on him, and it gave him a feeling of assurance. He just hoped he'd get there in time.

55

Hannah was inside Jez's office frantically searching for the evidence she needed. With trembling hands, she started on the remaining documents on his desk. She soon flicked through them. She was familiar now with the type of documents connected to The Gilded Cage and his other businesses, so she disregarded anything that wasn't important to her.

Next, she switched on the computer, her sticky hands leaving sweat marks on the keyboard as she tried to figure out Jez's password. She tried anything she could think of: the name of the club, Jez's name, Pake, Pake Holdings and the names of the two directors, but none of them worked.

Shit! she cursed, aware of the time and the fact that Jez could walk through the door at any minute. *The cabinet,* she thought. That might be somewhere he would hide documents he didn't want anyone to see. She tried one of the drawers. *Locked. Damn!*

Hoping that the key would be in the desk somewhere, she searched briskly, her heart pounding as the clock ticked away. There was nothing in the drawers. She surveyed the wreckage on the desk where she had tipped out the desk contents and sighed. Where? Where was the bloody key?

Something told her to feel her way around the desk. She didn't know where she'd got the idea, maybe in an old movie. But it did the trick. As her hand settled on something hard taped to the underside of the desk, she let out a breath of relief. She pulled away the tape and smiled as she looked at the key in her hand.

Aware of how long she was taking, she dashed to the door and searched the corridor. There was nobody around and she couldn't hear anything. *Good*. Hannah eased the key into the cabinet and opened the top drawer. All the files were headed, which made it easier to scan through them. But there were lots of them, so it still took some time.

When the top two drawers didn't yield anything of value, she tried the bottom one. Hannah couldn't believe her luck when she caught sight of a file headed 'Pake Holdings Ltd', the bold lettering staring back at her. She couldn't resist a peek and was satisfied when she saw letters connecting Jez to Pake Holdings. Wanting to be sure, she grabbed all the papers from the file and turned to go, a thrill of excitement pulsing through her. Hopefully she'd manage to cram them into her handbag in case Jez saw her leaving.

Hannah dashed to the door, eager to get to the staffroom and grab her things. She walked into the corridor. It had been deathly silent only moments earlier. But there, facing her, stood Jez, a wide grin on his face as he eyed the papers in her hands.

'I think me and you need to have a word,' he said.

Then he took her by surprise, shoving her inside the office and turning the key in the lock.

*

Using the chisel, Russ soon broke into the cellar hatch, but he'd known that that would be the easy part. The door to the club was secured by a bolt so he'd have to do a fair bit of chiselling before he could release it from its casing. And he'd have to do it as quickly as he could.

He passed through the cellar, which looked much as it had done the last time he had been there. It took him by surprise to find himself overwhelmed by memories. Bad ones. The vicious attack by Joel and the time spent there in the dark, terrified and in pain. He glanced at his scarred finger and shuddered. Then he recalled the tremendous relief on discovering an escape route followed by weeks of living in poverty, under the cover of a homeless man, and fearing for his life.

Russ forced himself to break free of the memories and concentrate on the matter in hand. There'd be plenty of time to dwell on all that later, but now Hannah was his priority.

He approached the door that led to the staff quarters and took out his chisel. But he couldn't remember whereabouts the bolt was situated. *Fuck!* That meant he could be chipping away for an age and still be no further forward. *Think!* he told himself, putting a hand to his forehead to help him focus.

Then he thought of a way that he could locate the bolt before setting to work with the chisel. Russ searched among the debris in the cellar and found a slim piece of card. Dashing back up to the door, he slid the card into the narrow gap between the door and the door jamb. He met with resistance about halfway up and knew that was where the bolt was situated. Dropping the card, he took hold of the chisel again and carried on whittling away at the wood.

Hannah staggered back, bumping into the desk. As she put out her hands to steady herself, the bunch of papers dropped to the floor and landed in a messy heap. She stared at Jez, her mouth agape.

A sly grin slid over his face. 'And what do you think you're doing with that lot?' he asked.

Hannah didn't have any defence, but she felt certain he knew anyway. A tremor of fear spread through her body and settled in the pit of her stomach. She stared at him in stunned silence, awaiting his next move.

After watching her squirm for several seconds, he changed tack. 'I fuckin' knew it was you! I expect you thought you were being clever, didn't you?' When she still didn't speak, he carried on. 'So, go on, tell me. What were you intending to do? Use those papers as evidence? Go to the police? Do you honestly think that would have achieved anything?' Without waiting for her to reply this time, he said, 'It's of no consequence anyway now.'

His words cut right through her. That must mean he was going to dispose of her. *Oh my God!* she thought, regretting not taking Russ's advice when he had told her not to search the office a second time.

'So, did you think you were avenging your grandmother?' he asked, a slight smile still playing on his lips.

Hannah continued to stare, but now she had a look of horror. He knew everything.

'Oh, if you're expecting a full and frank confession before I deal with you,' he continued, 'then you're mistaken. I just want you removing from the equation. You should have left things alone, things that don't concern you.'

Suddenly Hannah was filled with rage. How dare he say things didn't concern her. 'You killed my nana!' she yelled.

'It was her own fault. She should have got out while she could instead of being so fuckin' pig-headed.'

He took a step towards her, but Hannah was determined not to succumb to the same fate as her nana. Propelled by hatred and a need for revenge she pulled out the gun Russ had given her. Thank God she had had a change of heart and at least taken his advice about that!

'Back off!' she yelled, gripping the gun with shaking hands.

Jez laughed at her. 'You wouldn't dare!'

Then he rushed at her and thrust his hand forward to grab the gun. Hannah knew it was him or her. In an impulse reaction, she pulled the trigger, and a mighty bang filled the air. Then she gasped in horror as Jez yelled and gripped his chest. She could hardly believe what she was seeing when he slumped to the ground, his facial expression one of shock. A crimson patch formed on the front of his shirt as the blood oozed through his fingers. She really had done it. She'd shot Jez!

Russ was almost through the cellar door when he heard the shot. A feeling of dread assailed him. *Hannah!* He knew he couldn't afford to waste any more time, so he stood back and took a run at the door, landing a kick on the area near to the bolt. The wood gave way, and the door flew open.

He raced up the steps and through the corridor till he arrived at Jez's office. Peering through the glass, he saw Hannah standing, immobile, the gun still in her hand. He shouldered the door, but it didn't give.

'Hannah, can you open the door?' he yelled.

Then he watched through the window as she moved robotically towards him, and he heard the key in the lock. Russ pressed the handle and stepped inside.

It was obvious that she was in a state of shock, and as she stood there transfixed, he walked past her and approached the body on the floor: Jez. Russ checked for a pulse then turned to face Hannah once more.

'He's dead!' he announced.

Hannah became hysterical then, howling and in tears. Russ pulled her into a tight hug to calm her down. 'It's OK,' he said. 'I'll deal with it. It's OK.'

His mind quickly assimilated the facts. Jez was dead. Hannah was holding the gun. There were papers on his desk which looked as though they'd been disturbed and another stack on the floor a few feet from the body. Hannah's fingerprints and DNA would be on all of them. The cabinet was open too, so that would also probably have her fingerprints.

His own fingerprints were only on the door and in the cellar. That would be easy to deal with. He could soon wipe them off the door handle and explain his previous presence in the cellar, dismissing the broken door as something he knew nothing about. But he needed to come up with a way to cover up the evidence against Hannah.

He was just running through everything in his mind while also trying to calm Hannah down when he heard movement in the corridor outside. Grabbing the gun from Hannah, he turned around and his eyes settled on the enormous figure of a man, which filled the doorway. Russ recognised him as one of Jez's bouncers, and behind him was another. With Hannah in this state, there was no way he could fight off two of them single-handedly.

56

'Stand back, Hannah,' Russ ordered then he faced the bouncers. 'Keep back! I swear if you come anywhere near, I'll press the fuckin' trigger.'

The bouncer was stunned into stillness by the horrific scene of Jez lying dead on his office floor in a sea of ripe red blood and the splatters that ran up the walls. His colleague leant forward and peeped through the gap between the big guy's shoulders and the door jamb.

'Fuckin' hell! You've killed him,' he said, his tone incredulous.

'No,' said the big guy, finding his voice. 'He didn't do it. She did. He's just grabbed the gun off her.'

Russ heard a whimper from behind him and he reached back with his free hand, tapping it against Hannah to comfort her as he addressed the men again.

'Right, here's what we're gonna do. You guys are gonna stand well back and let us through.'

They took a tentative step backwards, but as they did so, the bigger of the two said, 'She'll never fuckin' get away with it!'

Russ felt he was probably right, but he couldn't think

of any other way out of the predicament. If he could get past the bouncers first, then he'd think about what to do next. He needed them to be much further away though before he and Hannah could make a run for it. Russ was just about to issue his orders when he heard someone else approaching.

He was shocked to see Dom stick his head through the office door and yell, 'What the fuck!'

'She fuckin' shot him!' said the first bouncer.

Then Russ heard another whimper from behind him before Hannah spoke, her voice trembling. 'He killed my nana. He frightened her to death so he could get his greedy hands on her home. Then he taunted me.'

She ended on a sob and Russ could see the changing expressions on the faces of the bouncers as they transitioned from hostility to sympathy. For a moment nobody spoke. Dom was the first one to break the silence, turning back to the two bouncers and addressing them.

'Look guys, you know what Jez was like as well as I do. He's fuckin' screwed us all over at one time or another. Do you really want a young woman sent to prison because he's driven her to this?'

Russ was amazed at Dom's depth of feeling and at the way he was taking control. He'd always seen him as a bit of a yes man, willing to do Jez's bidding and happy to accommodate Joel's blood lust. But maybe he had been motivated by fear back then. And now that Joel and Jez were gone, things had changed. Dom was finally stepping up.

'She still fuckin' killed him!' said the smaller of the two bouncers.

'Only because of what he did!' snapped Russ. 'He's been

fuckin' intimidating the residents on her grandma's street for the best part of a year. He even threw me out of the shop I was renting from him and then had me beaten up because I wouldn't help with the intimidation. And now look at me! I had to go in fuckin' hiding to get away from him.'

As if they had only just noticed his appearance and the putrid odour that emanated from him, the two bouncers screwed their faces in distaste. But neither of them spoke.

'We'll all be fuckin' better off without him,' said Dom. 'Look, lads, we can make this work. Nobody needs to know owt. We can just say we'd already gone home.'

'Cops will still know it's her,' said the big bouncer. 'What about fuckin' fingerprints and DNA and all that?'

'They won't,' said Russ, who had just thought of an idea. 'There's a way round it. All you guys need to do is say you know nowt. I'll deal with the rest.'

The two bouncers traded indecisive looks until Dom said, 'What have you got to lose, lads? This doesn't need to go any further than us five. As long as we all keep schtum, we'll be OK. And I know Russ and Hannah won't say owt, 'cos they're the ones with the most to lose. What d'you think?'

Finally, the bigger one nodded and said, 'Let's have a word in private.'

They walked a bit further down the corridor and Russ took the opportunity to check on Hannah, confident now that he could trust Dom if he turned his back to him. Russ put his arm around Hannah's shoulders, trying to soothe her as she sobbed uncontrollably.

'Don't worry,' he said. 'Everything will work out.'

Then the bouncers were back, the biggest one taking the lead. 'Alright, we'll do it. As long as you promise there'll be no comeback.'

They all had a brief discussion while they went over their cover story and Russ reassured them that once they were gone, he would lock the door after them all as though Jez had been the last person in the building. Then he would get back out through the cellar.

'I can't believe they've agreed to it,' he said to Dom, relief now flooding over him.

'I can. They fuckin' hated him just as much as we did. And don't forget, these guys operate by their own code. They don't always get the cops involved.'

'Thanks for everything, mate. I'll take it from here.'

'I fuckin' owe you one,' said Dom, 'after what happened in that cellar.' He shuddered. 'I never should have let him get away with that. I should have stopped him.'

'It's done,' said Russ. 'And you've more than paid me back.'

Then he addressed Hannah. 'I need you to go now,' he said. She stared back at him, panic etched on her face. 'The CCTV will pick you up. You too, Dom. When the police come sniffing, you're to tell them you left half an hour before you did. I should have told the bouncers that too. Will you make sure they know, Dom?'

'I'm gonna fix the CCTV. If I can't alter the time, then I'll wipe it. Don't worry, I know how it's done. A mate of mine used to work in electricals. Wait outside, away from the cameras, Hannah. Dom, will you wait with her? I'll be out in a minute.

'Oh, and put them papers in your handbag, Hannah. We're gonna need them.'

'W-w-why?' she stammered.

'Just do it, I'll explain later.

Russ took the latex gloves out of his pocket, glad that he'd thought in advance to buy a pair in case he might need them. Then he did what he needed to do.

57

They were at Hannah's flat. Russ had insisted on driving her back as she was too traumatised to get behind the wheel. By the time they arrived, she was a bit calmer and had offered to make them drinks.

'You can stay if you want,' she said.

Russ could tell the offer was made under duress. The place was spotless and there was no way she would want him messing it up. It was bad enough that he'd brought his smell of grime and stale sweat inside with him. And then there was that other business; he felt sure Hannah didn't want a repeat of their night of passion, especially with him in his current state. But he had a good reason not to stay.

'No, it's OK,' he said. 'I just wanted to make sure you got home alright. Besides, I need to get rid of the gun and I prefer to do it sooner rather than later.'

Hannah's features clouded on mention of the gun. It was as though the knowledge of what she had done hit her all over again. 'Jez knew who I was,' she said. 'He knew it was me who had already searched his office once. I wonder how he found out.'

'Samuel Sweeney, one of the directors told him according

to Dom. Apparently he got the information from a guy who worked for him called Pete.'

'Pete?' she blurted out and Russ could see the terror on her face.

'What is it?' he asked.

'He's my stepdad. I need to ring my mum!'

She grabbed her phone and frantically tapped at the keys, a furrow forming on her brow as she waited for her mother to reply.

'Maybe she switches her phone off at night,' said Russ.

'She might do. Shit! I need to tell her. I fuckin' knew it. He had shares in Pake. He'd bought them through Sweeney but when we faced him with it, he told my mum he'd known nothing about the intimidation when he bought them. But this proves he's not as innocent as he claimed. And I can't fuckin' believe he would sell me down the river like that. My mum needs to know what she's married to.'

Russ could see she was getting worked up again. 'It's OK,' he said. 'You can talk to her first thing, but tell her she needs to be careful.' Then he drained the last of his drink and stood up. 'Hannah, I need to be off now. I've got things to tend to. Just try to stay calm, and I promise you, everything will be alright. Put those papers somewhere safe because you're gonna need them. I'll talk to you again tomorrow.'

She stood up too, her eyes filling with tears as she said, 'Russ, I can't believe you'd do all this for me.'

'You should know by now that I'd do anything for you, Hannah.'

He leant forward, hesitantly at first, but when she smiled

weakly, he saw it as a positive sign and took her in his arms, smoothing her hair as she cried out her anguish.

'Don't worry,' he said. 'Just do as I say, and I promise you, everything will work out.'

Hannah had had a dreadful night's sleep, not only because of all that had happened that night but because of her imminent conversation with her mum. She had to go round there anyway to collect Kai so she decided to wait until she knew Pete would probably be out playing golf.

All the way to her mum's, Hannah willed herself to stay calm. It would be easy to break down in front of her mother considering what she had done, but she needed to hold it together. Her mother must never find out that she was a killer. It would be impossible to disguise her troubled countenance altogether, but she would try to attribute it to what she had found out about Pete.

Hannah drew up outside her mother's house and took a deep breath. She was just about to knock on the door when it opened and there stood Pete with a wide grin on his face.

'Hello, Hannah. You're early,' he said.

Hannah was so tempted to tell him exactly what she thought of him. But she had to think of Kai. It wouldn't be good to create a scene in front of her young son.

'I couldn't sleep,' she said, through gritted teeth.

They went through and Pete offered to make some drinks while her mother greeted her with a warm hug and Kai flung his arms around her legs.

'Hannah, you're shaking. What's the matter?' Jill asked.

Checking Pete was in the kitchen, Hannah whispered,

'Mum, I need to talk to you. It's about Pete and it's not good. Is he going out?'

'Not today, no. He's doing jobs around the house.'

'Well, come back with me then. Make up some excuse. I need to speak to you urgently.'

Half an hour later they were back at Hannah's flat.

'What is it?' asked Jill. 'It must be bad if you couldn't tell me in the car.'

'I don't want Kai to hear,' Hannah whispered.

Waiting until Kai was settled, Hannah told Jill all about how Pete had tipped Jez off about her searching his office. The distressed look on her mother's face tore at Hannah's heart. She hated to do this to her.

'But why? Why would he do that?' asked Jill. 'And why would you put yourself at risk by searching his office? Who told you anyway?'

Hannah told her mother a diluted version of events claiming it was her friend from the club who had told her about Pete but omitting to mention what had happened when she had gone to search Jez's office again.

'Sorry, Mum, but you needed to know. But please tread carefully. If he's capable of putting me in danger by tipping Jez off, then I don't know what else he's capable of.'

'Don't worry about that,' said Jill. 'He's not a violent man. I think he's just got in over his head. He wouldn't dream of hurting me, but I need to speak to him. I want to know just what the hell he's been up to.'

Hannah felt bad. She could tell that her words had just destroyed her mother's world.

58

The following day, Hannah was on the phone with Russ. 'I can't believe they got me in so quick for questioning,' she said.

'Well, it doesn't surprise me,' said Russ. 'They don't mess about in a murder case, and it would be pretty obvious from looking at Jez that he hadn't died of natural causes.'

'Alright!' snapped Hannah who was still having difficulty coming to terms with what she had done.

'Did you keep your cool?' asked Russ.

Hannah moderated her tone now, feeling guilty for snapping at Russ. 'Yeah. They mentioned the fact that the CCTV had been interfered with, so they had no record of me and some other members of staff leaving the building. And they said that was why they'd pulled me in. I kept to the story about what time I'd left, and they seemed to buy it. Then they asked for my fingerprints so that they could rule me out of their investigation.'

'That's fine, it's what we expected,' said Russ. 'They'll have you back in, they're bound to but just stick to the story. Keep telling yourself the tale we discussed, and by the time they pull you in again, even you will believe it.'

Hannah let out a loud breath. 'I bloody well hope so.'

'You will, Hannah. You just have to keep your cool, and it'll be OK.'

Hannah laughed. 'You're unbelievable.'

'Yeah, but I'm bloody good.'

When they'd finished the call Hannah's thoughts went to her mother for the umpteenth time since she had told her about Pete. She hoped she had handled it alright. Hannah had wanted to ring her, but things had been frantic. Between the police interview, catching up on sleep and looking after Kai, she hadn't had much time.

When she did have a spare minute, she had decided, instead, to wait until her mother contacted her. Surely, she'd give her a ring once she had something to tell. But it had been a whole day now and Hannah was becoming worried. She wondered how Pete would have taken it when Jill faced him with what she knew. Hannah didn't think of him as a violent man, but you never knew.

Finally, she gave her mother a ring. 'Mum, I've been worried about you. How are you? Did you tell him?' she asked.

'Yes, I've told him,' said Jill.

Her voice was soft, resigned even, and Hannah realised how difficult this must be for her, especially coming so soon after the death of her mother.

'And? Are you OK?'

'As well as to be expected, I suppose. He's gone, Hannah.'

'Oh, I'm sorry, Mum.'

'Don't be. We're getting a divorce. It's the best thing under the circumstances. He, erm … he said he was sorry.

Apparently, the whole thing spiralled out of control. He didn't realise it would get that bad, or so he said.' Then she sighed. 'Trouble is, I don't know what to believe anymore.'

'Oh, Mum, I'm so sorry,' Hannah repeated.

'It's alright, love. I'll be OK. And don't worry about the money from Mum's house, you'll still be getting it. I had a feeling ages ago that things would end like this, back when you told me about his involvement with Pake Holdings. I thought there was more to it than he was letting on. That's why I had the funds from Mum's house transferred into your name before I split up with him. I want you and Kai to have a home, Hannah, so you won't have to worry about finding the rent every month. It'll help you get on your feet till Kai's in school when you can go back to the career you love.'

'Thank you so much, Mum,' said Hannah.

Elation wasn't quite appropriate under the circumstances, but she was relieved Pete wasn't going to get his hands on her nana's money. It was a bit of good news among all the bad things that were happening. And she couldn't help but feel a certain admiration for her mother. She'd always thought she got her strength of character and feistiness from her nana, but perhaps some of it had come from her mother after all.

Then another thought occurred to her, and she felt guilty for getting so carried away in her thoughts. 'What about you, Mum? Does that mean you'll lose your home in the divorce?'

'No, not at all. Pete didn't sell his shares in Pake after all, even though he'd promised he would. That was just another deception. But at least it means he won't be after part of the house. Apparently, the shares are worth a fortune now the development's progressing, so he'll be fine. But I don't want any part of his blood money.'

'Oh, Mum,' said Hannah. Without reiterating how sorry she was once more, Hannah didn't know what else to say.

'I saw the news about your boss,' said Jill, changing the subject. 'He's been killed, hasn't he?'

'Erm, yeah,' said Hannah, shocked that her mother knew. She didn't realise it had hit the TV news headlines already, and she wondered how to play it. She quickly decided on what would be an honest reaction had she not been involved in his death. 'To be honest, Mum, I won't be shedding any tears, not after what happened to Nana.'

'Me neither. I wonder who did it though.'

Hannah was glad her mother couldn't see the guilt written on her face. 'Search me,' she said, aiming for nonchalant. 'He had plenty of enemies, that's for sure. 'And if he was behind the other deaths in Nana's street, then it could be any one of a number of people.'

'Well, let's hope that's the end of it. I've been worried sick about you, Hannah. You were too involved.'

'It is the end of it, Mum. It's over. Things can only get better from now on.'

But Hannah knew that, for her, things weren't over yet. She was still under suspicion for Jez's killing but she wasn't going to share that snippet with her mum.

59

For the past two weeks Hannah had been constantly on edge, her sleep disturbed and her stomach upset. She was struggling with the enormity of what she had done that day, but she was also dreading the imminent second interview with the police. Following Russ's advice, she had gone over her cover story every day, talking to herself out loud to make it feel more convincing.

When the police appeared at her door, their visit wasn't unexpected. Even before they showed their ID, she knew who they were from their smart suits and their incongruous presence on the rundown estate. They were both middle-aged, both balding, and what little hair they had left was dark in places but peppered with grey. The thing that set them apart was their difference in height. Where one stood at almost six feet, the other was about three inches shorter.

'Hannah Conway?' asked the taller of the two.

'Yes,' said Hannah.

'I'm Detective Inspector Carlisle. This is Detective Sergeant Pleasance. We'd like to take you in for more questioning.'

'OK, but I need to drop my son at my mum's on the way. You'll have to wait while I get ready.'

The police officers agreed to wait outside in the car. As she helped Kai to put his outdoor clothes on, Hannah's hands were shaking. Now that the moment she'd been dreading had arrived, she didn't know if she could handle it. What if she broke down and confessed all? But then she remembered how Russ had primed her, and she gave herself a stern talking-to. If she could handle this, then things should get easier.

At the station the two detectives were polite, offering her a drink and allowing her to settle down before they started questioning. They began with innocuous questions at first: name, address, place of work and so on. Then, after they'd verified that she was in work on the night in question, DS Pleasance asked her where she was at around 2.30 a.m.

This was it. She had to stay calm even though she was quaking inside. She looked fixedly at the officers, her body language telling them she had nothing to hide. Hannah did some quick mental arithmetics. She knew Russ had scrubbed the tapes for that evening, so they had no record of her or anybody else leaving The Gilded Cage. Any information they had would be from questioning other members of staff. And they would have told the officers that Hannah was still in the building when they had left for the night.

But it wouldn't pay to be too precise, so Hannah replied, 'At around that time I'd probably be setting off for home.'

'Probably? You don't know for sure?'

'Well, I normally get out around twenty past. Obviously, I don't always check the time when I leave. But I know it was later than usual because I stayed behind to do some tidying.'

'Were you the only member of staff who stayed behind?'

'On that bar, yes. I'm not sure what was happening on the other bar because I can't see it too well from where I work.'

'So why was that?' asked Pleasance.

'Why was what?'

'Why were you the only member of staff who stayed behind when the others had left?'

'Oh, I let them go. It's like that. We all get along and we do each other favours.'

'And are the management happy with that situation?'

'Yeah, as long as it's all left clean and tidy at the end of the night, they're not worried who's last to go.'

'But if there was only one person cleaning the bar, wouldn't that mean the management would have to wait longer before they could shut the club?'

'Oh, it was only for the last few minutes that it was only me. Everyone else was there up to that point.'

DI Carlisle stared pointedly at her now and Hannah squirmed, sensing that he was preparing to go hard on her.

'So, when you stayed behind and were the only member of staff at that bar, where was Jez Reilly at that point?'

'Erm, he came over while I was clearing up to check everything was OK. Then he went to the foyer.'

'And did you see him come back from the foyer?'

'No.'

'OK, so what did you do after he'd gone to the foyer?'

'It wasn't long after that when I went to the staffroom to collect my things and go home.'

'So, are you saying you went straight home?'

Hannah nodded. 'Yes.'

'Are you sure you didn't stop off at Jez Reilly's office on the way?'

This time Hannah shook her head. 'No, I didn't.'

Carlisle's pointed stare became even more intense. 'Then can you tell me, Hannah, why your fingerprints are all over Jez Reilly's office: his door, the desk and even the filing cabinet?'

Hannah reached into her handbag, zipped it open and pulled out the paperwork she had lifted from Jez's office that night. Placing them on the desk, she said, 'Because I'd been in there earlier that night looking for these.'

The officers shared confused looks, and without waiting for them to come at her again, Hannah told her story.

'I was searching for information tying him to Pake Holdings. I knew he was connected to the company, which meant he was also connected to the intimidation that was taking place in Rovener Street, including wrecking my nana's home and harassing her so much that she suffered a fatal heart attack.'

Carlisle held up his hand. 'Steady! This is all assumption. There is no proof that Pake Holdings were behind the intimidation of Rovener Street residents.'

'That's only because you haven't been able to find it yet,' replied Hannah, emboldened by her anger at the mention of her grandmother's death. 'My friend Russ Coles has further evidence, so has Dom Slater and we've spoken to Connor Davis who has agreed to testify against Pake Holdings too.

'Between that and what's contained in those papers there, I think you should have enough not only to prove that Jez was connected to Pake Holdings but to nail the two company directors too.'

The two officers gazed in amazement at Hannah. She knew that this was the proof they'd been waiting for. Nailing the perpetrators of the Rovener Street incidents was probably even more important to them than finding out who killed Jez, because innocent victims were involved. Nevertheless, she knew they had a job to do so she left them with a parting shot, confident that they would soon bring the interview to a close.

'That man had a lot of enemies and any one of them could have been responsible for his death. I think you'll soon establish that once you start digging a bit further.'

Hannah looked at the two men, resisting the urge to breathe a sigh of relief. She'd done it! She could tell from their facial expressions. She'd taken the heat off herself and hoped they would now investigate the two directors of Pake Holdings Ltd. Because, currently, Samuel Sweeney and Thomas Markham were still at large and living the high life on the profits of other people's misery.

60

Six Months Later

Hannah knocked at the door of what used to be her flat, smiling broadly when Russ answered. He was dressed smartly in fitted jeans and a t-shirt, and he smelled fresh and clean. Hannah knew he had come a long way from the Russ who had been forced to live on the streets only months previously, and she was pleased for him.

For a while he had moved in with her but slept on the sofa. Hannah didn't want any more complications in her life. Her focus now was rebuilding life for herself, Kai and her mother, and she didn't want anything to complicate that. When the money from her nana's estate had come through, Hannah had bought a two-bedroomed apartment in a nice area and Russ had taken over the tenancy of her old flat. She and Russ had kept in contact ever since.

'Come in, I'll put the kettle on,' he said.

She followed him through to the kitchen, and they chatted while he spooned coffee into two cups and brought some biscuits out of the cupboard, handing one to Kai who chuckled and said thank you.

'How's things?' asked Russ.

'Not bad. Mum's gradually getting better, but I think she still misses Pete as well as Nana.'

'And what about you?'

'Oh, y'know …'

'Still having the nightmares?'

'Not as often.'

Russ put his arm around her. 'It will get easier y'know. You had no choice so don't be feeling any guilt for him.'

Hannah shrugged. 'It's not so much guilt for him but, well …' She glanced at Kai before continuing. 'It was a bad thing to do, wasn't it?'

'You had no choice, Hannah,' he reiterated.

'What about you anyway?' she asked, glad of a change of subject. 'Did you get that shop you were after?'

Russ beamed. 'Yeah, come on, let's go in there and I'll tell you about it.'

They settled in the lounge, Hannah fishing a puzzle out of her bag and handing it to Kai.

'I take over next month. I've bought a cheap van too out of that money you lent me, and I've already been checking out house clearances so I can have it well stocked by the time I open.'

'Where will you put all the stuff?' asked Hannah.

'In the bedroom. I've only got a bed and a rail in there at the moment. I've moved the bed nearer the door, so I don't have to climb over all the stuff to get to it. Once I've got the shop, I can store it there, and then I can get some more bedroom furniture for myself. I might even come across something when I start clearing houses out.'

'I'm really pleased for you,' said Hannah, but then she couldn't resist adding, 'Are they the only goods you'll be selling?'

'Definitely. I've told you, Hannah, I'm putting that life behind me. From now on I'm on the straight and narrow. There's no way I want to go through all that again.' He paused for a moment before saying. 'Actually, that's not strictly true. There is someone I've been in touch with.'

Hannah bristled. 'Oh yeah? Who's that then?'

'It's not what you think, Hannah. It isn't someone from the criminal world; it's a guy I met when I was homeless. He's just a kid really, called Luke. He was good to me when I was on the streets, and I want to pay him back.'

'How?'

'Well, he's on drugs, but he's a smart guy. It's just sad to see him wasting his life. I'm trying to persuade him to get help. Then, once he's off the drugs, he might stand a chance of getting his life back.'

Hannah had simmered down a bit by now. 'Be careful, Russ,' she said. 'It isn't easy to get off drugs. He's got to want to do it for himself.'

'I know. Don't worry. I will be.'

Hannah nodded and as she looked at him, she became carried away in her thoughts. Russ might not be the best-looking guy in the world, but he had something about him. He'd been so good to her and now here he was trying to help somebody else too.

The mutual attraction was still there, and Russ had told her he would like to make a go of things together. But, with a young son to think about, Hannah was unsure about the less savoury aspects of Russ's past. It would take time to see if he really would stay on the straight and narrow. And, if he did, who knew what the future might hold?

Epilogue

Three Months Later

Hannah was sitting in the public gallery at Manchester Crown Court with her mother on one side and Russ on the other. The last nine months had seen a change in all of them. Hannah was still trying to come to terms with Jez's death and hoped that in time she would be able to accept it as easily as Russ seemed to do.

Russ was going from strength to strength and finally making a living as an honest man. Hannah couldn't feel prouder of him, and they were still good friends. Jill got along well with Russ too, although she had no idea what actions both he and Hannah had taken in the past, and Hannah preferred it to stay that way.

Jill had struggled in the early days after Pete had left, but she was steadily getting better thanks to Hannah's support. Nobody had seen anything of Pete after he had left, and once the divorce settlement was sorted, all contact had ceased. It was the best way, Hannah had told her mum. Even if Pete hadn't known about the intimidation, he had still lied to them when he'd retained his shares, and he'd also sent word to Jez that Hannah was onto him.

Today's trial was important to all three of them. Hannah and her mother wanted justice for the death of Pat. But

Russ also wanted justice. Hannah was aware of his history with Thomas Markham and knew how badly he had been hurt by the killing of his best friend, Bryce. The fact that Markham had escaped justice for the death of Bryce had always troubled Russ. He had confided in her late one night after a few drinks.

It was now the third day of the trial of Thomas Markham and Samuel Sweeney for intimidation of the residents of Rovener Street. The evidence against them had been overwhelming. Not only had Hannah, Russ and Dom testified against them, but the court had presented evidence via video link from Connor Davis, and some of the previous residents of Rovener Street had also given evidence.

Pete hadn't been called as a witness, but Hannah wasn't surprised. She had deliberately kept his name out of things, knowing that if he admitted feeding Samuel Sweeney information about her searching Jez's office, it might put the focus on her again. The police had previously closed the case relating to Jez's murder due to lack of evidence, and she didn't want to risk them reopening it. Hannah had persuaded her mother to go along with her request on the basis that none of them would benefit from having Pete's reputation tarnished in public.

Although the trial wasn't concerned with Jez's death, Hannah had been on edge when Samuel Sweeney was questioned in case he revealed anything that would incriminate her. But fortunately, he had kept to the required answers, and Hannah was relieved when the court finally reached the summing-up stage.

Now that the nerve-wracking part was over for her, Hannah felt restless as the prosecution and defence barristers summarised the evidence for and against. Finally, it was time for the jury to give the verdict. Hannah glanced first at Jill then at Russ. They both looked as keen to see the end of it as she was.

'Guilty,' pronounced the foreman of the jury and they all gave a collective sigh of relief.

'Thank God for that!' muttered Jill.

Hannah smiled weakly then glanced at Russ. To her surprise his eyes were filled with tears.

'Are you alright?' she asked.

Russ took a deep breath to calm himself, and Hannah could see he was embarrassed at his show of emotion. 'Yes, I'm OK. I've waited a long time to see that bastard sent down. I know it'll never bring Bryce back, but at least justice has been served.'

Hannah gave his hand a squeeze then turned back to her mum. Unlike Russ, Jill was smiling.

Hannah smiled back and asked her mum the same question she'd asked Russ, 'Are you alright?'

'Oh yes, I'm more than alright. It was great to see those two so-and-sos get their comeuppance. In fact, I'm beginning to enjoy watching court cases. I might just make a hobby of it.'

Hannah recognised the excuse she'd given Jez last time she and her mother were in the public gallery of a courtroom and, seeing the irony, she flashed a satisfied grin.

Acknowledgements

THANK YOU to my publishers, Head of Zeus, who have been with me since the start of my career. I appreciate all the support you have given me over the years. Particular thanks go to Laura Palmer, who has always backed me and helped to develop my author brand. Thanks also to Martina Arzu, Bethan Jones, Ian Rutland, Matt Bray, Peyton Stableford and all the Head of Zeus staff who have worked on my novels.

I recently signed up with a new agent, Francesca Riccardi of Kate Nash Literary Agency Ltd, who has been an absolute joy to work with. Big thanks to Francesca and to Sam Brownley for the introduction. The rest of the staff at Kate Nash have been really welcoming too so I would like to say thank you to all of you.

Thank you to the wider crime reading community including book bloggers, reviewers and all the people who give up their free time to run social media groups where crime readers and authors can connect and share their enthusiasm and recommendations for crime novels. Thanks also to my readers, many of whom have become regulars who read every book I publish. I am eternally grateful.

I am also grateful to my author friends. The author community is very friendly and supportive, and I feel privileged to be a part of it.

Lastly, I would like to thank Kerry and Pascoe, for being a sounding board for my ideas, and my family and friends for their continuing support and for always being there for me. Particular thanks go to: Phil, Baz, Diane, Karen and Mary.